To: Lisa

Enjoy

Emily's Quest

Cora Alyce Seaman

Cora Alyce Seaman
10/07

This is a work of fiction. Names, characters, places, and incidents either are the product of the author's imagination or are used fictitiously. Any resemblance to actual events or locales or persons, living or dead, is entirely coincidental.

ISBN 0-7414-2972-1

Cover artwork is by Pauline Holtz.

Published by:

INFINITY
PUBLISHING.COM

1094 New DeHaven Street, Suite 100
West Conshohocken, PA 19428-2713
Info@buybooksontheweb.com
www.buybooksontheweb.com
Toll-free (877) BUY BOOK
Local Phone (610) 941-9999
Fax (610) 941-9959

Printed in the United States of America

Printed on Recycled Paper

Published January 2006

Acknowledgments:

I gratefully acknowledge the patience of my faithful editor, my husband, Don. I could not have completed this project without him.

My thanks to my friend, Jackie, who told me this story.

Chapter 1

Back in the winter of 1908, the Doctor had arrived in his carriage at the home of Guy and Camilla Whitfield on a bitterly cold winter day. Winters were always cold in Peterborough, Ontario, Canada, and that December was no different. Guy had sent for the Doctor because Camilla was in advanced labor and would soon deliver her baby. She was having a difficult time trying to get the baby's cooperation. It was as if he/she was fighting the right to enter this world. Labor had started in the wee hours of the morning and continually became more intense. Naturally Camilla was praying it would soon be over. This was her first child and, at this moment, she determined it would also her last. This was not something she wanted to repeat; at least not anytime soon. When the Dr. came into the birthing room, he instructed Guy to begin to bring hot water and towels. The impending birth would be momentary. Guy had no knowledge about such things. He had spent his life working in the Hershell Shoe factory. He was an only child who had never been a part of babies or pregnant mothers. His mother never discussed such things with him. It was the custom of the day that any subject pertaining to the female anatomy was never discussed in polite conversations. To be faced with assisting the birth of your own child was a totally new experience. He was both elated and terrified. He could hardly handle the sounds of labor from Camilla. He was helpless to comfort her and he felt totally responsible for her condition. At the rest periods between labor pains, she tried to assure him this had been a joint effort. She wanted him to understand that together, they would raise their baby.

Suddenly the Dr. gave out an excited shout. Guy quivered at the sound, fearing the worst, but the Dr. was near hysteria when he announced the FIRST baby was born. All at once, both Guy and Camilla understood the news…there was more than one child. Dr. Hoover had already discovered that there was another baby. Camilla did her best to make the births happen, and it was soon apparent that the Whitfields were the parents of two precious baby daughters. Dr. Hoover was aghast. He had never delivered twins before.

Dr. Byron Hoover was a general practitioner who had recently set up his medical practice in Peterborough. He had selected this town since their only Dr. had decided to retire before his 90th birthday. Most of the folks in Peterborough had doctored with the old doc for their entire lives. When he retired, they were delighted to have Dr. Hoover move into his office and assume his duties. The new Dr. was pleased to be able to take over a practice that was so well established. However, he was young and inexperienced. When Mrs. Whitfield had come to him and he had established her pregnancy, he had followed her progress regularly. He felt she was in good physical condition and would deliver a healthy baby. Little did he know what a surprise it would be for the Whitfields as well as for him. He quickly handled the birth process and handed Guy his newborn daughter. Before he could wiggle her around in his arm, Dr. Hoover handed him the second one. This procedure was more than Guy could handle. He asked the Doc to help him bathe one and then the other. After bathing them and wrapping each one in a blanket that was ready for them, Guy held one and Camilla took the other one. She was very tired and could only enjoy this moment for a short time before she lapsed into a deep sleep. The babies settled down and snuggled next to their mother until they could be fed.

Guy left the room with the Dr. and as they stood in the hall, he consulted with the doc about his next move. How could they handle twins? Could Camilla possibly nurse two babies at one time? Would he need someone to come in and help her? Camilla had no family in Canada and his mother was not well herself. Dr. Hoover assured him he would check on the family each day for a few weeks. He suggested that Guy check with the folks at the Parish House of St. Anthony's Catholic Church to see if there was a lady who would assist Camilla in handling the babies for a couple of weeks. Guy mentioned that he would be able to pay a little bit for this service. He had been with the Hershell Shoe Company for four years and had worked himself into a good salary. Then he realized that he needed to discuss money with Dr. Hoover. No mention had been made about the cost of his services before he was blessed with two wonderful children all in one day. Dr. Hoover told him that because this was his first set of twins, he would only charge him for one! Guy laughed to think he got a "two for one" bargain. And the total bill would be only $20.00. He went to his desk and carefully counted out $20.00 from the cash he had been saving for this occasion. Guy was a good money manager. He was able to save a small amount from each paycheck and Camilla was frugal in her spending. He really wanted her to be able to go back to school, but right now that seemed to be a pipe dream. She could hardly go to school and handle two babies, too. He would have to cross that bridge when they came to it.

Guy returned to the bedside of his wife, who was still sleeping, and smiled at his good fortune. He had three beautiful girls in his life and he felt as rich as Craesus. He studied them intently for a few moments. These babies were his creation. How could he be so lucky? Camilla was his lovely bride who, only one year ago had consented to marry him. She was tall and thin. Her dark shining eyes matched her brunette colored hair. She was gregarious and outgoing in her personality and she loved people. That trait alone made her a desirable catch for anyone. Guy had loved her from afar, but she paid him "no mind". She was alone and lived in a rooming house with other girls. She had been attending school to become a teacher. She was too busy in her own life to consider having a beau. She had dreams for her life. Her parents had left Ontario and moved to Texas when she was young leaving her alone in Canada. Her father had been working for a refinery in Ottawa and was transferred to Texas where he was offered what he hoped to be a better job. Unfortunately, shortly after he arrived on the job, he was struck by a falling beam on an oilrig and was killed. Her mother was unable to handle the trauma of his death and lost her mind. She was unable to face reality and since the mother was so far from her only child, there had been no one to assist her. She had to be committed to an institution where she was cared for on a long-term basis. Many days she hardly knew her name. Camilla was devastated that her beloved mother was so ill, but she also knew that there was little she could do to help her. She often thought she should bring her back to Peterborough but she wondered how she could afford to keep her. She was barely able to support herself. When she thought about this predicament, it made her sad. Nevertheless, she knew that if she could get through her training school and become a teacher, she would be able to earn enough money to bring her mother home.

Chapter 2

Meanwhile, Guy returned to the birthing room and gazed at the miracle before him. The babies were identical, beautiful, and looked like their mother. Their hair was dark and curly. Both of them had lots of curls on top of their head. Their features were pristine and pronounced. Each had dimples, little button noses, fair complexions, and dark curly hair. Although Camilla had been in labor for several hours, the twins showed no signs of any struggle. As Guy stood over the bed, he marveled at the tiny little bundles before him. He wondered how anything so tiny could live to adulthood. The Dr. had estimated their weight at about 4 pounds each stating that this was a good sign. He predicted they would have healthy lives.

Camilla was beginning to awaken. She seemed a bit groggy at first, but when she realized that her dream was true, she really did have twins, she began to cry. Guy was distraught. "Why are you crying" he asked? "They are tears of happiness", she replied and the two of them held a baby apiece and the tears continued to roll down their cheeks splashing on the babies. "What shall we call them"? Camilla wondered aloud. Guy could not respond because of his emotions. "We will decide that tomorrow," he said, once he was able to compose himself. "Tonight you must learn how to feed them and I will go to see Father Paul about someone to help you". Camilla nodded in agreement while she trying to coax baby #1 to nurse. It was not an easy job. Her breasts were sore and the baby was hungry. Suddenly, baby #2 began to cry. Oh, how will I manage this, she thought. I can't possibly do this myself. She began to pray to the Blessed Virgin Mary for some help that would make all this easier. Before Guy returned with the lady from the Parish, Camilla was able to get both babies to nurse a little, but she was exhausted again. Mrs. Perkins, from the Parish, immediately took over. She hustled around the bed and cleaned up the mess. No one had even noticed the pan of water and towels still in the room. The babies had stolen all their attention. Mrs. Perkins drew some warm water and proceeded to sponge off Camilla's face trying to get her to relax a little bit. The babies would need to be fed again soon, since they had not been satisfied with the first feeding.

Mrs. Perkins could see it would be a long night trying to keep the babies happy and Camilla rested enough to continue to manufacture milk for the babies. She promptly went to the kitchen and put on a kettle of soup. Everyone would soon need to be fed. Guy was still wandering around in a daze. He hardly knew what to do. Suddenly he decided he should go to see his mother and share his good fortune.

Camilla had managed to make it through that first night with the help of Mrs. Perkins. It had been a long exhausting night, but the babies finally learned to nurse and their mother learned to relax a little. Guy was still in a state of shock but was so proud of himself for having been a part of creating twins. He left for work very early the next morning but not before Mrs. Perkins had a chance to fix him a good breakfast. She packed him a good lunch and filled his thermos with some of the hot soup left from the night before. She mumbled something about taking care of the new father. As Guy was leaving he kissed Camilla goodbye and agreed that they would have to come to some agreement on names when he returned in the evening. The day passed as quickly as it began and Mrs. Perkins continued to handle all the routine problems at hand. She was a jewel to have around to help. However, time would soon reveal another side of her.

Guy returned home in the evening with stories of how his good fortune was received at the factory. All of the men decided they should make a pair of shoes for the babies, but Guy assured them they had no "lasts" the size of the babies' feet. It would be a long time until they would grow enough to fit into any of the "lasts" they had at the factory.

After dinner that Mrs. Perkins had prepared, Camilla came to the sitting room with the babies and announced they would name each one of them. Both twins had dark hair and long eyelashes. One of them had more auburn hair than the other one and that would be the only way they could be identified. They were very fair skinned and had dimples. It was hard to tell them apart. Emily Marie was the name chosen for the older of the two darling little girls, and Charlotte Antoinette was the name chosen for the other one. Both of the girls slept through this experience as if it really didn't matter what their names were.

Several weeks later, the twins were christened in St. Anthony's Catholic Church. Their names resounded throughout the sanctuary as Dr. Hoover and the Parish Priest; Father Paul took part in the ceremony. Dr. Hoover had agreed to be the godfather to the girls since he was so proud of himself for delivering his first set of twins.

Chapter 3

Emily and Charlotte soon became the town cherubs. They were not the first twins born in Peterborough, but they were the youngest. It seemed the whole community surrounded them and made them the object of their affection. Camilla, as an experienced seamstress, was able to dress the girls in the latest fashion. She spent many hours at the sewing machine making dresses, coats, bonnets, and petticoats. She vowed they would be the best-dressed children in town. Guy and Camilla doted on their twins as time progressed and they grew. Camilla continued to curl their hair in long curls each day and taught them impeccable manners. They would curtsy when meeting an adult stranger. At mealtimes the girls learned to set the table as if for a banquet and they were taught to ask a blessing before eating any meal. Camilla wanted Guy to think he was a king so each meal was treated as if the royal chef had prepared it. She and Guy were as happy as any family could be. While they were not considered wealthy, there was adequate income to support them and the twins in fine style.

Emily became the tease of the two. She was constantly playing tricks on Charlotte, who was the more subdued. Sometimes Emily would be so mischievous that Charlotte would cry and run to her mother for consolation. One day when they were playing in the yard Emily spied a big worm crawling on the walk. Knowing that Charlotte was deathly afraid of any kind of worm, Emily picked it up and put it in the pocket of Charlotte's apron. As the worm got warmer in his ominous hiding place, it began to crawl out and up her apron. When Charlotte discovered the worm, she went into fits of screaming and crying. Emily thought the whole event to be humorous but when her mother discovered her dastardly deed, Camilla forced Emily to stand in the corner for an hour while she consoled Charlotte. Such punishment rarely cured Emily of her devilment, although it seemed to work for the moment.

The twins loved animals and their parents allowed them to have a kitten. Owning a pet was considered a way of teaching the girls the responsibility of caring for it. One of their chores each day was to feed their kitten, Lily, before they went out to play. She was a snow-white kitten with lots of fluffy fur. A bowl of milk and some scraps of meat or eggs were gleaned from the table and put in another bowl for Lily. If she had messed in the house, the girls were forced to clean up the mess. Emily would take that chore in her stride but Charlotte had a difficult time with this procedure. It seemed that anything that smelled bad made her ill. Camilla would often come to her rescue knowing it was better to clean up one mess rather than two. The kitten was playful and loving to the girls but they constantly fought over whose turn it was to play with her. Lily loved to play with the girls' stockings that they usually hung on the back of a chair in their room each night. Once when the parish priest, Father Paul, had come to visit the Whitfield family, Lily came dragging one of the girls' stocking into the parlor and deposited it at Father Paul's feet. It appeared an invitation for him to play with her. Camilla was mortified at such an affront to good manners. Father Paul laughingly picked up the stocking and proceeded to do just what Lily wanted. When the girls discovered what had happened, Emily quickly retrieved the kitten and her stocking and hastily retreated out of sight.

The girls were enrolled in a catechism class at St.Anthony's Catholic Church. They were too young to go to the public schools, but their parents considered the classes part of their education. They studied hard with the Sisters and Father Paul and soon had completed their studies. They were ready to be confirmed and accept first communion. They were only six years old but they felt that they were 15!

After they had completed their confirmation and had enrolled in school, Camilla felt that they should also receive some musical training. The old piano that stood in the corner of the parlor had belonged to her mother. When her father and mother had moved to Texas they had been unable to take the Upright Baby Grand with them and had left it in the boarding house where Camilla lived while attending school. When she and Guy were married the landlady gladly allowed her to take it to her new home. Camilla had played the piano a little bit when she was young, but had never mastered the skill. However, she felt the girls should be exposed to this experience as part of their education. A teacher from the school agreed to come once a week and give them piano lessons. On Tuesday afternoon Emily would be the first to get her lesson. She loved the lessons and practiced daily. She progressed through the piano books with ease and soon could play the little tunes the teacher gave her to do. Charlotte was shy and didn't like the routine of playing. She had a difficult time with the finger exercises and tended not to practice when she was told. Camilla decided maybe she needed a different instrument so she promptly retrieved the violin that Guy's father used to play, from the attic. If she could find someone who could teach Charlotte the violin, perhaps that would be more to her liking. After several weeks of enduring the squeaking of the violin and listening to Charlotte complain, Camilla decided that perhaps she was not a musician. Emily continued to excel on the piano and soon could play for anyone who would come to the house.

The School at St. Anthony's Catholic Church was not a real Catholic school. The Province of Ontario supported it but it was Catholic by nature. The teachers in the school were pious Catholic women and the men were actually laypersons. The girls were enrolled in the school as soon as the Church had confirmed them. It didn't take long to for the teachers to discover that they were very bright. The school welcomed them and they quickly began to attract attention since they were the only twins in the school. Guy and Camilla insisted they take their studies seriously and they conferred with the teachers often. Emily was the gregarious one and Charlotte tended to be more withdrawn. She depended on her sister to be the leader and she seemed content to follow. One day in the spring of 1915, Charlotte came home from school with some papers on which she had drawn in class. When Camilla looked at the papers she noticed the accurateness of the animals that she had drawn. She had drawn a picture of a tiger that they had seen at the zoo the previous summer. She had the stripes placed correctly and the claws at the end of the paws were so realistic looking that Camilla cringed. The big eyes of the cat seemed to peer right into her eyes. She called Charlotte to her side and asked about the big cat. Charlotte announced that she loved to draw and the teacher had encouraged her to draw something that she saw last summer. She decided that the big cat was the prettiest thing she had ever seen. Camilla wondered if Charlotte could repeat this experience with something else. She quickly gave her large stack of paper she had been saving to write letters on and a few pencils. If she could draw in pencil, then maybe she could color them later. Charlotte ran to her room and disappeared from sight for several hours. Finally when she joined the family for dinner she had drawn Lily, the cat, with a great deal of detail, she had drawn the barn out in back of the house, and had started drawing the doll that sat on a chair in her room. When Guy came home from work, Camilla shared the discovery with him and he too, was awestruck at the apparent talent. Camilla wondered if she could ask the teachers at school again for someone to help Charlotte with her artwork. The family still had someone teaching piano and perhaps an art teacher for Charlotte would be available. Camilla met the girls after school the next day and stayed to talk with the Headmaster. She explained her plight to him. He seemed very encouraging, but there wasn't anyone who was an accomplished artist on staff. As an alternative, he suggested that Camilla go to the newspaper office and get a stack of paper or a small roll of newsprint and just let Charlotte draw to her hearts content. Camilla understood that they would be able to get more art supplies on their next trip to Ottawa since Peterborough had no such facility. Once the paper was in Charlotte's hand she regularly hurried to her room and had to be called for mealtime. She loved to draw and could see beauty in almost everything she saw. Guy and Camilla could hardly believe the two prodigies they had on their hands. They embraced each other and gave God the credit for giving them such wonderful girls.

Chapter 4

In 1916 Canada was still a Dominion of Great Britain. The First World War was raging in Europe and troops had been called to serve from all the Provinces of Canada. Many of the neighbors of Guy and Camilla had been called to service in the King's Navy. The Whitfields prayed daily that Guy would not have to go off to war. He had been deferred because of his family for a while, but if the war continued on very long, he would surely be called to serve. The United States was still neutral, President Woodrow Wilson having been re-elected with the slogan "he kept us out of war". However, when the Germans sank the Lusitania the States immediately entered the war in order to protect their own interests.

All of Canada wanted to help the war effort in any way they could. Many of the women gathered to prepare "care" packages for the troops. Camilla had the ladies come to her parlor to pack and get ready for shipment the various items the men needed so badly. It was cold and wet in many of the areas where the intense fighting was taking place and the men desperately needed extra socks and warm underwear. Some of the women could knit and make the warm woolen socks while others like Camilla could sew and make the long drawers from woolen fabrics to be sent to the front. Some of the women made lye soap to include in the packages. The soldiers in the front lines had complained about the vermin that lived in the trenches and the lye soap would help to cure any kind of infections they might get. The ladies of Camilla's group of friends also baked cookies and fruitcakes to be sent in the packages. The school children rolled clean rags into bandages for the wounded. Emily and Charlotte thought this to be great fun and they were willing to give up their petticoats for the cause. However, Camilla would only allow each of them to give up one petticoat since she knew she had little time to make them more. Their school wrapped a record number of bandages and received an award from the Royal Palace for their efforts in fighting the war.

Chapter 5

Mrs. Perkins had continued to help Camilla on a weekly basis with all the household duties. She would come on Thursdays and help do the baking and cleaning for the weekend while Camilla would do the marketing. She would prepare the girls clothes for the coming week of school. She helped to mend anything that they managed to tear or rip, and for Emily that seemed to be a never ending chore. Charlotte was more sedate and rarely tore her clothing, but Emily could be seen climbing trees and playing stickball with the boys so her stockings and jumpers were in constant need of darning. Mrs. Perkins had a disdain for mending Emily's clothing. She thought her to be too much of a tomboy. She would scold her when Camilla was not in earshot. Once, when she caught Emily alone she pulled her ears and told her she was a bad girl. Emily carried that admonishment with her to bed that night, but did not mention it to her parents. She thought to herself that she would simply stay out of Mrs. Perkins way and everything would be okay. However, since Mrs. Perkins did not receive a rebuke for her misdeed, she felt she had managed to escape any detection. Emily was true to her word and stayed an arms length away from her. But, even then it seemed she couldn't avoid confrontation with Mrs. Perkins on all occasions.

When Camilla was gone to the market on another Thursday, Mrs. Perkins found Emily in the parlor playing the piano. She crept up behind her and slammed the piano lid down on her fingers, screaming that the constant piano playing was annoying her. Emily ran to her room and nursed her aching fingers and wondered if she should tell her parents. She wondered to herself why Mrs. Perkins had such a dislike for her. She seemed to favor Charlotte, but why did she mistreat her? Charlotte was busy drawing a picture of the School of St. Anthony's and looked up when Emily entered their room crying. Emily related the tale of the cruelty by Mrs. Perkins to Charlotte. They tried to decide in their own way what to do. Emily was not convinced she should tell on her because their mother needed her help, but she didn't intend to be the object of Mrs. Perkin's anger either. Charlotte, being the peacemaker, suggested that they let the issue go one more time. If something happened again, they would need to tell the entire story to their mother and father. Emily was never one to keep a secret very long but she did promised to keep quiet for the moment. Of course, the line of action the girls took only gave Mrs. Perkins perceived permission to continue her harassment.

Mildred Perkins needed the job at the Whitfield's home and they needed her assistance. She was confident in her position and felt she could do as she pleased with the girls since she was enjoying some 7 years of service. However, she failed to recognize the ingenuity of Emily. Mrs. Perkins often did the laundry for Camilla early on Thursday mornings. She hurriedly completed her Thursday morning chore so she could get the ironing finished before leaving in the afternoon. Emily knew she normally paid a lot of attention to what she was doing and could not watch the busy little girl in the background. So, on a given Thursday, Emily went outside and into the flower garden and dug a pail full of fresh dirt. When she found Mrs. Perkins outside hanging laundry on the clothesline, she quickly scurried inside and dumped the pail of fresh dirt into the wash water turning it into a muddy mess. Mrs. Perkins returned to her chore of doing the next tub full of clothes and found the mess Emily had made. Mrs. Perkins knew in an instant where the blame lay for this deed. Emily stood in the kitchen doorway calmly watching to see if Mrs. Perkins would say anything to her as a reprimand. Not a word was spoken. It was obvious that Mrs. Perkins got the message conveyed by the muddy water. Needless to say, Mrs. Perkins emptied the water and started over with her laundry and never again wreaked her ill temper on Emily.

Charlotte continued to have a problem with strong odors. When her mother would cook cabbage the smell would permeate the entire house. Charlotte would hide in her room knowing if she came out into the kitchen she would be sick from the smell. Often when they were in the garden there would be odors that were offensive to her, and she would run inside to get away from the offense. Only Emily seemed to understand the frailty of Charlotte and there didn't seem to be an answer about what to do. No remedy proffered seemed to make much difference. It was just accepted that Charlotte did not handle strong odors well and the family respected this idiosyncrasy.

Guy's mother, Mamie Whitfield lived very near them in a small house of her own. She was getting on in years but the children loved to visit her. She had a small flower garden that she managed to tend on her own. When the girls came over, she would ask them to help her pull the weeds. She would tell them stories about when she was young. She could remember how the States were putting in a railroad across their own country from 1867-69. That same railroad would eventually expand into Canada. "Grammy" Mamie talked about the first time she had seen an "iron horse", as she called it. It seemed to belch smoke and sparks as it rumbled across the tracks going from one town to the next. She also told them about the 1890's when the women dressed in fine clothing and went to grand parties at the biggest hotels in Ottawa. She could remember the story about the great fire in Chicago in 1871 that was started when Mrs. O'Leary's cow kicked over a lantern. Mrs. O'Leary was milking the cow when it became startled and kicked over the milk bucket and the lantern. It set the barn on fire and the flames spread to everything around the farm. The fire raged out of control because the only method of fighting fires at that time was with horse drawn tanker wagons. It caused the biggest fire in history at the time as it burned nearly all of Chicago to the ground. She remembered reading about such a disaster in the local newspaper that came from Ottawa. Emily and Charlotte loved going to visit her and swinging in the porch swing while she told them endless stories. They called her Grammy because it had been too hard to say grandmother when they first learned to talk. They were her only grandchildren so she doted on them as well. She always seemed to have cookies and cold milk available for the girls when they came to visit. She lived near their school so they could stop by to see her after school when Camilla gave her permission for them to be late getting home from school. They would remember going to Grammy's house even after they were grown.

Chapter 6

Guy Whitfield had been a faithful employee at the Hershell Shoe Company for nearly ten years. His job was secure because he had become quite an asset to the company. While he did not have the title, he had been supervising a number of inexperienced workers and teaching them the trade. The factory had gained a contract to manufacture boots that soldiers were wearing in the war and the factory had hired a number of older men who had not had steady jobs for a while. The young men had all gone off to war and left the older men behind. Many of the plants were forced to close when the young soldiers left for war. Guy had been able to hire some of the older men who were previously without jobs. They proved to be excellent workers. First of all they were delighted to have a job and secondly they were mature enough to be conscientious about their work. Several of them had sons on the front lines so they had another interest to make the best boots they could make because they might go to their own sons. One afternoon as Guy was leaving the plant, the owner, Jake Hershell stopped him before he could get out the door. He called him into the office and asked him to become the manager of the plant. He offered him a considerable salary increase and an afternoon off per week. Guy was ecstatic. He could hardly believe his good fortune. He fairly walked on air all the way home and burst through the door with the good news for Camilla. This increase in salary meant she could go back to school and finish getting her teaching certificate. The girls were now 7 ½ years old and they could be of a lot of help in the household. Mrs. Perkins could come after school and stay until one of the parents returned home each day. Camilla would be able to develop a training schedule that corresponded with the school hours for the girls. It was such a wonderful bit of news, which was included in the blessing offered at dinner that evening. Guy remembered to thank God for his continued favor on the Whitfield family. Camilla could hardly wait to begin her studies again.

This also meant she would soon be able to have her beloved mother come and live with them. She would not have to be in the sanitarium any longer. It would be great for the twins to have both grandmothers become a part of their upbringing.

The following Monday morning Camilla went to the nearby Teacher Training College to see what she would have to do to enroll again. It had been eight long years since she had been in school. The Dean informed her that her previous studies were in order and she would only need to complete the few courses required for a teacher's certificate. These courses consisted of advanced mathematics and a class of history. She should be able to complete those in one year, he told her. What a boon, she thought. Before her girls were nine years old she would be a real teacher. If she could get a job at St. Anthony's Catholic School it would be good, but if not she would take a position in the public schools. Camilla returned home exuberant and relieved to know she could continue her studies without much expense and would soon have earned her certificate.

Before Camilla started back to school Father Paul came to the house one evening and told Guy that they had found his mother in her home. She had passed away in her sleep. Guy had not been to see his mother for several days, and he was overwhelmed with grief. He wanted to blame himself for his perceived inadequate care. Father Paul said she had died peacefully and had not suffered at all. Most of the neighbors reported that she had been in her yard picking up sticks the day before and appeared to be in good health. Guy felt guilty but tried to realize that she was 81 years old and had lived a full and prosperous life. He simply was having trouble accepting the inevitable, that she would not live forever. Emily and Charlotte also had a difficult time understanding that Grammy was gone. They had loved her so.

On the following day a funeral was held for Mrs. Mamie Whitfield. She was laid to rest in the St. Anthony's Church cemetery. She was buried beside her husband, Guy Sr. The twins had never been to a funeral and because they were very close to their Grammy, it was an experience that mystified them. They loved the beautiful music and the lovely interior of their church but it was very difficult to see their father weep. Emily tried to comfort him by holding onto his arm and Charlotte leaned into him and whispered how much she loved him. Guy tried to put up a good front. He knew that he would have to mourn his blessed mother on his own time. He owed his attention to the girls in helping them cope with the experience of losing someone they loved. He wasn't sure they really understood the process but he wanted to comfort them if they needed him. No mention was ever made of any relatives of Mamie that lived in the States even though she did have one sister still living.

Chapter 7

Monday morning came in the Fall of 1916 and Camilla marched off to school to complete her work for a teaching certificate. The girls had gone to school and Guy had gone to work. They all departed the house and left Lily in charge. Camilla was so excited to be able to go back to school. She knew she could work hard enough to finish her requirements in one year and then teach. The twins came in from school and were greeted by Mrs. Perkins. She had a nice piece of cake for them and a glass of cold milk. She no longer seemed to be at odds with Emily. Charlotte had remained her favorite, but Emily had managed to maintain peace with her ever since the muddy water incident.

They had many stories to tell about the days in school and she listened as patiently as she could while she was preparing an evening meal for Camilla and Guy. The girls scampered to their room and changed their clothes. Emily went to the piano and Charlotte found her drawing pad and scurried off to a sunny corner to get all the light she could before it began to fade into evening. She was drawing a picture of Grammy's house complete with the porch swing. She would draw a little bit and then her tears would roll onto the paper. She missed her Grammy so much.

When Camilla came in there were more stories to be told about her first day at school. The girls thought it funny that mother had school just like they did. Guy listened to her talk about all the things she had to do and finally he was able to tell about his day at the shoe factory. They had received a new order for 300 pair of combat boots to be sent to the war in Europe. He was happy for the business but sad to think the men would not be coming home very soon.

Mrs. Perkins cleaned up the kitchen and hung her apron by the door bidding them goodnight until the next evening. She was hardly noticed in her leave-taking because of the clamor of voices coming from the parlor. It was not a long walk home and she quietly left them to themselves. As she walked, she thought about how much she loved her job and the entire family. Sometimes she wondered what was in store for them in the future.

Chapter 8

Camilla had nearly completed her education by the spring of 1917. The girls were about to be nine years old soon and she hoped to have time to give them a party to celebrate. She had managed to get the Headmaster of the Public School in Peterborough to promise her a position with the school in the fall. She was trying to prepare for this new stage in her life. She had her family at home and she would also have a career helping other children to learn. Of course, in the back of her mind she carried the thought that she would soon be able to bring her mother home to live with them. Camilla thought that in being her caregiver, she could help to pull her out of this long-term depression. Hopefully, she would no longer need to be in a sanitarium. The fall of 1917 saw Camilla beginning her teaching career. She was able to get the position of teaching the youngest classes at the Peterborough Public School. Every day she was prepared to meet their shining faces having worked on her class plans most of the night before. The classes were full of energetic children anxious to learn what she had to tell them. It was a dream come true for her and she was expecting to put all her efforts into making the job a success.

Guy was so pleased to see her dream finally become a reality. He felt he had encouraged her to become what she wanted to be and the twins had given their blessings to her continued efforts by agreeing to take on more chores at home as they needed to in order to help their mother prepare for the next days' lessons. Evenings became a fun event as the entire family gathered around the big dining room table to work together in getting Camilla's lessons ready. Charlotte always wanted to illustrate the lesson plans as a way to boost Camilla's spirits during the day. She had become very good at drawing cartoons featuring animals.

The winter of 1917 was a particularly severe winter for those living in Peterborough, Ontario. Many of the businesses were forced to close on several different days because of so many absent workers. A deadly strain of influenza was rampant in the city and in the entire province. It seemed to know no distinction of persons. It ravaged families taking with it the parents and children leaving one or two children as orphans. The troops in the military service were also severely affected by this demon-malady. Fever, chills, and complete fatigue were the culprits that robbed whole families of their ability to survive. Many of the servicemen had been sent to the hospitals with symptoms so severe that there didn't seem to be any hope for recovery. Unfortunately, Guy was not excluded from this curse. He came home from work one evening with a very high temperature and chills. He immediately went to bed in hopes that it would not be transmitted to Camilla or the girls. Camilla called Dr. Hoover and he came by with a tonic he thought might help with the symptoms. Guy took the medicine and immediately fell asleep. Camilla stayed by his side sponging off his face hoping the fever would go away. By morning she, too, was experiencing the chills and fever. Mrs. Perkins came to help get the girls off to school. She was terrified that she would get the same illness, so she did nothing to help Guy or Camilla. She tidied up the kitchen and washed the girls clothes, but totally ignored the parents. For three days Guy and Camilla lay in their bed unable to sit up or get out of bed. Guy's fever was so high he was talking about all kinds of things that Camilla had never heard of, but she was too sick to care. Around midnight on the fourth day, Guy reached for Camilla in the bed and muttered through his deliriousness that he loved her. She grasped his hand and begged him not to die but to no avail. Guy died in his delirium on December 6, 1917. Camilla also took the tonic that the Dr. had given them. He came to the house every day hoping to see some change in Camilla. Unfortunately, the change didn't come and two days after Guy died, Camilla joined him, leaving the girls without parents.

Mrs. Perkins was suddenly left with two nine-year-old children to care for and no knowledge of where a family member might be found. She assured the Dr. and Father Paul that she would stay long enough for them to locate any family members who would take the girls. If no members could be found, the girls would have to go to an orphanage to live. She shuddered at the thought.

Chapter 9

Immediately, Father Paul began to do some inquiring into the background of The Whitfield family. Mr. Hershell only had a recollection of an aunt and uncle he had heard Guy mention one time. It seemed that they lived in the States somewhere like Pennsylvania or New York. He wasn't sure of a name but he thought there had been a relative of Guy's, possibly his mother's sister and her husband. Father Paul began to inquire of those who knew Mamie Whitfield to see if someone remembered her having mentioned any family living in the States. He then went to the postal authorities to see if they could remember mail coming for Mamie from somewhere other than Canada. Because of the difference in the postage, any mail from the States would be obvious. The postmaster remembered mail coming from Pennsylvania and he thought the city was something with a "ville" on the end. A lady from the aid society in St. Anthony's Church remembered that Mamie had occasionally mentioned her sister from Meadville. Now Father Paul seemed to have it all and he could begin his search. Emily quickly came to the rescue when she mentioned her Grammy talking about her sister called Margaret who lived in the States but she had never heard where. Father Paul had the parts, he only needed to put them together. He contacted the Catholic Church in Meadville with the information he had gleaned from all his sources to see if he could find a family connection that would be the only living relatives of the twins. The Priest in Meadville checked his roster of parishioners and found no one with the name of Margaret who had a sister in Ontario. He, too, began a search of all the persons around town whom he knew who might have known about a family with relatives living in Canada. One day as he was walking on his daily walk, he chanced to meet a lady from the Quaker sector of town. The thought occurred to him that she might know if such a family existed Father John questioned the lady regarding her possible knowledge of anyone named Margaret with a sister in Ontario. She replied that she knew one family named Margaret and Russell Garland who lived near her and attended the Society of Friends Church.

She then offered to take him to their home where he could talk with them directly.

As Father John went up to the door he noticed the home was very austere. It did not resemble the other well cared for homes in the neighborhood. He felt sure the husband was a miner but he couldn't be positive. He could see in the backyard a chicken pen and the evidence of what had been a well-kept garden. He knocked on the door and a middle-aged woman came to the door. She appeared to be a very busy housewife. He quickly stated that he was looking for a family with relatives in Canada. The lady of the house invited him in and led him to a room off the kitchen that appeared to be a parlor. He related the story of the family in Peterborough who had passed away and left two girls orphaned. Their names were Camilla and Guy Whitfield, and he wondered if she were any relation to this family. She immediately began to cry. Through her tears she related that her nephew did, in fact, live in Peterborough. She also knew her nephew, Guy, had twin girls. However, she had not yet received the news that the parents had been victims of the flu epidemic. Father John attempted to comfort her as he explained that the family had been victims and their passing had been quite sudden. He assured Mrs. Garland that he would get in touch with Father Paul and relate to him that he had found a missing family member. She rose as he departed and thanked him for his kindness but wondered in her heart what in the world would she do with twin girls to raise. Father Paul received the confirmation from Father John that the lost relatives had been found and he corresponded with the family of Garlands about the possibility of their taking the girls to avoid sending them to an orphanage.

Mr. & Mrs. Russell Garland replied that they would decide in the near future about whether or not they could take the girls. They needed to discuss the situation with their pastor at the church. Once the elders could have a meeting and pray for guidance, they would be able to make a decision on their position. Since the Garlands had no children of their own, the possibility of having two girls at one time sounded like a gift from God. It would be a wonderful blessing to be able to enjoy parenthood although their birth parents were both deceased. Russell could hardly sleep at night because he was so excited about the impending opportunity for fatherhood.

Russell Garland was 54 years old. He and Margaret had been married for sixteen years but had had only one child who died in infancy. Margaret had never completed the grieving process related to the loss of her one child. Russell was a family man and loved children. Though he never complained to Margaret about their inability to have more children, he secretly yearned for a family of his own. He loved to go to the park just to watch the children play. He was the oldest of four children himself so he was experienced in handling little ones. He missed the frivolity and gaiety of children around him. Margaret, on the other hand, was more subdued. She was the younger sister of Mamie Whitfield so she had no experience with young children. She ran a rather stern household and insisted that everything be in its proper place. When she thought about what two nine year olds would do to her house and routine, she had her doubts about the total picture. However, these were blood relatives and she must do what needed to be done at the time. If the elders of the church felt it was God's will, she and Russell would welcome the girls into their home and raise them as their own. Three days after the visit from Father John, the elders of the Society of Friends paid a visit to the Garland home. They initially asked to pray with them, then they announced that the church body felt it was in the best interest of the girls that the Garlands be made the guardians of the orphaned children as soon as possible. The elders were certain that life in an orphanage would not be beneficial to the girls. Margaret and Russell were ecstatic about the decision of the elders. They made arrangements immediately with Father Paul to send the girls on the train from Ottawa as soon as possible. Margaret and Russell hustled to make their room ready for the girl's arrival. They could hardly imagine how this newfound family would change their lives.

Margaret Garland was 53 years old and was the younger of two girls. Her older sister, Mamie, had raised her since her mother had passed away when she was only 10 years old. Margaret had never known a real mother. Her father never remarried, thus the only model she had for parenting was Mamie. She had been a stern taskmaster, insisting that Margaret do more than her share of the chores to be done. When Margaret was 12, her sister married and moved away leaving Margaret in the care of her father. He had always been a heavy drinker and had paid little attention to Margaret. On many nights he had come home too drunk to talk to her and would stagger to bed without saying a word. Some nights when he had come in, he was abusive to her. He would whip her or slap her for only small infractions of misbehavior. For most of her life, Margaret had always avoided contact with him. However, his behavior had left its mark on her.

Needless to say, she was never sure what a normal childhood was. She and her sister almost raised each other. When the opportunity to marry came to each of them, they jumped at the chance for a normal life. Of the two Margaret was the last to marry, but prior to her marriage, she had the opportunity to take a job as a domestic for a wealthy family. She took the job as a way of escaping the tyranny of her father. She had kept the house of the wealthy family up to the proper Victorian standards and met the demands of a socialite mistress of the house. While working for the family, her father literally drank himself to death. His body had been found in a gutter where he had fallen and was unable to get up to go inside. Margaret was never sure how she felt about such a travesty. She had loved her father in her own way, but somehow she felt perhaps it was better that he died than to live a tortured life.

After Margaret married she had become a busy and efficient housewife. She always kept an immaculate house. She ran her home as if it were a business. Everything had to have a place and she expected things to be put back in their place. When she met Russell he was a breath of fresh air in her life. Marriage had meant that she could leave the drudgery of keeping someone else's house and concentrate on her own home. She was not a patient woman and sometimes she got impatient with Russell. He, however, had a heart of gold and overlooked her abruptness. He never mentioned it if she was short with him. He simply dropped the subject and said no more. She had become a member of the Society of Friends and expected to stay with them until her death. Russell also was a Quaker. It had been easy when they married to agree to attend church, as their faith demanded. Her church had been the only stabilizing effect in her earlier life, and following her marriage they both worshipped together every opportunity they had.

Suddenly the impending arrival of the twins caused Russell and Margaret to have a serious discussion about how they would handle a very impacting situation. There never was any doubt about their Christian duty. What Margaret would do with two girls in her household on a daily basis remained to be seen. She had never been around young children, and she certainly was not experienced in handling nine year-olds. On the other hand, she felt she could use their help around the house. They were certainly old enough to help with the laundry, the cleaning, the gardening and tending to the chickens. Little did she know they had never had any training in such domestic skills, but Margaret and Russell both knew that honest work was a good teacher, too.

Chapter 10

Meadville was a medium sized town in the middle of Pennsylvania. It was a coal-mining town. All the businesses in the town catered to the coal industry. The business district was situated around a town square and the businesses were located as if they were gates around the town holding in the residents. On one side of the square were three saloons. They all did a booming business because almost all of the miners who worked deep down in the mines stopped in one of them each evening to get a liquid refreshment before going home to face the rigors of a poverty stricken lifestyle. Because the miners worked far below the surface digging and loading coal, when they came to the surface and stopped in the saloons, they presented a strange picture. Their faces were black with coal dust with only white lines around their mouth and eyes. They almost all wore metal hats on their heads that protected them from any falling rock. On the front of the hat was a small light that was used to light the way in an underground tunnel. The lights were called "carbide lights" after the substance used inside the light as a fuel. The men were sweaty and dirty so the atmosphere in any of the saloons was one of stale body odors, black dirty faces, and stale beer, and the faint odor of carbide on all their caps.

A hardware store located on the south side of the square functioned as the gossip mill for the town. The owner, a crotchety old cuss, named Hobart Hopkins, knew all the news for miles around. He could sell you a pick or shovel, or the seeds to plant in a garden in the spring. With the purchase he would also dispense his version of the latest happenings; who died, who gave birth, and who got married. There was no charge for his verbal account of the news. In many cases, he interspersed his own opinion with the news, making himself a "commentator extraordinaire" long before news commentators were ever heard about. He had kerosene lamps for lighting homes, and he even had a few of the "new-fangled" ALADDIN lamps in stock. These new lamps gave off a brighter, whiter glow than their counterparts since they had a white "mantle" that fit over the flame. The mantle was little more than ash, once the covering was burned away with the first lighting. However, the Aladdin lamps were very desirable if one could afford them. They also used kerosene as a fuel and the original cost was about $2.00 higher than an ordinary kerosene lamp. Once you had purchased your lamp, Hobart would sell you the kerosene to put in it. He also carried the mantles for the Aladdin lamps for five-cents apiece. If you owned an Aladdin lamp, it was wise not to let a child try to fill the lamp. If you touched the mantle, once the covering was burned off, it would leave a hole in it, and it was virtually useless for light. Many a child was reprimanded for wasting the five-cent mantle after he/she had tried to light the lamp but couldn't resist touching the interesting "mantle" only to see it crumble before their eyes.

Meadville also had a resident Doctor. His name was Dr. Dennison. He had been practicing medicine there for about 40 years. He had delivered every baby for miles around and the story was that he had not lost a one. However, that was rumor not fact. He had lost a few babies along the way, but through no fault of his own. In the early twentieth century most babies were born at home. Many times the facilities were not conducive to helping a struggling baby survive. If the baby was premature or sick at birth, it was almost a foregone conclusion that it would not live. However, Dr. Dennison mourned every one of them. He was a very compassionate man. Dr. Dennison had usually been the first one to arrive at the mine disasters that occurred in Meadville. Quite often there had been an explosion at the mine that would require a Doctor's presence. Sometimes when the coal dust would ignite, it would blow everything in front of the explosion to the surface. He would comfort the injured and treat the broken limbs as best he could. Many times it was his lot to comfort the survivors with just his presence and his bedside manner. He handed medicine to those he felt were in dire need of it, knowing full well that he might be too late with the hopeful cure. Everyone in the community loved him and it appeared that the love was returned.

In the back of the businesses on the east side of town was a livery stable. Ebert Hoskins ran the only blacksmith shop for miles around. He boarded horses for those who did not have a barn on their property or for persons just passing through town. He also shod most of the horses in town and kept wagons and carriages on hand for the use of the residents. He was a hard working man whose wife, Maude, helped him run the business. She could be seen riding the horses around town, which she insisted, was to give them exercise. Many of the town folks felt she wanted to be a cowgirl and this was as close as she would ever get. Maude had read about Annie Oakley and Wild Bill Hickok and their exhibit at the Columbia Exposition in Chicago in 1893. She had dreamed of attending the event, but money was much too hard to come by for her to use it to go to a sideshow in a faraway city. Maude had had to be content with the image of Annie Oakley in her mind regardless of that the other towns' folks thought. Aunt Margaret would not let Uncle Russell board their horse at the livery stable. She didn't like Maude because she didn't think she acted like a lady, so they erected a makeshift barn on the back of the yard and housed their horse there. She also complained about the fact that it cost $3.00 per month to board "old Roger" and that was too much money.

Meadville had a wonderful library that had been built with money donated by Andrew Carnegie in the early 1900's. Mr. Carnegie had become a very wealthy man in the steel industry. He wanted to share his wealth with as many people as he could so he began to develop libraries in Pennsylvania. Once the libraries were built, they were stocked with many books. Most libraries contained books from the classics as well as newspapers from larger towns around. A person could go to the library and read the New York newspapers. Even though they were mailed to the library and the news was a day old, it was still the only way many people could obtain any information of the outside world. In many cases, one day mattered not to most of those who went there to read. Most of the news was about the Great War and the immigrants who were flooding into Ellis Island.

Politics was not of much interest to folks around Meadville. Their political scene centered around the events at the mines.

The funeral home rounded out the business district. Henry McSwain was the undertaker. He carried an array of caskets on hand since the burial business in any coal-mining town seemed to be a thriving business. He had a fine carriage that he would use to carry your loved one to the cemetery. He owned a beautiful black stallion that he would hitch to the carriage, invite the grieving survivor to ride up front with him, and they all rode up the hill to the cemetery in a blaze of glory. In the back of his establishment he had a number of gravestones that he would sell you and even engrave them to your satisfaction. His wife, Mildred, would sew the grave clothes if the deceased had not owned a proper burial outfit. She could easily turn them out in one day, since she once commented that the deceased only needed the front. She was sure they weren't going to back into Heaven.

Most of the residents of Meadville worked for Pennsylvania Consolidated Coal Company. It was virtually the only business in the area. Since the coal industry employed most of the able bodied men in town, they also maintained a "company store". Almost any commodity could be purchased at the store on a "ticket". At the end of the week, prior to the miner's receiving his pay, the amount he had put on a ticket would be deducted from his pay. The "company store" carried everything from groceries, milk, butter, eggs, fuel for their lamps, feed for their horses and chickens, and almost anything else the miner's family might need. If a miner was not extremely careful, he would owe more at the store than he made for the week. Many of miners were not good managers with their income and would spend many years working for nothing. The coal companies were very ruthless. Their records were not accurate and many of the miners were simply cheated out of a just wage. It was a very depressing lifestyle for a hard-working man with a family to raise, and no hope of escaping to a different way of life. Uncle Russell occasionally ran a ticket at the Company Store, but Aunt Margaret would not allow him to charge anything on the ticket unless they were absolutely out of money. She simply could not conceive of Uncle Russell working for nothing.

Chapter 11

Father Paul visited Mrs. Perkins at the home of the girls. The funeral arrangements had been on hold until the disposition of the girls could be finalized. Now there was no doubt where the girls would go, so a simple memorial service was held at the St. Anthony's Church. Mrs. Perkins dressed the girls in their finest dresses and curled their beautiful long curls just like their mother had done every morning before they left for school. They donned the coats and bonnets anticipating a cold trip to the church. The memorial service was short but very moving as several people spoke of the loyalty of their father in his work and their mothers' determination to become a teacher. Emily and Charlotte held hands and fought hard to hold back the tears. Charlotte could not contain herself and Mrs. Perkins cradled her in her arms to ease her sobbing. Emily was determined to be strong. She would just have to cry later, she thought. It was a fiercely cold day in December as the hearse pulled away from the curb to travel up the hill to the cemetery. The hearse was a new Ford but it had difficulty negotiating the hill through the snow. When they finally arrived at the gravesite, suddenly Emily was also overcome in grief when she realized the finality of it all. She could not bear the thought of putting her mother and father in that hole. Father Paul and Mrs. Perkins tried every way possible to console the two grieving girls, but it was nearly impossible. Finally the Priest took them into his buggy and held them both in his arms tightly until they could control themselves. He would later remark that it was the hardest job he had ever had as a Priest.

The girls returned home with Mrs. Perkins. She made them some hot soup and offered to play a few games with them. If they could play, surely they would mend their spirits that way. The girls politely refused her efforts and quietly went to their room to be alone. Emily sat beside Charlotte in their window seat and talked with her about their next move. She wanted Charlotte to know that she would always be by her side. She assured her they were a pair and nothing could separate them. They talked to their mother as if she were present. They promised their daddy that they would stay together and remember their religious vows as long as they lived. They wanted their parents to know that they loved them and would always love them no matter what happened. Then, they promised that when they got to Aunt Margaret and Uncle Russell's house they would mind their manners and do as they were told. As the sun was going down on the horizon, they held each other and cried together, remembering all the things they had experienced with their "real" parents. They could not imagine what life would be like in Meadville.

Chapter 12

As the car carrying the twins approached the train station they saw the huge locomotive on the tracks. They could remember the stories Grammy Mamie told them about the "iron horse". They were completely mystified by such a big piece of machinery making such awful noises. Father Paul explained to them how it worked. The fireman on board shoveled coal into a huge furnace that made the train run. There would be a conductor on board to take their tickets and make sure that they connected with Aunt Margaret and Uncle Russell when they arrived in Meadville. Father Paul also talked about their crossing the border between the United States and Canada since they would be going from one country to another. It all sounded exciting to the twins. They could hardly wait.

When they went to the train station in Ottawa, Mrs. Perkins and Father Paul had accompanied them. They were taken in the horse drawn carriage that belonged to the priest. It had been a cold ride since they had left very early in the morning to meet the train that was scheduled to leave at 9:00 AM. As the carriage rumbled along over the hard ground, Emily continued to ponder what might be ahead for them. Since she had left her kitten, Lily, with Mrs. Perkins, she wondered if Aunt Margaret would let them have a kitten. She also wondered if they would have a room of their own. She did not mention her apprehensions to Charlotte because any unanswered questions always caused her to weep.

As the train pulled into the station in Meadville, Pennsylvania, the girls pulled their coats tightly around their necks and tied their scarves even tighter. Their bonnets sat on top of their long dark curls but served to keep their ears warm. They knew it would be cold because it was January, but part of their reaction was fear itself. The other passengers were trying to get off the train as quickly as possible. Most of them were carrying large bags as they lumbered down the aisles. Some of the women held their little children by the hand to guide them down the stairs from the train. Emily and Charlotte seemed very lost at that moment and could not understand what they were expected to do next. They carried only a small carpetbag with their belongings in it and there was a trunk full of their possessions in the baggage car. When they came down the steps from the train, their eyes glanced around the platform looking for an answer. Maybe someone would meet them inside the station. Besides, it would be warmer inside. They had no idea what their aunt and uncle would look like and no one had told them what to expect. Mrs. Perkins had put them on the train in Ottawa. They had been told that Uncle Russell would meet them when the train got to Meadville. They were prepared to go home with him since there was no one else to take them. The girls hardly knew what to expect from this transition. In their hearts they longed to be home in Peterborough but there was no one there for them. Two nine-year-old girls could hardly make decisions on their own. To ride a train on such a long journey seemed cruel, but there didn't seem to be an alternative plan for the situation. The only other alternative for them was to go to an orphanage in Ottawa if their Aunt and Uncle had not come forward and offered them a home. Naturally, they were so afraid and often fought hard to keep the tears from flowing.

When they gathered their bags from the train, they came down the steps to the station looking all around for Uncle Russell. They had no idea what he looked like, but surely he would look for them. Suddenly a very large man approached them and called them by name. As they looked up they saw a kind face with a sunny smile. Their fear quickly dissipated. He embraced each of them and assured them he would gladly take them to their new home. Meanwhile, Aunt Margaret stood on the sidelines looking stern and cold. She grabbed their hands and tugged at their coats mumbling something about their clothes looking too prissy for common folk. Emily pulled back somewhat and tried to hang onto Uncle Russell, but he had to let go of her hand in order to pick up her suitcase. Charlotte reached for Aunt Margaret's hand and docilely walked with her through the stationhouse. Many thoughts were running through Emily's head. She wondered just what this was all going to mean to her and Charlotte. It certainly wasn't what she expected. Oh, if only she could have her daddy back. He was so kind and gentle. Would Uncle Russell be like him?

They were loaded into the horse drawn carriage and the bags were put in the back. As they rode through the city streets, they noticed the streetlights flickering in the night. The streets were narrow and dark. Not many people were out at this time of night. It seemed the businesses were closed for the night and some were shuttered to keep out the cold air. As they rode toward home, the girls could not help but notice how much different Meadville was from Peterborough. In their hometown, it was always bustling with people coming and going. Meadville seemed to already be asleep for the night. Maybe tomorrow would be different.

Aunt Margaret and Uncle Russell had a small home in Meadville. They lived near the library and the park. Emily and Charlotte envisioned being able to play in the park on winter days. Maybe it would also have a lake where they could ice skate. They had learned to skate on the lake in Peterborough and they had remembered to bring their skates with them. If the library was like the one at home, they might be able to go there and read the books that they loved so much. Their father and mother had taken them to Mass every Sunday, and they loved their church. It was a beautiful church with lots of pretty colored windows. Father Paul chanted the mass in Latin, also the music was so good, and they loved the ceremony of attending church. Surely Aunt Margaret and Uncle Russell would take them to church.

Morning came all too soon for the twins. They had slept together in a big bed in an upstairs room. It seemed so empty and so far away. Aunt Margaret had taken them up with their bags the night before, telling them they would discuss some things when morning came. Charlotte cried most of the night. She couldn't understand just what was happening to her. Emily tried to comfort her but was somewhat mystified herself. Their new home was not what she had expected. When daylight came, the twins got up, put on their clothes and went downstairs. Aunt Margaret was fixing breakfast for them. Uncle Russell was nowhere to be found. Finally, Emily asked where he was only to be told he had gone to work a long time ago. Breakfast, consisting of a scrambled egg and a piece of toast, was put before them. Emily asked for a glass of milk, but Aunt Margaret replied that the milk was for dinner. The girls were bewildered, but ate in silence. As soon as they had finished with their breakfast, it was time to do their chores. First they had to clean up the kitchen from breakfast. Then, Aunt Margaret called them to come to their room. She considered the room a mess. They would be expected to clean their room before lunch. They were to put their clothes in the wardrobe and their undies were to be put in the bureau drawers. Shoes of which they seemed to have many pairs, according to Aunt Margaret, would be put neatly under their bed. Following lunch, they would again have to help clean the kitchen. Then, they would take a bath and wash their hair. Aunt Margaret did not like their hair. Camilla had taken such pride in the girls' long curls. Their hair was dark and hung beautifully in curls down their back. Their mother had curled it every day and had dressed them in their nice dresses each morning. Aunt Margaret had cast a disparaging look at their clothes. She was not impressed by what she called their "finery". She would have to make them some common clothes, she exclaimed. No one in her family had ever had such a vast wardrobe of unsuitable clothes for work, she said. She considered it too much of a chore to comb and curl their hair. And they might as well know that they would no longer be the objects of everyone's attention. After all, the Garland family was a working family. Aunt Margaret did not look upon a schoolteacher as a working occupation. Each time Aunt Margaret demeaned their mother the girls would nearly be in tears. Their mother had been a saint in their eyes, and they could hardly handle anyone criticizing her.

Emily and Charlotte cringed at the chain of events that Aunt Margaret laid before them. Never in their life had they taken a bath in the middle of the day. However, Aunt Margaret left little chance for a discussion. It appeared that the girls were expected to do as she said without a word of dissent.

Early in the morning on the second day they were in Meadville, Aunt Margaret took the girls to the nearby school. It was a rather small building, built on a high foundation and, much to the surprise of the twins there were many other children in the school. They had not seen children in their neighborhood so they were delighted to know there were other children in Meadville. Emily spied a piano in the back of the room and asked the teacher, Mr. Gray, if she would be allowed to play it? Aunt Margaret admonished her for talking to the teacher, but before she could say any more, the teacher took her to the piano and asked her to play her favorite piece. She quickly sat down and played a piece from Chopin so beautifully that even Aunt Margaret was impressed. The teacher and the students clapped their hands in admiration.

Mr. Gray assured her she could play for class each day as they had time for music. Emily immediately liked Mr. Gray. Charlotte stood by the edge of the teacher's desk and said nothing. Mr. Gray noted her reticence and questioned her about playing the piano, too. Emily quickly spoke for her saying that she was an artist. Charlotte grinned and Mr. Gray informed her she would have lots of chances to draw in his school. Of course, he recognized that Charlotte was a very shy child. He knew nothing of the reason why they were in Meadville, but he was soon to find out.

On their first full day of school in the Meadville School No.3, the twins arose very early and dressed. When they had finished breakfast and cleaned the kitchen, they waited by their bedroom door for Aunt Margaret to curl their hair. She took one look at it and said it would be braided for today. She was not going to curl hair every morning. The girls had never had braids, but on that day they did. It seemed so strange to them. They couldn't keep their hands from feeling them. Aunt Margaret had placed a big bow on the end of the braid so it really didn't look bad. It just looked funny to the girls. As they scampered off to school, they laughed at each other.

After school they hurried home to see if Aunt Margaret would let them go to the park and play. There were swings at the park and many girls and boys their age seemed to be playing there. Aunt Margaret met the girls at the back door and told them it was bath time. The trip to the park was quickly put aside for later. Emily and Charlotte each took turns taking a bath and washing their hair. When they came out of the bathroom, Aunt Margaret was standing in the doorway with the biggest pair of scissors they had ever seen. She stood them by the wastebasket, put a cereal bowl on their heads and cut off the long curls. Both girls were mortified. It was cruelty beyond their wildest dreams. Their hair had been their crowning glory. How could she do this to them? They ran to their room to hide. They hated this "bowl cut". Both girls stayed in their rooms crying over their loss until Uncle Russell came home. He came to their room to see if he could console them. They were near hysterics over the loss of their beautiful hair. He held them close to him and let them cry it out. He then tried to explain that Aunt Margaret didn't know how to curl their hair as their mother had done. He promised them a trip to town on Friday where he would buy them some candy at the shop where they made lots of good things to eat. He hugged them and asked about school. Both girls rattled on and on about their first day at school. He, then, asked Charlotte to draw something for him on the paper he had brought her. She quickly drew a picture of Lily and explained to him that she had been their pet kitten when they lived in Peterborough. He was impressed with her work and quietly assured them both that he might see if they could have a kitten in Meadville.

The girls had always been very happy at St. Anthony's Catholic Church. When they came to Meadville they had asked about church. They remembered the beautiful stained glass windows and the lovely music that was so much a part of their worship. Aunt Margaret and Uncle Russell attended the Society of Friends Church, which was of the Quaker faith. They took the girls to church with them, and it obviously was not the same. The church was very austere and plain. There were no stained glass windows and no musical instruments. The pews were hard and straight. The only music was the singing of the congregation. Because Emily played such beautiful music, she mentioned to Aunt Margaret that she would play for the people in church if they wanted her to, only to be admonished about such sinful ideas. The messages were given in English, unlike the ones in their home church that had been in Latin. At least they could understand what the preacher was saying. One day when the preacher came to visit at the house when the twins were home, he talked with them about their beliefs in God. They quickly told him about their catechism classes and their confirmation before starting school. This ritual didn't impress the preacher one bit. He reminded them that they would need salvation before they could get into heaven. Emily wondered about such a conversation, and it quickly brought on the tears in Charlotte. As soon as the preacher had gone from the house, Emily asked Aunt Margaret about what salvation meant, only to be told she was too young to understand. The question simply remained unanswered.

Chapter 13

Uncle Russell had always been a coal miner. He worked for the Pennsylvania Consolidated Coal Company. They mined "hard" coal from deep shafts and sold it to the steel mills in and around Pittsburgh. It was a dangerous job, and he worked long hours. The miners would go into deep shafts sometimes as deep as 3000 feet under the ground. A crew of workers had already dug the pits in order to get to the coal seam. The dirt above the seam had to be removed before the coal could be exposed. There were steam driven lifts that would lower the miners to the bottom of the pits. When the coal was ready to be brought to the surface, the lifts would bring up the coal. The men would enter the pits and follow the coal seam, removing the coal and loading it on cars. More dirt covering the coal seams had to be removed before the miners could continue to dig the coal. Sometimes the tunnels that were dug were not very high. If there was enough headroom, they would lower mules into the shaft and use them to pull the coal cars along rail tracks that had been laid. If the tunnels were too small the men would have to crawl on their bellies to continue the removal of the coal, loading it onto the rail cars for its trip to the surface. The tunnels often contained methane gas that was highly explosive and could be ignited by a spark from the wheels on the rail tracks. In order to test for the presence of methane, they would release canaries into the mine tunnel. If the canaries died, the miners knew it was not safe for them to go into the area. The steam-powered fans would be lowered to attempt to remove the gas from the area. Many times, in spite of all the efforts of the mining companies, the miners were forced to proceed into dangerous territory with only their faith to sustain them. Even though the dangers were imminent many generations of miners had continued to go into the shafts and mine the coal for the steel industry on a daily basis. Mostly, there were not many other opportunities for work in the Meadville area.

Once when Uncle Russell had been working at a nearby mine, a large explosion occurred. He had been ready to be lowered into a very deep shaft at that mine to start his workday when the methane gas exploded. It blew the entire opening, equipment, and 34 miners to the surface. Many of his friends that he had worked with for several years were blown to bits right before his eyes. It affected him, emotionally, for a long time; however, he felt he was not capable of finding another job to support Margaret and himself. He had been at the mine for 22 years and as far as he could figure, he would be there until the day he died. He had no way of knowing that a man named John L. Lewis would make some changes in the mining industry in the foreseeable future.

In the evenings when Uncle Russell would come home to eat, he looked so funny that the girls would laugh at him. He wore a funny looking hat that had a little light on the front. He told them it was a "carbide" lamp that was named for the fuel used in the lamp. He used it in order to see inside the tunnels as he proceeded deeper and deeper into the mineshaft. His face would be black all over with just a little white line around his mouth and his eyes. His clothes were always black with coal dirt, and his hands were rough and sometimes bleeding from handling a pick and shovel all day. Aunt Margaret met him at the door and asked him to change his clothes on the porch before coming into the house. She didn't want all that black dirt inside the house. The girls were sent to their room while he removed his clothes lest they should see him in his underwear.

Dinnertime at the Garland house was a busy time for everyone. Russell had stories to tell about the mine, and the girls rattled on and on about their experiences at school. Aunt Margaret surely felt left out of all the discussions since her day consisted of doing the household chores and cooking for her growing brood. Cooking was her specialty. Everyday she made homemade bread, which the girls found irresistible especially when she put some fresh jelly on it. Charlotte continued to have an aversion to strong smells and Aunt Margaret seemed to love to torment her with this frailty. She quite often cooked cabbage or turnips and the odor of them sent Charlotte into a fit of nausea. She would try to run outdoors for fresh air or to her room when she could get away. However, if Aunt Margaret caught her trying to escape, she forced her to come back into the room and suffer. Charlotte could hardly handle this dilemma and even though Aunt Margaret might have felt she would get accustomed to the smell, it amounted to a form of abuse for such a frail child.

Aunt Margaret also had a garden in the back of the house. She raised all sorts of vegetables that were used to feed the family. In the early spring she would plant the vegetables in her garden. The girls seemed to think it was fun to drop the seeds in the furrows or set out the plants in the soft dirt. When the seeds began to sprout and as they began to grow, they would need to have the dirt loosened around the root system so they could absorb the spring rains and grow larger. This process was called hoeing. Aunt Margaret expected Emily and Charlotte to take part in this exercise. It was hot and hard work for two girls who had never experienced any kind of physical labor. It was not long until they had developed blisters on their hands from holding the rakes and hoes. Aunt Margaret treated the blisters with an ointment, then insisted they wear gloves until calluses began to form. Emily and Charlotte hardly understood what was happening to them, but they were being transitioned into working class girls.

There was also a pen for chickens in the yard. Uncle Russell periodically brought home a crate of baby chickens that had to be fed each morning and each evening. This was another chore that was relegated to the girls. They loved the baby chickens and considered them their pets. They talked to them every day as they were feeding them. When they were forced to clean the little house where they were kept, their love for these critters began to fade. It was a disgusting and dirty job. Suddenly Emily began to wonder who did all this dirty work before they came to Meadville. She knew that there was no need to question Aunt Margaret about such activities. Her standard answer would always be for the girls to stop complaining about hard work. She added: "after all, you could be in an orphanage".

The girls' wardrobe of clothing that was brought from Peterborough had always seemed unsuitable to Aunt Margaret. She called it "finery", not suitable for working girls. She used the sacks that the chicken feed came in to make the girls replacement clothing. The sacks were printed with flowers and patterns of geometric design. She would wash them, iron them, and then sew them into pinafores or straight dresses for the girls. They really were nice little dresses, but a far cry from the embellished dresses they had worn in Peterborough.

Aunt Margaret continued to bake cakes and pies so that there were lots of sweets to put into Uncle Russell's lunch bucket. The twins thought his lunch bucket was strange since it said "Landry's Lard" on the outside of it. Aunt Margaret explained to the girls that nothing was ever thrown away and using the old lard bucket was a way of saving money. She was trying to change their way of thinking about the world around them. Since they had come from a more affluent background, it was a real awakening for them to be plunged into a more frugal family.

By 1920, the girls were eleven years old and had acclimated themselves into the Meadville lifestyle. They had learned the value of hard work as prescribed by Aunt Margaret. She continued to be harsh with them and continually made snide remarks about their parents. Even though Guy had been her nephew, she had a great deal of disdain for him. Eventually she would admit that she had only seen him twice in his lifetime: once when he was a tiny baby and once when he and Grammy Mamie came to visit Margaret on his 12th birthday. She hardly knew him, but seemed to have this hidden dislike for him. Even though their parents had been gone three years, the girls continued to talk about them almost daily, but their conversations were limited to the times they spent together, privately since Aunt Margaret would not allow them to talk about their past with her. She felt the girls had not had a proper "raising" since they had never learned to do hard work. She constantly berated Charlotte for what she considered a "big waste of time" when she saw her sitting in the window drawing on anything she could find. Charlotte was admittedly moody and spent a lot of time just staring into space. Sometimes when Aunt Margaret would scold her she would burst into tears and flee to her room. This reaction to a reprimand was more than Margaret could bear and she repeatedly spanked Charlotte for what appeared to Emily, to be nothing. Emily had a stronger constitution. She would take any admonishment meted out by Aunt Margaret in her stride and try to do better. If the punishment was deserved, she accepted it. If she felt it was not a valid misdeed, she would simply listen quietly and then go on her merry way. And, if Charlotte were unnecessarily punished, Emily would hold her in her arms and comfort her trying to make amends for Aunt Margaret's cruelty. However, the abuse never abated. It continued on a daily basis. Charlotte seemed to be the object of Aunt Margaret's anger from the moment that she awakened until Uncle Russell came home. Strangely enough she never picked on either of the girls when he was present. He never knew about the verbal and physical abuse. Uncle Russell loved the girls and spent as much time with them as possible. Naturally, Margaret seemed to always have work for him to do when he was not at the mine. So his time with the girls consisted of only a few hours each week. Occasionally he would read to them in the evening after dinner before bedtime. If Aunt Margaret felt slighted, she would complain that he was burning up the oil in the lamps and would send the girls to bed.

Aunt Margaret eventually managed to convince Uncle Russell that Charlotte was becoming a problem. No one was ever privy to those discussions. Either she had fabricated certain stories about Charlotte or Uncle Russell was an easy mark to convince. Before long Emily noticed that Aunt Margaret began making more dresses for Charlotte than for her. She also noticed that she had made her new underwear and had also knitted extra stockings. All of this extra effort was a mystery to Emily. Little did she dream what the next step might be.

One day, after the girls came in from school Emily noticed a carpetbag resting by the door. Before she could ask any questions, a large black car pulled up in front of the house, and a matronly woman came up the walk. She had papers in her hand and Aunt Margaret hustled to the door. She inquired if this were the Garland home and was there an eleven-year-old child in the house by the name of Charlotte Whitfield. When Aunt Margaret replied in the affirmative, the woman promptly took charge of Charlotte holding her by the hand, gathered up the carpetbag and swiftly walked back to the awaiting car. Emily never saw Charlotte again.

Emily was devastated. Where had they taken Charlotte? When would she be back? She ran to Aunt Margaret for the answers to her questions, but Aunt Margaret simply said Charlotte had to go away. Emily cried herself to sleep. She refused to eat dinner with the family. She went to school with little or no breakfast, and when she asked the teacher at school what had happened to Charlotte, he simply replied that Aunt Margaret would have to tell her. When Uncle Russell came home that evening Emily met him at the door asking the same questions that she had been asking all day. He only shrugged his shoulders and mumbled that she need not worry, she would be taken care of. Nevertheless, Emily needed answers. Where was her family? First her mother and father were taken and now Charlotte. Would she be next? She worried about going to sleep for fear she would not awaken. She didn't even want to leave home, afraid that she would never return. She was terrified of Aunt Margaret. She believed that if she were to incur her aunt's wrath, she, too, might receive an unwelcome ride in a black limousine. So many questions, so few answers.

Chapter 14

After the supposed abduction of Charlotte, Emily became the apple of Aunt Margaret's eye. She lavished more attention on her than the girl could ever have expected. Aunt Margaret baked cookies for her and cooked her favorite meals. Emily was now allowed to go to the park to play without any fuss. Aunt Margaret appeared to be a changed woman. Uncle Russell continued to give Emily all the attention that he could muster. He spent evenings reading with her or telling her stories about World War I. One evening, on his way home from work he found a stray kitten. He picked it up, placing it in his coat pocket and presented it to Emily as he came through the door. It was snow white with black paws. She thought it looked like Lily after she had walked in black paint. She named her Snowball. Aunt Margaret even let the kitten sleep in the bed with Emily, which pleased her very much.

Although Emily continued to miss Charlotte, she had ceased asking about her on a daily basis. Snowball had become the object of her affection. In the early spring of 1921, Aunt Margaret went to Emily's school to ask about the music that was available to the children. The teacher told her that Emily had been playing the piano for everyone almost every day. Emily was very talented. Aunt Margaret asked if anyone knew where she could get a piano for their parlor? The teacher responded by telling her of an elderly lady who had a piano but no longer was physically able to play it. Perhaps she would sell it to the Garland family. Aunt Margaret promptly went to the woman's home to inquire about the possibility of buying the piano.

The very next afternoon Aunt Margaret and Emily stopped by the Thompson home. Mrs. Thompson was, indeed, too infirm to play anymore but wanted to hear Emily play. Emily stepped up to the piano and played some of her very best pieces of music for her. Mrs. Thompson cried tears of joy. She, then, shared her story with them about how she had purchased the piano for her daughter back in 1902. That talented prodigy daughter at 4 years old, had been able to play music. Tragically, in 1910, while she had been riding a horse, it became frightened by a passing horse-less carriage. She had been thrown and her neck was broken. She died in her mother's arms. Thus the piano had stood silent for all those years. Mrs. Thompson was more than glad to give the piano to Emily in memory of her daughter. Emily jumped from her chair and ran to Mrs. Thompson's side and hugged her. She wanted to blurt out all the heartache she had endured in her short life, but Aunt Margaret was admonishing her for being so bold. Mrs. Thompson invited Emily to visit her any time that she wanted and her visit didn't conflict with chores to be done at home. On many occasions thereafter Emily would hurry through her chores and run over to Mrs. Thompson's house to visit with her. They became good friends just like Grammy Mamie had been to the twins. Emily shared her story with Mrs. Thompson about her parents and the mystery of Charlotte. Mrs. Thompson held her in her arms and assured her that Charlotte was taken care of and that someday she would find her again, all the while wondering how anyone could be so cruel as to give away a child.

Chapter 15

Emily continued attending Meadville Public School #3 through the eighth grade. She was now going to move on to High School. It would be in a different building, and it was called an "Academy". She wasn't the least bit apprehensive about attending since she had excelled at the elementary school. She had continued to play the piano at school. Mrs. Thompson was delighted that she could give to Emily the piano that had once belonged to her daughter; however, they had not yet moved it to the parlor at Emily's house. Emily continued to stop by Mrs. Thompson's house and play for her almost daily. Emily was sure that going to the Academy would mean an opportunity for her to explore more and different types of music. She often wondered what had happened to Charlotte. Maybe she would be at the Academy, too.

When school opened in the fall Charlotte was not to be found. Nevertheless, as Emily was growing into a teenager Uncle Russell had become more and more attached to her. He told her often how much she had enriched his life. He took her to the library when he could and to the Vaudeville Show when it came to Pittsburgh. It was not the kind of show he particularly enjoyed, but he wanted Emily to be exposed to public presentations of music and drama. He lavished gifts on her when he could afford them. As a coal miner, his wages were not very high, but he was happy, even fortunate to have a job. He could not have loved her anymore if she had been his own flesh and blood. Aunt Margaret had also softened considerably since Charlotte had been taken away, but she sometimes appeared to be jealous of Emily and Uncle Russell. She complained bitterly if he spent too much time with Emily. Whenever possible she would always find a way to thwart his plans if she had enough advance notice of what they were.

The pastor of the church came to visit the family often. He was interested to see if they were in need of any assistance from the church. Emily wanted to run to him and tell him that sometimes Aunt Margaret was cruel to her and her kitten, but there never seemed to be a moment when she was left alone with the pastor. Aunt Margaret usually would tell her to go to her room. Children were to be seen and not heard, she often said. Emily wanted to ask the pastor about Charlotte, but there was never an opportunity. One night after every one had supposedly gone to bed, Emily heard Aunt Margaret and Uncle Russell arguing. She crawled close enough to the wall to hear what the discussion was about. Aunt Margaret was talking about money, that there was never enough to support all of them. Uncle Russell raised his voice and insisted that she be a better manager. He was certain she was spending money foolishly. Emily began to feel guilty thinking that the reason there was no money might be her fault. Suddenly their voices became louder and louder. She heard Aunt Margaret screaming at Uncle Russell that he simply spent too much money on Emily and not enough on her. She accused him of spending more time with Emily than he did with her. Her parting words were that she could get rid of Emily just like she did Charlotte, if he didn't change his ways. Emily wanted to hear no more. She slid down the wall and fell into a heap in the floor. How evil she felt Aunt Margaret was. She couldn't believe her ears. Now she was convinced that Aunt Margaret had something to do with the disappearance of Charlotte. She also felt that Aunt Margaret knew where Charlotte was, but how could she find out? She crawled into her bed and cried herself to sleep. Would she ever see Charlotte again?

Chapter 16

Emily was growing up. She would soon be 14 years old. She was developing and maturing. The morning that she had awakened and found her bed soaked with blood frightened her beyond words. She quickly ran to find Aunt Margaret feeling that she would soon die from some unknown ailment. Aunt Margaret calmed her down and explained that she was now a woman and that she could expect this event to happen every month. She showed her how to take rags and fold them for a pad to wear in her drawers. She was told that the "period" would last about 5 days. Each morning she would have to scrub her "pads" with soap and let them dry, to be used again. Emily was mystified, but listened carefully. A few weeks later she noticed that she was developing breasts. She looked at herself in the mirror and winced at her bobbed haircut. She was now a full-grown woman and she wanted a woman's haircut. However, she didn't know how to do her hair. She pondered who could help her fix her hair in a different style.

Emily stopped by the library to look at pictures in magazines and rotogravures that were there. She saw styles with waves and curls. She wondered just how she could do all that. When Emily asked Aunt Margaret for some help in doing her hair, she was shocked when her Aunt took a comb and some water and made waves in her hair. Emily liked the look and asked for some gel that she had seen advertised in the magazines that cost ten cents. It promised to make the waves stay in your hair for a week. Aunt Margaret gave her the money and she ran to the corner department store to buy some "wave-jel" that she had seen advertised. From then on, Emily practiced, daily, making the waves just like she had seen in the magazines.

During this crucial time of development, Emily was becoming conscious of the people around her. She also began to notice the boys in her school. She wondered if they liked her hair. She wondered if they knew about the "periods" that she would be experiencing. During her "periods", Emily noticed a foul smell associated with "the event". She was concerned that someone else could smell it, so she constantly used rose water that Aunt Margaret had given her to bathe her body, hoping it would disguise the odor. She noticed her clothes did not look as stylish as the other girls did and she wondered if she might be able to make different clothes.

Emily repeatedly went back to the library for more information about fashions. She perused magazines for hours getting ideas. When she asked Aunt Margaret for some fabric to make new clothes, she met with a big argument. Aunt Margaret accused her of being vain and self-centered. Emily only wanted to look like a woman and not a little girl. In desperation, she went to see Mrs. Thompson. She asked her how she could buy fabric for new clothes. Mrs. Thompson offered her clothes that she had not worn in many years. She told Emily to take the clothes, if she could use the fabric in them to make something new. Emily was so excited she could hardly catch her breath. She hurried home, finished her chores as quickly as possible, and headed for the pantry and the old sewing machine. She would have stayed up very late sewing, but Aunt Margaret said she was burning too much oil, so Emily went to bed with new clothes ideas swimming around in her head. She got up at daylight and started sewing again. She made dresses, jumpers, coats, hats, and purses over the course of a few weeks. She loved her new wardrobe and she knew that, among her other accomplishments, she had decided that she could do almost anything by putting her mind to it. She continued to wonder about Charlotte. Did she have pretty clothes? Did she have friends at school? Many, many times she silently wished to talk with Charlotte about lots of things that girls talk about to each other.

School activities at the Academy were exciting. She found that learning, in most classes came easily. She also found the students to be a lot different than the ones in the elementary school. The girls seemed to have a lot of friends and gathered together in groups of two or three. She had never had a lot of friends and she assumed that it was because she had to hurry home each day to get the work done that Aunt Margaret had assigned to her. She had never had the opportunity to go to the library with the girls or even stop at the park. Most afternoons she had had to go straight home after school. Emily also noticed that the boys in the Academy were paying attention to the girls. When there was a break in their studies, Emily was usually surrounded by boys. She could laugh with them and enjoy their company. Because she had been reading since she was quite small, she understood the topics they talked about. She was aware of current events and had some interest in the political scene. The boys seemed aware that she was also interested in music. This piqued their interest and they questioned her about her musical ability. Because she could excel in music, she continued to practice the piano and listened to the music that they offered in the school. Even though there was a band at the school, it only had brass instruments in it, so she had no opportunity to play the piano as part of the band. The Academy always had plays in the spring, and Emily was asked to play the background music for the drama department.

In 1926, Emily was nearly eighteen years old. She was ready to graduate from the Academy. She wanted to go on to college and study music, but she wasn't sure just how she could accomplish that. One of the teachers at the school talked with her about maybe getting some financial assistance from the college where she might attend. However, attending college had not been approved at home as a future option for Emily. Aunt Margaret was adamant about not spending any money for more schooling. She had expressed to Emily many times her belief that Emily needed to stop all that foolishness about music and find a husband. Aunt Margaret felt that she needed to settle down and get married. Music would certainly never make her any money.

Since Emily knew she would not be able to go to college short of a miracle, she reconciled herself to waiting. Besides she had also found a friend in the Academy that she felt was interested in her. She had discussed her new found friend with Uncle Russell, and he seemed pleased that she had found someone to take care of her.

Her new friend had walked her home from school on several occasions, but she never invited him in. His name was Eustis Carmichael. He was living in Meadville with his parents. He had several brothers and sisters so life at his house was crowded. He and his family attended the Catholic parish in Meadville, the same parish where Father John was still the priest. Eustis was a shy young man. He was the oldest of six children born to the Carmichael family. His father had always been a coal miner, too. He had worked in the mine all his life and had no intention of ever leaving, even though it was dirty and dangerous work. Eustis had worked around Meadville for various farmers and businessmen since he was 10 years old. He could do the work of a man by the time he was 12. He had driven a team of mules that plowed farm fields nearby, walking behind the mules from sun-up to sundown. He was also learning to be a carpenter and helped to put up many barns for local farmers. He had helped put on a roof for several people when the temperature outside was nearly 100 degrees but feeling about 10 degrees hotter on the roof. One summer he had worked breaking in horses for a farmer in a nearby town until he suffered a broken leg. When he was unable to work for the rest of that summer, the family really missed his extra money. Normally, he had paid all of his wages to his mother to help raise the little ones. He was a sensitive young man. He was very considerate of others, especially of Emily. He would look for a secluded corner at school where they could talk to each other privately. He loved his family and frequently commented about how he felt sorry for his mother because she had to work so hard to raise all the children. He was a good Catholic. He attended mass each week and sometimes even spoke to some of the confirmation classes at the Church. His grades in school were very good even though he spent many hours working and had little time to study. He had always worked evenings after school and had still managed to keep his studies well above average. He had taken a liking to Emily Whitfield because he saw that she was very bright. He certainly loved her musical ability and he knew she would also excel in whatever else she did. The two of them had talked a lot during breaks at school. Occasionally Eustis would walk her to the park on their way home from the Academy. Of course, she had shared her story of how she came to live in Meadville. He was very interested in hearing her tell about her life in Peterborough. She had never had the courage to mention Charlotte to him. It was still too painful for her to talk about even to Eustis although it had been six years since she had been taken away.

By 1926-27 work at the mine had changed in its pattern. They were digging deeper into other tunnels, and it was long hard work. Uncle Russell would be completely worn out when he came home in the evening. Emily still found humor in the face of Uncle Russell with the white line around his mouth and eyes. And, of course, he was still wearing the funny little light on his hat. It seemed that he had less energy than before. Now he also had a hacking cough when he walked with Emily. She wanted to spend as much time with Uncle Russell as possible because she loved talking with him about many things. She tried not to antagonize Aunt Margaret because she feared she could endure the same fate that Charlotte did.

One evening after Uncle Russell came home from work and as they were eating supper, she asked if she might bring her friend to the house on the following Sunday for dinner. She wanted them to meet him. Both of them agreed that it would be a good idea; however, Emily would have to help with the preparations.

On the prescribed Sunday at noon, shortly after church, Eustis Carmichael came to call on Emily. She introduced him to Aunt Margaret and Uncle Russell. As they had gathered around the table to eat, Eustis complimented them on their fine home and the lovely meal before them. The compliment impressed Aunt Margaret. As they bowed their heads to say "Grace", Eustis made the sign of the cross on himself as was the custom in his family. The act of crossing himself did not go unnoticed by Aunt Margaret. The conversation around the table centered on what was happening in the community. Uncle Russell discussed the coal industry and asked Eustis what his plans for the future were. He replied that he wasn't sure, but that he had always worked. He did not rule out working in the mines. He also explained that he might need to continue assisting his family with some finances since there were several mouths to feed. The men adjourned to the parlor and the women quickly cleaned up the table. Emily could hardly wait to get Aunt Margaret's opinion about Eustis and she was delighted when she approved. Naturally, she expressed displeasure about his religious affiliation with the Catholic Church. Emily reminded her that she had been born and raised a Catholic before coming to Meadville. That statement did not meet with Aunt Margaret's approval as she calmly snorted that all the Catholics were bound for hell. Emily shuddered and wondered if she would ever learn what to say so as not to arouse her ire. She often longed for someone to share her thoughts with about any number of subjects. In fact she was a very lonely girl living in a crowded world. It seemed each time she tried to talk to Aunt Margaret, she would criticize Emily for whatever was being discussed. She was sure that she could never please her no matter what she said or did. She also knew that if Charlotte were here, she could talk to her about everything and there would be no criticism of her at all.

Emily and Eustis graduated from the Academy that spring of 1926. Shortly after graduating, Emily announced that she and Eustis were planning on a wedding in the Fall. She wanted to have the wedding in the Catholic Church but Aunt Margaret and Uncle Russell would have to give their permission since she would not be eighteen until December. She vowed to herself that if they didn't give their blessings, she would just wait a year. Then she would not need their permission. She hoped to have a very simple wedding with Father John performing the ceremony. Uncle Russell had immediately agreed that he would be delighted with the entire event as Emily proposed. Aunt Margaret began to mumble about having a Catholic wedding done by a priest. She declared that they would need to consult the Elders at the Society of Friends church for their input on this event. Emily was distraught over this announcement. She felt this was her big day and if she wanted a wedding in the Catholic Church it should be permitted. As she retreated to her room, she made an agreement with herself that if she couldn't do the wedding as she and Eustis had planned, they would quietly have their vows spoken by Father John at the small Altar on her 18th birthday. "Oh, if only Charlotte could be here to see me get married", she thought. "I wonder where she is?"

Summer was upon them and the garden was at its peak. It was all she and Aunt Margaret could do to get the vegetables picked and preserved for the winter. They were busy "canning" as many of them as they could. Some of the fall vegetables would always be wrapped in paper and stored in the root cellar. The chickens were growing and soon it would be time to begin killing them and preparing them for the winter table. This was a process of cooking the chickens then pouring the hot grease over the meat after it had been carefully packed into glass jars. The jars were put into a big tub of water over a hot fire out in the yard. Once the water came to a rolling boil, the jars would need to be boiled about an hour. This meant that Emily always had to tend the fire to make sure that the water continued to boil rapidly. The temperature outside was hovering near 95 degrees, so tending the fire was a very hot job. However, Emily had been doing it for the last few years. She had the procedure down to a routine. As she was tending the fire, she vowed that when she had a home of her own, she would never can chicken again!

Emily had some concerns about what kind of a dress that she would need for her wedding. Aunt Margaret had already announced that she would have nothing to do with a Catholic wedding. Emily wondered just where she might get enough money to buy the fabric for her dress. She thought about how it was nearly impossible for her to make money because she never seemed to have a spare moment. If she ever seemed idle, Aunt Margaret would dream up a job for her to do. Emily knew how to sew. She had taught herself to operate the old treadle sewing machine that stood in the pantry. She had been making her clothes for quite sometime from the feed sacks that the chicken feed came in and sometimes she would make a skirt from an old coat that Uncle Russell no longer wore. She had made herself a complete wardrobe from the clothes Mrs. Thompson had given her; but a wedding dress? Where would she get the finery to do that? For some time Emily had been thinking that she could teach other children to play the piano. Mrs. Thompson still had the beautiful piano in her home that she had allowed Emily to play. In fact, Emily had played that piano nearly every day since she had met Mrs. Thompson. Perhaps she could convince Mrs. Thompson to allow her to teach children to play the piano in her parlor. If she could get a student or two, she might make enough money to buy the fabric for her wedding dress.

Emily ran all the way to Mrs. Thompson's house one day with her plan to teach piano to the children from her school or from St. Andrew's Catholic Church. She quickly laid out her plans for earning money for her wedding before Mrs. Thompson. She listened carefully and made a few mental notes as Emily was rattling on about her idea. When Emily finished with all the details, she waited for Mrs. Thompson to give her blessing to the plan. It didn't occur to her that she might say no! When Emily had finished outlining how she could make a few dollars to buy the fabric for her wedding dress, Mrs. Thompson asked her if she might be willing to accept a dress already made that had only been worn one time. Emily was flabbergasted. Mrs. Thompson hobbled to a wardrobe in the spare bedroom and brought out the most beautiful dress Emily had ever seen. It was lovely Algonquin lace over ivory colored peau de soie. It featured a high collar and rows of seed pearls sewn on the bodice. The bustle in the back was made of even more ivory satin and featured a train of the Algonquin lace. Algonquin lace was an imported fabric from Ottawa woven by the Indian tribe that once inhabited the area. Emily could not even imagine wearing such a beautiful dress. When Mrs. Thompson urged her to try on the dress to see if it would fit, Emily began to cry. She thought of how her mother would have loved to have been a witness to seeing her wear such a dress. She also wondered if somehow she could convey to Charlotte, wherever she was, how beautiful she would be in the dress that Mrs. Thompson had worn in her wedding so many years before. Emily stepped out of the dressing room with the dress fitted to her perfectly and Mrs. Thompson gasped at the beautiful sight before her. Oh, how she wanted Emily to be like the daughter she had lost. Could she ever tell Emily how much joy she had brought to her life in her old age? Would Emily ever understand how happy she had made her by playing the piano for her, and now how she loved to see Emily in her dress? The two held each other and wept silently for two different reasons.

Naturally, Uncle Russell was delighted that Emily had a beautiful wedding dress even though it had come from Mrs. Thompson. Aunt Margaret frowned with disdain that Emily had imposed on the old lady's generosity. Uncle Russell was enthralled to hear Emily talk about the plans she and Eustis had for their wedding. Since they were both Catholics they could be married at the High Altar of the Church. Emily had written a letter to Father Paul in Peterborough and invited him to attend. His response came much later stating that he would be unable to travel so far since his health was failing. He also informed her that Mrs. Perkins had passed away during the winter of 1925. Emily bowed her head and prayed for her hoping that she had not suffered in her illness. And asked her for forgiveness for any animosity she had ever felt for her in the past.

Emily and Eustis made plans for their wedding to be on September 15, 1927. They had decided to wait an extra year for two reasons. The primary reason was that they would not need the permission of Aunt Margaret and Uncle Russell. Secondly, if they waited a year, they would be able to save a little money to buy things that they would need for their first home. Eustis' had part time jobs at the funeral parlor and at the livery stable. He had been unable to get a full time job at either establishment so he worked a few hours for both of them.

Aunt Margaret and Uncle Russell had not offered them a place at their house to live, and Eustis' family had no room. Emily and Eustis had to look for a home following their wedding. They were looking for a rooming house where they could stay. Before Emily said her vows, she insisted that they have a good place to live. Finally, Eustis found an apartment over the hardware store that was for rent. They would have to share the bathroom with another couple who lived in another apartment on the same floor. They could start housekeeping there and he could walk to work at both his jobs.

Plans for their wedding continued, and as the day drew nearer, Aunt Margaret seemed to be sorry that she had not been included in the plans. When Emily told her about Mrs. Thompson offering her wedding dress, Aunt Margaret seemed upset that she had not been asked about a dress. Her own wedding dress hung in her closet having been worn only once. Emily never felt comfortable sharing any of the wedding plans with her. On the other hand, Uncle Russell was fascinated by all the excitement of the event and continued to quiz Emily about each little detail. She asked him if he would walk her down the aisle of the church during the ceremony and he excitedly said yes. Aunt Margaret cautioned him about his involvement in a Catholic wedding and tried to infer that it was sacrilegious to attend such an event in a different church. Emily was distraught. She just couldn't understand why this could not be as big a day for Aunt Margaret as it was going to be for her.

Chapter 16

On the last Sunday in September, 1927, Emily became Mrs. Eustis Carmichael having been married in St. Anthony's Catholic Church at the High Altar. Father John had officiated in the sacrament of marriage. Uncle Russell had walked Emily down the aisle with the biggest smile on his face, and he told all his friends at the mine that it had been the proudest moment of his life. Aunt Margaret chose not to attend the wedding but did agree to host an afternoon tea following the ceremony in their parlor for their invited guests. The guest of honor at the wedding and the tea was Mrs. Thompson. She had shed tears of joy that only she and Emily understood.

Emily and Eustis had moved into their apartment above the Hobart's Hardware Store and immediately began to set up housekeeping. The apartment was furnished even though it was sparsely so. For Emily, it was a relief to be out of Aunt Margaret's grasp, but she did miss Uncle Russell and his humor. Eustis missed his little brothers and sisters, but he vowed to take them to the park as often as he could in order to spend time with them.

It wasn't long until the newly wedded couple had settled into their new home. Emily knew nothing about being married. On her wedding night she and Eustis had to get to know each other intimately. No one had ever discussed the ritual of making love to her and Eustis seemed as equally inexperienced. He had little brothers and sisters so he was aware of the procedure. Emily was completely mystified and had to have it all explained. She found the act of intercourse to be painful and disgusting, but Eustis was patient and explained to her that it would not always be so difficult. He was right, as time went on Emily began to really enjoy Eustis' attention. Finding someone who loved her for who she was was another new experience.

All her life Emily had been put aside for someone else. Now, it was her turn to be the center of someone's affection and Eustis was the one to do it. Emily really loved being loved. As time went on Emily began to look forward to the times when she and Eustis could be intimate. She even began to prepare for his arrival early in the afternoon and she found the ritual of taking a bath in the middle of the day, as Aunt Margaret had insisted, was not a bad idea after all. Emily was as happy as she had ever been since she left her childhood in Peterborough. Naturally she still missed Charlotte, and had wanted her to be part of her wedding, but it was not to be. Emily prayed to her patron Saint, St. Theresa that she would watch over Charlotte and bring them back together someday.

Mrs. Thompson decided to give the piano to Emily and several men had moved it upstairs so she could give piano lessons to some of the children from the schools around, including St. Anthony's. It became a way for Emily to earn money for the family. She only charged .25 cents for a lesson and most of the neighbors could afford to give their daughters a music lesson. Eustis continued to give his mother $3.00 per week for her family so he and Emily had to struggle to make ends meet for themselves. They managed on a tight budget but they had each other, and they knew that their struggles would eventually lead to a more prosperous life.

Chapter 17

In 1929, the stock market crashed in New York City and Western Europe. It affected business all over the world. Pennsylvania Consolidated Coal Co., who had been supplying coal to the Pittsburgh steel mills, had their orders cut back drastically. The steel mills had lost many of their standard orders that were from the on-going boom of the Automobile Industry. The steel mills simply didn't need the coal for shut-down pot-lines. The coal companies, as a result, didn't need nearly as many employees. Uncle Russell lost his job. His health had been beginning to fail him, but he had continued to work every day.

Now Russell Garland had no job. He was forced to take whatever work he could find. He walked several miles every day trying to find some work. He dug ditches, plowed those same fields that Eustis had worked the previous summer, and even helped roof a barn. But Uncle Russell was a lot older than Eustis so the work was much harder. He also worked at the funeral parlor helping the undertaker but the chemicals used for embalming made him deathly ill. When he returned home from working so hard each day, Aunt Margaret would have to put him to bed. He could hardly get his breath. He had begun coughing until he was coughing up blood. It was a dire situation for the Garlands. The Society of Friends Church came to their rescue and tried to help with food for them, but the church had other families out of work too. There didn't seem to be enough money to go around for everyone.

Work also was getting more and more scarce for Eustis as well as most other men in the area. Many men, who had been put out of work, had been known to commit suicide because they could no longer face the fact that they couldn't support their families. Eustis knew he had an obligation to Emily and to his family, and he refused to give up hope. His father had not been laid off at the mine but his hours were cut somewhat. He was still working part of the time. Eustis wondered just what else he could do to bring in money for all of them.

Emily and Eustis frequently had been going to the library to read in the evenings. One night, as Eustis was reading a New York newspaper, he read that the U.S.NAVY was looking for able-bodied men to train. The promise was being made that if you joined the Navy, you would receive regular pay. You would also be able to work anywhere on a body of water, building bridges, ports, and steel reinforced buildings, or go to sea for the adventures of your life. Eustis immediately showed the newspaper to Emily and announced that he could send the money home to her and his family while learning to be a sailor. What an opportunity this appeared to be! The article stated that men could sign up for the Navy in Philadelphia, Pittsburgh, or New York City. He had decided he would leave the next day for Pittsburgh, since it was the closest city.

Since they didn't have a buggy or a horse, Eustis went to the livery stable and offered to ride the meanest or the feeblest horse they had and return the same day. Ebert deferred this decision to Maude who promptly gave him the meanest horse that she could find. She told Eustis that if he could ride "ole Thunder", he could ride anything.

Early the next morning Emily had packed his lunch and sent him on his way. She wished him well and promised to wait patiently for him to return. As soon as he was gone out of sight, she began to wonder just what this would mean for her. Would she be all-alone? Would she be able to go with him? Was he going to be in danger? Where was Illinois? As soon as she could she quickly went to the library and looked up some more information about the Navy. She discovered that sailors were assigned to build bridges and dams over large bodies of water. They were also trained to navigate huge ships on the oceans. The sailors were used in all sorts of industries that had been shipping products to and from the United States. Since she had spent all day pondering all that she had learned, Emily began to wonder if it was such a good plan. It was nearly midnight when she heard Eustis coming up the steps.

He burst through the door and grabbed her up in his arms. He had joined up and had a job that paid him $30.00 per month. He would have to leave Meadville and go to the Great Lakes Naval Station in Illinois. He would be working out of the dock there and would not be home except once every six months. Emily cringed at the thought of Eustis being gone all the time. She didn't know how she could manage by herself and she couldn't imagine being without Eustis. She had always been around Aunt Margaret or Uncle Russell and she pondered what life would be like alone. Too much of her life had been spent alone but Eustis did not have to leave for two more weeks.

Eustis could see the reality of leaving Emily alone. While visiting his mother one sunny afternoon, his mother suggested that he take Emily to his grandfather's farm in Kentucky while he was gone. His grandmother had passed away the previous summer and his grandfather was alone on the farm. Emily could stay with him and keep house for him. Then neither of them would be alone. It all sounded like a good plan. Eustis hurried home to tell Emily the good news. They could travel to Kentucky before the end of the week, if she agreed.

Eustis agreed to go to the train station and inquire about a ticket on the next train going to Kentucky. They would be able to load up their belongings into the two trunks they owned and be ready to leave by Thursday. It was about 350 miles, so it would be a long trip. His grandfather would love to have her and Eustis could go to the Navy without worrying about how Emily was doing at home. He promised that when he got a chance to come home, he would come to Kentucky to visit her there. Emily stood in awe at this plan. She wasn't sure she wanted to leave her students and what would she do about the piano that Mrs. Thompson had given her? Meanwhile, what would happen to Aunt Margaret and Uncle Russell if Emily left Meadville? It all seemed too fast to imagine, especially by the end of the week. When she and Eustis sat together discussing the total picture, it seemed there just wasn't a better solution. There would not be enough money for her to stay in Meadville. Frankly she didn't really want to be there if Eustis wasn't going to be with her.

Very early the next morning Emily went to see Mrs. Thompson and discussed the move with her. She assured Emily that she should do what her husband asked her to do. Mrs. Thompson convinced Emily that this move would simply be a new experience. She assured Emily that she would have a wonderful time wherever she went. As for the piano; Mrs. Thompson suggested that if the piano couldn't be taken with them, Emily could bring it back to her house until she could return to Meadville. That was the best news that Emily had heard. She would try to take her beloved piano with her to Kentucky, if they could get it on the train.

Next, Emily went to visit Aunt Margaret and shared their plans with her. Aunt Margaret wasn't very excited about the whole event, but she assured Emily, as Mrs. Thompson had done, that she should do what her husband asked her to do. After all, Kentucky wasn't very far away and she could come back and visit sometimes. When Uncle Russell came home from helping to roof a barn, he was tired and hungry. Aunt Margaret had fixed him a nice meal, but he fell asleep before she could share the news of Eustis and Emily and their trip to Kentucky. Emily had already decided that she would not leave without telling Uncle Russell goodbye. So the next day she went back to the house prior to daylight to see him before he left for work. She hurriedly told him of her plans and about Eustis going into the Navy with a job that paid $30.00 per month. He hugged her and told her it was a good plan.

As for the Garland family, Uncle Russell wasn't sure how long he would have a job. He reminded Emily that all the canning of the vegetables and chicken that she had done the previous summer helping Aunt Margaret, was all that they had to eat and he didn't know how long he could continue to find work. He hoped that the mines would hire again soon.

As Emily said her final goodbye to him, she still was bubbling with excitement about her new trip and she seemed oblivious to his problems. He lovingly and patiently stood in the doorway watching her bounce down the street just full of excitement. As he watched her disappear around the corner, tears rolled down his cheeks. She was his little girl, and he wasn't sure he would ever see her again. Emily didn't notice his tears or how feeble he was. She was so full of anticipation about her impending move.

Chapter 18

Kentucky, here we come!

If Emily had had even the remotest idea of what an excursion she was going to be taking, she hadn't expressed it. As Eustis and his friends were loading the baggage car, including Emily's piano, Emily had been busy preparing lunch for them to eat along the way. She packed as much food as she possibly could into the picnic basket thinking she would not be on the train very long. She carried extra bread that she had baked and fresh lemonade for them to drink as they traveled along. Finally, all of their possessions were loaded and the travelers were ready to leave.

The train was not scheduled to leave until 6:00 A.M. on Thursday morning. Emily insisted that she go to mass before leaving on such a trip. She had wanted to say goodbye to Father John, and they both had wanted to take the holy Eucharist before they left. She and Eustis had entered the church and bowed before the altar to ask for divine guidance and protection. True, they were not only going into unknown territory, but they had no idea of what awaited them in Kentucky. Father John had joined them in prayer and assured them he would pray for them every day until he heard that they were safe. He also expressed his pleasure that Eustis had joined the Navy. Father John felt sure there would be a meaningful career path for Eustis once he completed his initial training. He told Eustis that he might easily become a real ENGINEER by the time he finished his enlistment.

Eustis and Emily arose before dawn on Thursday. They had packed the things they would need for the trip as well as the lunch that Emily had prepared. The trip was about 350 miles long. They would be going through several cities and towns along the way. The train would have to stop for water and coal as it pulled its own weight through the mountains. Their first stop was going to be in Pittsburgh, Pennsylvania. The conductor had told them it would be about noon before they reached Pittsburgh. It had not occurred to

Emily or Eustis that it might take more than one day to get to Eastern Kentucky. As the train pulled out of the station, Emily glanced around the platform searching the faces to see, for one last time, if she could see Charlotte. Where oh where had she gone? Would she ever see her again?

As the couple settled into their seats, reality finally set in. If this journey were to take more than one day, where would they sleep? They didn't have enough money for a pullman car, so Eustis and Emily would have to sleep in their seats. What a new experience this would be for her! She and Charlotte had come from Peterborough to Meadville, many years earlier, but she had not remembered much about that trip. On that excursion, she only remembered the fright she experienced at having to leave their home.

The train had arrived in Pittsburgh at about 1:20 P.M. as scheduled. The city streets were bustling with people but they all seemed to be going nowhere.

Emily thought it was a very interesting city. They had eaten their lunch and had consumed all the lemonade. They were still in Pennsylvania and all that was left of the lunch she had prepared was the bread that by now was beginning to get hard. Emily began to wonder what they would do the next day. As the train pulled out of the station in Pittsburgh, Emily and Eustis snuggled down in their seats holding onto each other and wondering about the next leg of their journey. As the conductor came through the car and checked to see about everyone, he told them they would arrive in Morgantown, West Virginia, about daybreak the next day. Since there were no meals served on second-class tickets, they would need to find breakfast quickly while the train was stopped to take on water and coal. Eustis hoped that there would be "food stops", however he wondered if he could find a place to eat and if his money would hold out. Their tickets had been $3.00 each and he needed a roundtrip one that was $1.50 more. Altogether they had spent $7.50 of his original $41.00. He had only $32.50 left and it had to get him to the Great Lakes Training Center.

When the trained pulled into Morgantown, Emily discovered that she had slept reasonably well through the night in the sitting position. She was hungry, she scrounged through the picnic basket looking for the extra bread she had brought. Much to her surprise, she found a few crusts of the bread that she and Eustis ate as quickly as they could. Eustis left the train to see if he could find food for them to eat for lunch. There had been a small lunchroom near the train station where he could purchase something to eat. He bought a large sweet roll, two bottles of milk, and two beef sandwiches for $.45 cents. That would have to do for the rest of that day. He had hurriedly boarded the train as it was getting up steam to pull out again. While he and Emily were sharing the sweet roll, the conductor advised them that they would be in Charleston, West Virginia, about 6:00 P.M. for a short stop before going on to Huntington, West Virginia. It would just be getting dark when they arrived in Huntington. There they would need to change trains and board another train that would take them to Pikeville, Kentucky. The conductor did not know anything about the train to Kentucky. He was a conductor on the Baltimore and Ohio train routes with no knowledge of local train service.

Eustis and Emily had saved their sandwiches to eat for dinner and before they came to Charleston. When they arrived in Charleston, Eustis went into the station to see if he could get information about the local train to Pikeville. The ticket-master told him the train only ran on certain days and that he wasn't sure which days they might be since he did not have that train schedule. Eustis had quickly boarded the train but did not tell Emily the bad news. He decided to just wait until they got to Huntington to get better information. While he was in the station at Charleston, he was able to get each of them a cup of coffee.

Their arrival day was a cold one in West Virginia and Emily could see snow on the mountains. The train seemed to be moving at a snail's pace. She was anxious to get to their destination and get off the moving monster. Each time they came to a road crossing the train blew a loud shrill whistle. Emily had heard it so often since leaving Meadville; it seemed to haunt her. She swore to herself that she was hearing that whistle even when it wasn't blowing. Finally, the train pulled into Huntington where they had to change trains. She gathered up her things and prepared to disembark. Meanwhile, Eustis had already gone inside to inquire about the train link to Pikeville. The stationmaster at Huntington told Eustis that the local trains only ran on Monday, Wednesday, and Thursday to Pikeville. Unfortunately it was Friday, meaning the train would not run again until Monday. Their baggage was unloaded on the platform outside the station, but the piano was a big problem. How in the world would they ever get Emily's piano to Papa's house?

Eustis went inside the station, glanced at the clock and realized it was already 7:30 P.M. Since Papa had no idea that they were coming, he would not have known to meet them to take them to his house. If Eustis' mother had written to him, it might have been possible that he would have received the letter; however, it would not have mattered since he could neither read or nor write. Someone would need to read it to him. Eustis assumed that this had not happened. He would need to figure it out for himself. As he was pondering his own dilemma, an elderly man came into the station and asked about the piano on the platform. Quickly Eustis explained their predicament and asked for the man's help. Jasper Baker introduced himself to Eustis and told him that he was a neighbor of his Grampa in Sandy Fork. Mr. Baker had come to the station to pick up a package of fabric that his wife had ordered from the catalog. He agreed to take them to the farm even though he only had a wagon. They soon discovered that they would have to leave the piano at the train station. Eustis wondered how he could tell Emily that her beloved piano must temporarily stay in Huntington. Tears came to her eyes, but she knew they had no other choice. Besides, she determined that she could come back and get it soon. She asked the station master to roll it into the train station. She then pulled up a chair and played "My Darling Clementine" on the piano as if it would be the last time she might have a chance to play her most prized possession. All the folks in the train station immediately gathered around the piano and sang as she played. Emily sadly played one more song and then, with great trepidation, she assured the ticket master that she would be back to claim her piano as soon as possible.

They loaded their belongings on Jasper's wagon and ventured down a dark muddy road toward Sandy Fork, Kentucky. Little did she know that there was not a good road anywhere in that part of the country. The roads were rutted, muddy, narrow, and almost impassable in some places. They would have to cross a stream of water that the horse did not like. Mr. Baker had to severely whip the horse to get him to go on. The water wasn't very deep, but the horse didn't seem to believe that he could pull his load across the stream. Emily cringed each time he struck the horse, with the whip, remembering the times she had been whipped by Aunt Margaret. She was tired and hungry from traveling for two days. It seemed a lifetime to Emily. She had no idea the country was so big, and that the trains would seem to go so slow. And now she was in the rickety wagon going over an impossibly bumpy road. She wondered if she would ever find a home again. She hardly thought about the fact that Eustis would soon leave her for awhile. Tonight she only wanted to get to Papa's house.

It was nearly midnight when the wagon and its cargo lumbered up a long and rutted lane to a cabin on the hillside. There was no light to be seen and as the wagon drew nearer to the house, a huge hound dog began to bark. Soon there were several dogs in a chorus of barking that announced their arrival. When the wagon was within 15 feet of the front door, a man appeared in the doorway with a lantern and a shotgun. He stepped onto a creaky porch and shouted for some identification of the trespassers. Eustis called out his name; Papa Percy, and announced that it was Eustis, your grandson. Pulling on his galluses of his bib overalls and stepping carefully in his bare feet, he came to the side of the wagon to help him alight. Eustis introduced Emily to Papa and quickly explained that she would be staying with him a while. He then turned to Jasper and offered to pay him for his services. Jasper quietly refused his money stating that he would come back the next day to help them if they needed. Eustis thanked him profusely for all his help, but most of all, for not taking what little money he had. Papa was busy getting the bags into the house and stirring up the fire in the old cook stove. He put the coffee on the front of the stove to heat. He checked the cupboard and brought out a piece of meat of unknown origin and some cold biscuits. Emily quickly agreed to eat whatever there was to eat and so did Eustis. It had been such a long time since they had eaten that the mere mention of food was the best news they had heard since leaving Meadville.

In the course of the evening Eustis told Papa about how he had already joined the Navy and would need to go to the Great Lakes Training Center in Illinois in the next few days. He wanted Emily to be taken care of while he was gone and thought it had been a very good idea to bring her to Kentucky. Papa listened carefully to all that Eustis was saying. He agreed that Emily would be good help to have around. Papa then told them they could take his bed and he would sleep on the cot in the kitchen for the rest of the night. Eustis and Emily agreed and could hardly wait to get into a real bed since they had been sleeping in an upright position for the last few days. They snuggled together in a strange bed, one that seemed to swallow them. Eustis informed her that it was a feather bed. She didn't care what you called it; she only wanted to get closer to Eustis because she was beginning to realize it wouldn't be long until he would be gone for a long time. It ended up being a short night, but one she would remember for a long time.

Chapter 19

Daylight was peeping through the windows when Emily heard Papa rustling the pans in the kitchen. He made several trips in and out of the screen door and each time it would slap shut with a resounding noise. Since she hadn't bothered to unpack anything the night before, she had to rummage around in their carpetbag for a robe so she could go to the kitchen. She asked Eustis which way was the bathroom. He smiled and said that it was about 40 feet behind the house. Emily looked horrified. She had never seen or heard of an "outhouse" before. She wandered through the kitchen, barefoot, and out the noisy screen door that closed with the familiar sound. She glanced around the cabin taking in all the things she had not been able to see the night before. She spied the decrepit looking shed at the back of the house. She assumed it was the right building. The door hung on two hinges, both of which looked like they might give out at any time. She went inside to survey the facility and found the odor disgusting. She knew for sure that it wouldn't take her long to do what she needed to do and get out of this shanty before the foul smell made her faint. She had forgotten to lock the door behind her with the huge hook that hung loosely on the door facing. It hooked between two huge bent nails forming a method of securing the door. While she was attempting to get her drawers pulled up the door popped open and there stood Papa. He was shocked to see her, but 'lowed as how a city girl might need to learn how to latch a door. He quickly closed the door and waited patiently for her to come out.

Emily could see that this was going to be an experience that she had not anticipated nor had she ever been involved in anything like it before. The weather was still cold and Emily soon learned that you needed to wear shoes if you were going outside for any reason. Papa had prepared breakfast for them while they were trying to get dressed. Finally they all gathered around a big table in the center of the room for a feast of biscuits, more meat of unknown species, gravy, and coffee to drink. The coffee was poured in heavy white cups with no handles. When she asked about the lack of handles, Papa informed her that she should hold the cup with both hands and it would warm her as she drank the brew. She wondered about the "brew" since it seemed black and thick enough to be used as shoe polish. She was sure she needed both hands to hold it or it would walk off the table!

After they had eaten, Papa informed Emily that she could clean up the kitchen and prepare "dinner" because he and Eustis were going to take a trip. She wondered what that entailed, but asked no questions. She went about cleaning the kitchen and was introduced to some real surprises. She soon found a "tea kettle" on the back of the stove that she assumed was used to heat water. Then she found a deep pan to be used for washing dishes, and rags to be used for cleaning. There were larger rags to be used to dry the dishes but there was no soap. She ran to the door as Papa and Eustis were leaving to ask about the soap to be used. Papa showed her a box of square pieces of something that he explained was "lye" soap. She gingerly picked up a piece of the substance as he was telling her that they would have to make some soon because that was all he had. Emily had a natural curiosity about making soap. How could she do that? No doubt the instructions would come later.

After she had cleaned the kitchen, she wandered about the cabin. It was a sight to behold. The floors were bare wood but were swept clean to a shine, even thought there were cracks in the planks that would allow a strong wind to blow through. The windows were pieces of glass loosely held in makeshift frames that, again, allowed the wind to come through. The curtains were the same type of feed sacks that Aunt Margaret had used for her dresses; however, these all had printing on them such as "Daisy Feed" or "Chicken Feed". Her first thought was that they were just hard to get the printing out, but upon closer scrutiny she realized that they had never been washed at all. When she tried to work with them the dust flew all over everything. She made a mental note that she would have to start cleaning soon. The closets, of which there were two, still had "mama's clothes hanging in them. She had been a large woman as it appeared from the size of the clothing. These items, too, had not been laundered in a long time. Then, she also wondered what to do about the fire in the stove. She didn't know how to fire a stove. She opened up the door in the front to find it was an oven. Well, where did the coal go, she wondered? She found a strange looking hook like thing that lifted the round lid on the stove. She then put a few pieces of coal in the stove and hoped it would work for awhile. Then she needed to take another trip to the little building in the back. She had to work up the courage to face that awful smell again. As she left the house on her quick trip, she noticed the porch was also a bit rotten and would need repair soon. As she stepped down off the porch, she ran into an old mother cat with her brood of kittens following her. They were as cute as they could be and she was reminded of Snowball. She stooped to pick up one of the kittens, but they were wild and untamed. They all ran away as fast as they could. On her way to the "outhouse" she again paused to glance around the yard and she spied several more small buildings. She wasn't sure what purpose they might serve, but she was sure that she would investigate them soon.

As Emily was perusing the property, she spied a garden plot. She easily remembered how she and Aunt Margaret had raised a garden and had canned the vegetables. In back of a grove of trees, she also saw what appeared to be a chicken coop. Her memories of having to can chicken quickly flooded her mind, and she remembered in horror what a chore that had been. She certainly hoped that she wouldn't have to do that again. Farther on down the hill she saw a big field where something had been planted. She wasn't sure what it was, but it still had stalks standing as though the crop had all been cut recently. As she wandered back to the house trying to think about what she might need to do for lunch, she saw another building farther up the hill. It was bigger than the other outbuildings. Maybe it housed more animals. Emily decided to investigate for herself in order to see what could be hiding in such a big building. The closer she got to the building the bigger it appeared. She soon realized it was a lot bigger than the cabin. Stepping inside the barn, she found a horse and a mule, a wagon, and some farm implements that she could not identify. She quickly went to the horses but since she didn't know much about horses, she decided she needed more instructions on what to do. Tied to a big shade tree behind the barn was a cow. She seemed friendly enough, but cows were another new experience for this city girl so she decided it was time to go to the house.

Back in the cabin's "humble" kitchen, Emily wondered what she could fix for them to eat. She was accustomed to having leftover food from the previous meal but she decided they had probably eaten the only left-overs upon their arrival in the middle of the night.

Emily hardly knew where to look for anything to fix. She had spied a metal box in the window earlier. It appeared to hang to the outside, held in place by the window frame. She carefully opened the box to discover a bowl of butter, a crock of milk, some meat that had already been cooked, probably "canned". She thought about that for a minute and shuddered. She looked behind another curtain that covered a space in the wall and discovered the makings of biscuits, some coffee, and many jars of canned vegetables. Smiling to herself she thought that she would impress everyone by putting together a lunch for them. She remembered how Aunt Margaret had told her how to do biscuits and she promptly opened a can of beans, put some seasoning, of which she only found salt and pepper, in them and put them on the stove to cook. By now her fire was dying down so she opened the lid again and inserted a few more pieces of coal. She went to the window box and brought out the meat and put it in the biggest skillet she had ever seen to try to cook it. She found a clean crock to make the biscuits and remembered to use the baking powder she had found, just like Aunt Margaret would have done. When she looked for the shortening, she couldn't find it so she used the butter. She knew there would be lard there somewhere, but she hadn't found it. As she remembered how she once laughed at how Uncle Russell's lunch bucket said "lard" on the side, and it brought back memories of Meadville. However, this was not a time for memories, she had lunch to consider. By the time she had the biscuits ready for the oven, she heard steps on the porch.

Eustis and Papa were back. They came in the house starving and were ready for whatever she might put before them. Emily proudly put her first ever lunch on the table that had been prepared in such a rustic kitchen. She poured the coffee although it didn't seem as strong as what she had the night before. When she brought the biscuits out, they had not risen very high, and Papa told her the oven wasn't hot enough. She had cooked the meat and the beans together so they would have a good flavor. She had boiled a pan of potatoes and flavored them with the meat grease. The men sat down to eat and devoured all that she had prepared. When she commented about fixing lunch each day, Papa promptly corrected her by declaring that the noon meal was "dinner" and the evening meal was "supper". They just didn't do "lunch" around these parts. Much to Emily's surprise, Eustis agreed with him although he had never corrected her before. From that point on she would need to refer to the meal eaten at noon as dinner. That was just one of several surprises in store for Emily.

When Emily started to clean the table and prepare to do the dishes, she asked Papa where she could get water. He took her outside to the side of the house carrying a bucket. He showed her how she would have to sink the bucket inside the well while being careful not to let go of the rope attached to the bail. If the bucket didn't sink into the water and fill, she would have to flip the bucket quickly trying to make it sink. Once the bucket was filled, she would have to bring it to the top of the well, carry it into the house, and then heat it in order to wash dishes. Emily tried to sink the bucket into the well. Looking down into the well at the water made her "woozy". She tried and tried again, all to no avail. She simply could not sink the bucket. Finally Papa took the rope and, with the first try, sank the bucket, drew it to the top and carried it to the house. She felt so inadequate and decided she would try again when no one was watching until she mastered the art of sinking a bucket in the well!

Chapter 20

All the while that Emily was adjusting to Sandy Fork, time was running out for Eustis. He was scheduled to leave the following Tuesday morning in order to report to the training center at Great Lakes on time. Eustis also needed time in order to re-route himself to Lexington where he could get on a train through Louisville and Indianapolis into Chicago where the center was located. He was certainly hoping it wouldn't cost any more money. He intended to leave a little bit of money with Emily in the event she might need something. With all the time demands, Eustis didn't have much time to discuss things with her. On Saturday night, when they went to bed in that cozy featherbed, he did tell her that he would send his money to her as soon as he got paid. He also told her that she should save as much as she could for when he got out of the service. His hope for the future was that they could buy a home of their own. Emily quietly vowed to herself that their future home wouldn't be in Sandy Fork, Kentucky. He also planned to send a little of his money to his mother to help with the children still at home. That all meant that he would keep very little for himself; because the Navy would provide everything Eustis needed as part of his enlistment guarantee. On that last night that Eustis was with her, Emily snuggled as close as she could to Eustis and cried softly to herself. She wasn't sure why she was crying except that she feared the unknown, and she was "losing" somebody close to her once again.

Sunday morning came and with it came the sun. Emily rolled out of the bed, put the coal in the stove and was busy fixing breakfast when Eustis got up. Papa was no where to be seen. When he came in the back door, he was carrying a pail of milk, nine eggs, and a package of meat wrapped in paper. She asked if he had been to the store, a comment that brought on a huge laugh. He assured her he had only milked the cow, gathered the eggs, and brought the meat from the springhouse. That was their "grocery store", he said. Emily took his admonishment good-naturedly and decided that she had a lot more to learn about living in the country.

Cooking in Papa's house was becoming an art for her. She had their hot breakfast on the stove and the biscuits were perfect, according to the men in the house.

She queried Papa about going to church. He informed her that he would bring the wagon around to the front of the house so they could go into town for services at the Landmark Baptist Church. Emily wondered if it might be anything like the Quaker Church or the Catholic Church. She hurriedly dressed in order to be ready whenever the wagon was brought around. The three of them rode in the one and only seat as the wagon humped and bumped over the ruts in the path they called a road until they reached the settlement in the lower part of the valley. The church sat on the side of another hill and the horse knew exactly how to get up to the church.

When they went inside, she heard music. What a wonderful sound, she thought. The windows were plain stained glass panels but they cast a beautiful hue across the inside of the church. An elderly lady was playing songs on the piano that she had never heard. They were melodic and spirited. The group of persons in the front of the church rose to sing and Eustis whispered to her that this was the choir. Emily loved it all. She wanted to hear more. The entire congregation rose to sing and then the Preacher prayed. She watched as the people bowed their heads and the men removed their hats to pray. They passed a brass plate around where people could put their money. Emily noticed that very few of the group had put in money and she wondered if that was all the Preacher would make this week. Eustis informed her that he was a neighboring farmer and he was also a preacher. He also told her that sometimes the members of the church paid the preacher in eggs, milk, and chickens. This was all so intriguing that she could hardly believe her ears. She loved the music, the people who had been so friendly, and the message the preacher gave; she couldn't take it all in and she wondered when they would come back to this church. It would be no surprise when they came to this church often.

Tuesday morning came and it was time for Eustis to leave. The train from Huntington would leave around noon and they would have to travel the hard road they had been down on the Friday when they arrived.

Emily could hardly stand the fact that Eustis was about to leave, but she knew it had to happen. He loaded his clothes into the carpetbag as Papa hitched the horse to the wagon and brought it to the front door. They all climbed into the wagon for the trip to the train station. It was a hard trip, and they prayed it would not rain until they got back. If it should rain, the road would get muddy and slippery plus the occupants of the wagon would be drenched to the skin. Emily had prepared a large dinner for everyone so they could eat as they traveled to the train station and still have something to eat before they arrived back at the house.

As they pulled into the train station, Emily was reminded of her piano that still sat in the lobby. The stationmaster told her that no one had played it since she left, but that he had told everyone about the young woman who had played it so beautifully. Emily considered that compliment an invitation to play it again. While they waited for the train to arrive, she entertained the crowd with her playing. She played everything she could think of, and when people asked for requests, she did her best. Eustis could join in on some of the songs she didn't know. Once he had given her the tone and the timing, she could play anything.

Soon the train came puffing into the station. As the crew loaded the coal and water for the next leg of their trip, Emily and Eustis said their good-byes. She was determined not to cry, but when she thought about the "unknown", the tears came involuntarily. He held her in his arms and told her he loved her more than anything in the world. He assured her that he was doing this for their future. He believed that he could not make a living for her in the workplace in any city in the nation at this time. He had to make enough money for them to live on, and this enlistment was the only way he knew how. However, he told her, they would soon be together again, somewhere. He muttered that Papa would take care of her and as soon as he could he would have her join him wherever he was stationed. It all sounded too unreal to her. She just wanted him to hold her one more time. He boarded the train and waved from the window as she clung to Papa. It would be a long time before she would see him again.

Emily and Papa piled onto the wagon after promising the stationmaster that they would return for the piano soon. The weather was too uncertain to risk the piano's getting wet on the trip back to the farm. Anyway, Emily just wasn't sure where she would put it in Papa's cabin. It was so overcrowded now that she could hardly find a place for anything. The trip back to the farm would have been uneventful except for the fact that about a mile from home, the sky clouded up and rained on them. They had been trying to eat a sandwich, but as the rain came, they concentrated on hurrying home. It was not a spring rain, therefore it was extremely cold. Eating became secondary to their mission of getting inside out of the weather. When they finally pulled up the lane to the house, Jasper Baker was in the yard. He had come to the house to help with the milking since he knew that Papa was going to Huntington today. He had milked the cow and gathered the eggs for them. Emily invited him in to eat with them but he 'lowed as how he needed to get on home before the weather turned ugly!

As Emily lay in the bed in the dark, her mind wandered to many things. Always when she was alone, she thought about Charlotte. If she ever found her, she would be able to talk for a long time just to catch her up to the happenings in her life. She also knew that Charlotte would have stories to tell too. She began to think about what life on the farm would be about. She had only been here three days and already she felt as if it were a lifetime. She wondered about the garden, the farm chores, milking the cow, cooking on the coal stove in the summer, drawing water at the well and what was planted in that field to the east of the cabin? She thought about "town" if there were such a thing. Surely there was a town somewhere. She wanted to get mail and be able to write to Eustis. Was there a library? She wanted to go back to church. As she began to drift off to sleep, she took the pillow that Eustis had slept on and placed it beneath her head; she could still smell his scent. Tears began to roll as she drifted off to sleep just before daylight.

Chapter 21

Morning brought a new day in the life of Emily Carmichael. Chores began at sun-up. Papa was ready to go out to milk the cow. Emily asked if she could learn how to milk the cow. He was more than willing to show her how if she had a "hankerin" to learn. They climbed the hill to the barn and he brought the cow from out in the back to the pasture. He placed a rickety stool beside the cow and showed her how to sit on it with the bucket between her legs. The cow had four "teats"; one was huge, one small, and two were just normal sized. He assured her that she could begin wherever she wanted but all four teats would need to be milked. She chose the big one to start with, but it took both hands to reach around it. She squeezed and pulled and nothing happened. Papa showed her how to make this plumbing work, and after a few tries she had success. When she had drained two of the teats, she decided that she would go cook breakfast while he finished the job. She would help again in the evening. She walked slowly to the cabin thinking how proud she was that she had learned one more thing about living on a farm in Sandy Fork, Kentucky, and there was so much more to come.

The days drifted slowly by with the chores of each day more and more time consuming. Emily perused the surroundings on the inside of the cabin. Mama had been sick for such a long time and unable to do much, Emily decided she would undertake the chore of cleaning up the cabin. She started with the curtains. She washed them in the "lye" soap that papa had given her. She made starch in a pan on the stove, like she had seen Aunt Margaret do, and starched the curtains. She hung them to dry on a clothesline stretched from the corner of the cabin to the nearest tree in the yard. When they were completely dry she "sprinkled them down" and rolled them in rolls so they could get evenly damp before she tried to iron them. Ironing those old feed sacks was a challenge. It seemed the more you ironed them the more wrinkles you caused in the fabric. It was coarse, but sturdy. It would withstand much washing, to say the least. She wiped down the plank walls of the cabin with a damp rag and hoped it would give it a fresh look. The old cook stove that stood in the corner sometimes belched out black smoke when you overloaded it with coal. The walls spoke of this experience and wiping them just wasn't enough. She made strong soapy water and found an old brush that she used to scrub the walls. They took on a completely different color. Papa had been outside during this entire procedure and was unaware of her efforts. When he came inside he was surprised to see what she had been doing. She felt the place was sparkling clean. He told her that he had been working the "ter-bakky" patch. Emily wondered what that meant. He proudly took her outside to show her what he had been doing. He showed her a plot of ground about 2 acres in size that he planted each year in tobacco. That was their cash crop for the year. If they had a good crop, there would be enough money to hold them through the winter. If the crop was not good, they really would have a hard time buying the things they needed for the next winter. Emily paused to think about what they bought, since, in her mind's eye, they either raised it or did without it.

She asked Papa about going to town. He informed her that they would go to town the next morning if she had a 'hankerin' to go. She finished her chores for the day, and as she had promised she went with him to the barn to continue her education in "learning to milk a cow". They finished milking and gathering the eggs. Emily hated chickens so she wasn't real anxious to be involved in that chore, but followed instructions as she was told. When it came time to prepare "supper", Emily asked about the meat that they had been eating. She had not questioned its source before. She just assumed it was beef or maybe pork. Papa explained to her that it could be almost anything. There was plenty of wildlife in this area. In the fall he would hunt for deer, badger, opossum, squirrel, or rabbit, but she could rest assured he never ate dog meat! Emily cringed at the thought and wondered how it was saved from spoiling. Papa explained to her that it was "cured". He would use a mixture of salt and sugar and rub the meat with it generously for several days, then he hung it in the "smokehouse" with a slow fire under it for several more days. Once it was cured, it would keep in the well house for a long time. She listened carefully to this procedure and hoped she never had to try it out for herself. Nevertheless she filed this information in that storehouse of knowledge right along with canning chicken that she had learned to do at Aunt Margaret's house.

Chapter 22

Spring was just around the corner. The days were getting longer and it seemed that warm weather would soon be upon them. As the weather got warmer Papa hitched the old horse to a plow and tilled the garden spot. For Emily that meant planting time had arrived, too. She asked about how soon they should plant the vegetables and Papa assured her they would plant by the "sign of the moon". He proceeded to get down the Almanac and look for the signs. She noticed how he had difficulty understanding what it all meant but seemed too proud to ask for help. She stood beside him and asked questions that he seemed unable to answer.

Finally she asked him if she could read it to him. He then confessed, with tears in his eyes, that he had never been to school and could not read or write his own name. Emily asked if she could teach him. Now that the days were longer they could study by daylight each evening. She would be able to help him learn, and she felt like she would be earning "her keep". Papa could hardly wait. The next morning Papa and Emily hurriedly milked the cow, ate breakfast, and cleaned the kitchen. Soon they were on their way to town and Emily was sure there would be a library or a school nearby where she could borrow some books to teach Papa to read. As they were going down the rutted road, she spied a schoolhouse over on the next ridge. She asked Papa about it and he mentioned that it was the only school for the whole area.

The teacher rode a horse to school each day to teach the children who came from miles around. Emily asked if they could go there on their way home? He agreed to take her there when they had finished their work in town. He needed to go to the feed store to get some seeds to plant in the garden. He also needed to get some feed for the chickens since the grass was not up high enough for their feeding, yet. And, he needed to get some more "terbakky" plants. Emily went into the hardware store only to find it was a general store that handled everything from candy for the "young-uns," to tools for the farm, to groceries for the lady of the house, and even yard goods for makings a new dress. Eustis had given her $10.00 when he left, and she felt she should use a little of that money for a new dress even though she had no time to make a dress now. Out in the back of the store was a pile of coal that you could buy if you ran out before the next load came and some small pieces of lumber to mend a fence. You could also buy kerosene for lamps or to mix with sugar to cure a cold the shopkeeper told her. Emily wondered what other bits of knowledge this area had in store for her.

As they started home Papa remembered to take her to the school. She had already discovered that there was no library in town. In fact the town was a loose term used to describe an area one block long. It had the general store and the feed store. A barn like building served as the Post Office where they could get mail if the carrier could not get to your house because the roads were too bad. In the spring when it rained many of the roads washed out and became impassable until someone with a blade that was pulled behind a horse would scrape the ruts full of dirt. The roads would usually last from one spring to the next spring after they had been scraped. Another building that defied all description because it looked as if it would fall if a brisk wind came through town, was the Elliott County Courthouse. All legal business was transacted in this ramshackled building. Papa tried to explain that the county had already planned to build a better one, but he wasn't sure when. Also, in the same block with the courthouse and the Post Office was the Elliott State Bank. The bank was a newer building with large pillars in the front. Many of the local farmers had deposited their money in this bank for years. Papa explained that he kept his money there most of the time. The bank had many depositors but most of their deposits were small. The tobacco farmers generated the only industry in the area. There was no need for the bank to loan money since the folks of Elliott County never borrowed money. Most of them had received their farms from their families and the land was just handed down from one generation to the next. People in Elliott County lived off what they could make either farming or selling chickens and eggs.

Brummit's café was the local eatery. Hardly anyone had the funds to eat in a restaurant very often, but each morning many of the local gentry gathered around the counter in Brummits to enjoy of cup of coffee and a homeade donut that had been fried in a skillet of hot lard, no doubt. The men could enjoy this delicacy for only five cents and be brought up to date on the community's happenings. Emily remembered the coffee that she had been served the first night she arrived in Sandy Fork and decided that this cup of brew would be no better. She watched from the wagon as the men came and went from the Café'. Each time someone came in or out of the double screen doors they made the same "slapping" sound that the door at the cabin made. Emily peeked in the window but Papa told her that women didn't go in this place. She could see stools in front of a counter where men were sitting. She didn't ask to go in but wondered why women didn't go in. She thought about that and then decided that one day she would go in. Maybe then she would find out just what the prohibition of women was all about. But Emily's "someday" would have to wait until she really could do her own exploring.

Two blocks over from the café' was the Landmark Baptist Church where they had attended, and next to the feed store was the Discipleship Pentecostal Church. The reality of the business district was that if the General Store didn't have it and the Feed Store didn't have it, you just couldn't buy it in Sandy Fork. And if you were hungry enough; a cup of coffee and a greasy donut could be your next meal. The next nearest town was twenty miles farther south but was very little bigger than Sandy Fork. Emily wasn't sure when she would get the chance to visit there, but silently she vowed to explore all the area when the first opportunity presented itself to her. Emily just couldn't take it all in at one time but she knew she would return when she had a chance to get away by herself.

As Emily and Papa pulled up to the schoolhouse door, it was just about dinnertime. The children ran out of the door like birds let out of a cage. Emily went up the stairs to go inside to meet the teacher. As she got to the door, he met her just inside the entrance. He was a tall man, big in stature, and foreboding but not much older than she was. She quickly introduced herself to him as she sputtered out her hope to borrow a book in order to teach reading and writing to someone else. He smiled a big smile and welcomed her inside. As she stepped inside a long hall that went across the entire building she saw coats and hats of the children hanging neatly on pegs. At the end of the cloakroom was a large cupboard type structure without many doors that held the lunch the children had brought. Some of them had lunch buckets, some had the familiar "lard" buckets, and some just had their lunches wrapped in paper. There didn't seem to be as many lunches as there were children on the playground. It bothered her to think that some of the children had no lunch. The teacher led her through a big door to the interior of the building. She saw a huge "pot-bellied" stove standing in the middle of the room. It was stifling hot in the room but she understood about coal stoves and how long it takes to cool down after you have built a roaring fire. She was sure it needed to be hot to compensate for the ill-fitting windows that she saw along the north wall. The teacher introduced himself to her as he walked to a huge desk in the front of the room. Mr. Hay was his name and he had 32 students most of the time. Some of the children didn't get to come to school every day because of problems they had at home. Some of the older girls were needed at home to care for smaller siblings and some of the bigger boys tended the family farms. Mr. Hay walked with her to the back of the room as he assured her he had such a book. Of course, he wondered just whom she planned to teach. She motioned to him that Papa was just outside and he was the one who wanted to learn. Mr. Hay questioned her as to who she was, and with a non-stop dialog, she rattled off most of her life story in short sentences from the time she left Peterborough to her time in Meadville. She told Mr. Hay that her husband had gone to the Navy leaving her with his grandfather for awhile. Mr. Hay let out a big laugh and placed his arm around her shoulders. She seemed so small to him. He took her to the bookshelf and offered to loan her anything she wanted even though his supply was small. She took three books with her and promised to return them in two weeks in exchange for more if that might be agreeable with him. He hugged her and granted his permission.

He watched her as she hurried down the path and climbed into the wagon, thinking to himself what a breath of fresh air she was to this area. He loved her spunk and ambition and prayed that she would never get discouraged.

Chapter 23

Emily tore into the books with a vengeance trying to grasp the method she needed for teaching Papa to read. She understood that he wanted to learn, but taking lessons from one so young might present problems. She wanted to do it right so as not to discourage him from trying. She also wanted to instill in him the desire to continue learning until he could read simple things like the Almanac or a newspaper. Papa saw her working at the books and asked when they would start "school" for him. "After supper", she had told him, "when the milking is done and the eggs are gathered".

They began sitting at the table and studying together while there was still light. It was an exciting time. Papa took his schooling very seriously. He quizzed Emily about why there were two identical sounds for the same letter like "c" and "s" and why did "c" also sound like "k". Emily didn't know the why's and wherefore's of teaching; she only knew the answers. She tried to explain to him that the English language had lots of quirks and puzzles in it, but everyone had to learn it the same way. By the end of the week, Papa could recognize his ABC's and could read short sentences. Emily knew that before summer was over, he would be reading like any one else. She also wanted to teach him arithmetic. He had a head for figures, but wasn't good at writing them. She assigned that project to herself; to teach him how to figure using multiple numbers.

Spring came quickly that year in Sandy Fork. There were many more chores to be done. Papa had the garden all plowed and the ground ready for planting vegetables. Emily knew how to do some gardening from her days with Aunt Margaret. She had asked Papa for a small part of the garden to grow some flowers. He grumped about using good land for frilly things but 'lowed as how a girl might need something pretty now and then. She had to have zinnias in her yard, and she explained how marigolds would keep bugs out of the vegetables if they were planted around the edge of the garden. On a bright sunny afternoon, Papa and Emily planted onions, lettuce, and radishes because the sign of the moon was right according to the Almanac. It was too early to plant root crops and other vegetables. The moon was not right according to Papa and the Almanac. Emily just smiled and let him believe whatever he wanted to. He took her to the barn and showed her his seedlings of tobacco. He had sown the seeds just before she arrived and soon they would be just right for planting. He had been preparing the "terbakky" patch for several days. It was a lot of work. The ground had to be plowed several times and then a smaller plow called a disk had to be pulled over the ground several more times. The soil had to be fertilized and Papa used the manure from the chickens, cow, horse, and the mule that he had carefully stored in back of the barn. Once the ground was ready and the weather was getting warmer; sometime around the first of May, they would set out the tobacco seedlings. He warned Emily that it was really hard work, but she was strong and could do the same work any field hand could do. Emily wasn't so sure that was a compliment, but she decided he meant well.

Daylight was coming earlier now that spring had arrived. Emily noticed that when she went to the outhouse so early in the morning the odor seemed to affect her worse than usual. For several mornings she had not been able to go inside the outhouse unless she put her apron over her face and held her breath. When she came out of the building, she began to vomit. She wasn't sick, or so she thought, but for some reason she was vomiting. The next morning she was unable to get to the outhouse before she was vomiting again. This time Papa happened to see her vomiting in a pan. He questioned her about what might be wrong, but she didn't have an answer. He smiled to himself and assured her that he would get her a "slop jar" to put by the bed so she could by-pass the trip to the outhouse for awhile. He brought in, from the barn, a wooden box with a heavy lid that lifted. When Emily lifted the lid she saw a white bucket type container that hung on a frame. Papa said she should use that and he would then empty it each morning while she prepared breakfast. She thanked him for this kindness and she was sure the vomiting would stop soon.

In just a few days Emily noticed that she had not had a menstrual period since Eustis left. That was more than a month ago. She also noticed that, as she was dressing, her breasts seemed sore to the touch. "What is wrong with me", she wondered? She had never before been sick enough to vomit, and her breasts had never been sore. Also, why hadn't she had a period? If Charlotte were here she might have some answers. She didn't say a word to Papa but he just smiled at her each time he realized she had been vomiting. One day, as they were doing their class in reading he took a pencil and wrote on his paper: B A B Y. At first Emily did not understand what he meant. He smiled his big smile and his eyes were filled with tears as he calmly said there would be one soon. No one had ever told Emily what the symptoms of expecting a baby were so she didn't know what to expect. She started laughing and began to ask Papa all about what was happening. Since he was a father to Eustis' mother, he explained the process to her. She was happy to be expecting a baby, but sad that Eustis was so far away.

Emily had adjusted to the early morning sickness and found that if she ate a small crust of bread as soon as she got up, she sometimes bypassed the vomiting. She noticed her appetite had increased and Papa teased her about eating for two. He encouraged her to drink lots of milk to help the baby's bones to be strong. She continued to help in the garden and anxiously awaited the spring planting of the tobacco that would be a new experience for her.

One day shortly after they had eaten dinner, Papa came running into the house with some good news. Emily had a letter from Eustis at the Training Center. She could hardly get it open fast enough for both of them to read it. She read aloud the contents of the letter:

My dearest Emily:

Life here is different. It is very cold and windy. We are on the water of Lake Michigan, working. Our training has been very hard and I have so little time to write. When the day is gone I am worn out and too tired to do much. I hope you and Papa are doing fine. I miss you very much and I hope to see you soon.

Write to me soon at the address on the envelope.

Your loving husband,

Eustis Carmichael

Emily began to cry out loud and Papa put his arms around her and tried to comfort her. She explained that she was crying tears of joy because she had a letter from Eustis. She also stated that there was so much to tell him that she would write back to him immediately.

Eustis quickly learned that life at the Great Lakes Training Center was rigorous to say the least. It was long hard work to learn how to be a Sailor. His basic training was virtually the same as any other enlisted man in the Armed Forces. Eustis was up very early in the morning and had to do marching drills. There were rules about how to make the bunk where you slept and rules about when and how often to take a shower. Eustis had never had a shower before and it fascinated him to be able to stand under the water and wash his hair then his body. Sometimes there wasn't enough hot water. The other men complained, but Eustis had not had hot water most of his life. He didn't consider this an inconvenience. He thought a shower under running water beat the experience of taking a bath in a wash tub behind the cook stove by a country mile. After the morning drills and breakfast, the men had to do more training. Some of the training consisted of obedience drills and some were strenuous physical exercises. Eustis could do all the drills and exercises. He had worked as a laborer all his life. The drills that fascinated Eustis the most were the firearm drills. He was very good at firing a weapon, since he had been a hunter when he lived in Pennsylvania. After the first six weeks of intense drilling, classes began for the next six weeks. The trainees had to measure and calculate the distance between the components of a bridge or the depth needed to drive a "piling" into the earth to make it stable enough to support a bridge. He found this training to be so exciting and easy for him that the teacher asked if he had been to a University before joining the Navy. Eustis enjoyed the marching drills and when he compared them to walking behind a mule plowing a field he decided that being in the Navy was a lot easier. He received a uniform that was white for the summer and a dark blue one for the winter. He was informed that he must wear these uniforms at all times unless he was on leave. His uniform included pants, shirts with a big collar, shoes, socks, undershirts, undershorts, a hat and a tie that was tied in a "sailor's knot". The clothes he brought with him from Sandy Fork seemed old and outdated by comparison. One morning, shortly after he arrived, he was told to don his uniform and have his picture taken. When the pictures came back from being developed Eustis was amazed at what he looked like in his new wardrobe. He packaged the picture and mailed it to Emily, immediately.

Meanwhile, Emily sat down and wrote a letter to Eustis informing him of all the happenings in her life. She hardly knew how to begin but after she thought about it for a moment she proceeded to give him the good news first.

Dearest Eustis:

I received your letter today and was so excited to hear that you are ok. Papa and I are doing fine. It is spring here and everything is turning green. I have gradually learned to do some of the things that need to be done on the farm such as milking a cow. We went to town last week and I was able to visit some of the stores there. We have been going to church regularly and I love the music.

But, I must tell you the most exciting news. You are going to be a father. I discovered that I was "in a family way" shortly after you left. I should have the baby sometime around Christmas. Maybe you will be able to come home at that time to see the baby. Papa is going to have a mid-wife come next week to talk to me about having the baby. I hope it is a boy so I can name him Eustis, Jr.

Oh, yes, Papa is learning to read. I visited the one room schoolhouse on the ridge near downtown and got some books to teach him how to read. He is a good student. Soon he will write you a letter too.

Write to me again soon and remember that I love you.

Your loving wife,

Emily

Emily sealed the letter and hurried to the mailbox to be sure it was there when the mailman came by. She wanted Eustis to have the news as soon as possible.

Chapter 24

It was getting warmer each day. The planting of the garden plot had become a big concern. Emily was outside planting as much as she could each day. She knew it was very important to plant as soon as possible in order for the crops to be ready by mid-summer. She knew that there would be canning of the vegetables to do but she felt confident that Papa would help her with this chore. Surely he would tend to the fire that Aunt Margaret had always made her do when she lived in Meadville. Papa was ready to set out the tobacco plants and he assured her the planting would begin next Monday.

During this time Emily began thinking about Mrs. Thompson and wanted to write her a letter. She knew that Mrs. Thompson would want to know about the baby. She cleaned the table after dinner and took down her paper and pencil to write a quick note before going back to the garden.

Dear Mrs. Thompson:

We arrived here several months ago. Sandy Fork is a very small town with not very many stores. We attended church at the Baptist church. It has lovely stained glass windows and music. I love the music.

Recently I stopped at the nearby school and borrowed a few books to read. I am teaching Papa to read and write. He is a good student. We also have been planting a garden and tobacco. I have also learned how to milk a cow.

The good news is that Eustis and I are going to have a baby. It should be due around Christmas time. I feel fine and am very happy to be "in a family way". Papa will have a mid-wife help me with the birthing. She will come next week to give me some instructions before the time comes.

I hope you are doing fine. I sure do miss visiting with you. I hope you will write to me soon. I really look forward to the mail.

Your friend,

Emily

Emily hurried to the mailbox and posted her letter to Mrs. Thompson. Suddenly she realized that she should also write to Aunt Margaret and Uncle Russell soon. That letter would have to wait. Right now, she had to help with the planting before it was time to prepare supper.

Papa's schooling was coming along fine. He was so anxious to learn how to read that he studied hard. He constantly asked questions about certain words that seemed to give him trouble. He had learned to write most of the lessons that Emily had assigned him. He wanted to write to Eustis and asked that they try to write after supper.

Dear Eustis:

I lerned to red an rite. Emily is havin a baby.

We plant baky today. It raned yestidy.

Papa

Emily addressed the envelope and placed it in the mailbox with her letter to Mrs. Thompson. The mailman would pick them up on his next trip past the house.

She hoped the rain would continue then they would not be able to plant the next day and they could go into town. She needed to go to the schoolhouse to trade her books for some with arithmetic in them so they could start learning to do figures. She was also anxious to meet with Mr. Hay again. He was a very nice man and she was sure he would help her with any questions she might have about how to teach Papa to do his arithmetic.

Papa had wanted to show Emily how to handle the horse and wagon since she seemed so anxious to learn everything about the farm. She was sure she could do anything that Papa could do even if she were small. She had already mastered milking the cow and sinking the bucket. When fall came, Papa had promised to show her how to cure meat since she had developed a taste for the cured meat. She no longer asked for an explanation of what she was eating. She was confident that handling a horse and wagon would be easy for her to learn too.

It really had continued to rain for three days. The roads were muddy and barely passable. The mail had not been delivered for a couple of days. Emily wondered just when it would be delivered again. Since she had been writing to Eustis almost daily, she watched for the mail carrier to bring her a reply from him. If the rain continued, the roads would wash out completely and it might be several days before they could receive mail. She hoped that Papa would go to town and pick up their mail.

On Friday of that week the sun came out as if it had never rained. Everything took on a bright glow because it had been washed clean by the rain. Papa brought the horse and wagon around to the front so they could make a trip to town. He showed Emily how to hold the reins and instruct the horse on what to do. The horse understood simple commands and by pulling on the reins on one side or the other gave the old mare the direction she needed to go. It all seemed like "child's play" to Emily. She changed her mind once she was in the seat to drive the horse; it seemed a little more complicated. She nearly had the horse going in a circle until Papa calmly showed her what she was doing wrong. Driving the horse took eye and hand coordination that Emily did not understand on her first instruction, but after a little practice, she maneuvered the horse with ease. She managed to get the horse into town over the muddy roads, making the ruts deeper as she went. Surely when the weather changed and the sun shined for several days, someone would "drag" the road to fill in the ruts again.

When they got into to town, Papa wanted to go to the bank. He informed Emily that he wanted to see his money. Emily didn't understand that request, but she soon learned what he meant. He went to the teller of the bank and asked to see his money. When the teller showed him a ledger book showing how much money he had on deposit, he was not satisfied. He demanded that the teller show him, in cash, how much he had on deposit. Befuddled, the teller went to the vault in the back and gathered up some cash, returning to the counter to show it to Papa. He was not convinced that was his money. The teller, then, took him into a small room, brought the ledger book showing his deposits totaled $5,440.53, and carefully counted out that amount of money in cash and displayed it on the table. Papa was convinced that his money was still there. No mention was ever made to the teller that Papa could not have counted beyond $20.00, but he needed the assurance that his money was still in tact. Emily was mystified at the whole procedure. It had never occurred to her what a bank was for, but now she knew that when Eustis sent her money, she could safely put it in the bank for safe keeping.

On their way home from town, she led the horse straight to the one room schoolhouse. She wanted to meet with Mr. Hay again. As she guided the horse onto the school lot, Mr. Hay spied them coming up the lane. He dismissed the children for a recess because he wanted to see this young lady again. Her innocence and determination intrigued him, and he wanted to see that she didn't lose her enthusiasm for teaching and learning. She entered by the front door and he met her just inside. She returned the books she had borrowed and asked for arithmetic books. He queried her about what she had been teaching Papa and how he was progressing in his studies. Her report to Mr. Hay was encouraging and he knew she was on the right track.

She inquired about the closest library to Sandy Fork. He told her the nearest library would be at Newfoundland, which was about 4 miles to the Northwest. However, it was on his way home, and he would be glad to bring her any books she would want to read. She asked him to bring her anything he thought she might like to read for pleasure, but for now, she needed arithmetic books for Papa. Mr. Hay went to the shelves and gathered the books for her and offered her his newest book by Mark Twain for her own enjoyment. He also gave her a copy of the Huntington News, a newspaper from the town where the train station was. Emily was ecstatic. She could hardly wait to get home to begin reading. The thought never occurred to her that she soon would be planting tobacco, hoeing her vegetables, and doing all the other chores as well. She did not tell Mr. Hay about the impending birth of her baby, but she wondered when she would get clothes made for her baby in addition to all the other events going on at the farm. For the time being, she was proud of herself that she had been able to drive the horse and wagon to town. As they were going home, they had met Mr. Baker on his way to town, too. Papa insisted that he stop by the house on his way home from town and “set a spell”.

Jasper Baker was a kindly neighbor whose farm hugged a nearby ridge. He had known Papa for many years. They had helped each other with farm chores when one was unable to work for whatever reason. One time when Mr. Baker had broken his leg while trying to break an old mule, Papa went over to his farm daily and tended to his chores. When Mama was so sick and near death, Mrs. Baker came to Papa’s house and cooked for them. She was sure that some good cookin’ would restore Mama’s health. When the tobacco had to be hauled to the auction barn, the two of them loaded their crop onto wagons and went together hoping that there would be more profit in numbers. Emily knew if Mr. Baker came to “set a spell”, Papa had something on his mind to share with him.

Emily had hurried in the house with all her loot from her visit to Mr. Hay. She was filled with excitement over the prospect of going into Newfoundland to the library. She remembered the library in Meadville and knew she could get more reading materials as well as more teaching books from a trip to the library, however it was about four miles. That was a long way from the cabin. Since she had learned to drive the horse and wagon, she wondered if Papa would let her go alone. Maybe if she packed a lunch, the two of them could go some day. When she had a chance she would discuss the possibility with him, but for now she needed to be content with what she had received from Mr. Hay.

She hurriedly fixed dinner for them and cleaned the kitchen. She settled in the rocking chair with the newspaper. She began to read voraciously. She read about the new President, Franklin D. Roosevelt. He had a lot of new ideas to help those who had been so badly affected by the Depression. Many businesses were still not functioning at the top of their capabilities. The President had come up with a plan he called the New Deal. She began to read about all the plans he had for the unemployed. Her thoughts turned toward Uncle Russell. Would he qualify for some financial help? She got her pad and pencil and wrote to them shortly after reading the newspaper.

Dear Aunt Margaret and Uncle Russell

I was reading in the Huntington News today about the new program that Pres. Roosevelt has designed that would help the people who were affected by the Depression. It seems he has a lot of new ideas. I am hoping some of the benefits of his program would benefit you. I am sending the article to you so you can check to see if you can receive these benefits.

Everything here in Sandy Fork is fine. I have learned to do a lot of things since I came here. I can drive the horse and wagon to town, milk the cow, churn for butter, and we have planted a big garden.

Papa is doing fine, and I have been helping him in the garden. We have planted two acres of tobacco that we will harvest in the fall and sell for money.

Eustis has written to me about his life in the Navy. He likes it very much. We are going to have a baby in the winter of this year.

I hope you are all doing fine. Please try to come and visit me soon. I miss you very much.

Love,

Emily.

Emily had read the article in the newspaper that had outlined the new Social Security Program. It was a program designed to help older citizens who had been affected by the Depression and those who had not been able to save money to sustain them when they were no longer able to work. She was sure it would apply to Uncle Russell. The last time she had seen him he had seemed to be more frail than usual. She was concerned about his health. She had been gone from Meadville almost a year. She had not had time to realize how much she missed Uncle Russell. She didn't want to admit that Aunt Margaret had always made her uncomfortable. However, she loved Uncle Russell as if he were her real father. She didn't want to believe that he might not be well. Maybe she would be able to go to visit Meadville in the fall if the crops all came in right. She had no intention of mentioning it to Papa since he would not want to see her go on the train alone.

Jasper Baker stopped by the cabin on his way home from town one Thursday afternoon. He and Papa sat on the steps and talked a while, then Papa brought him inside to talk with Emily. Papa outlined what he wanted to do, but needed to discuss it with Emily before he proceeded.

Papa's plan was to build a room on the side of the house since there was going to be a baby there soon. He wanted Emily to have a room for herself and the baby. Since arriving she had been sleeping on a cot in the kitchen. Jasper said he would help with the building and he 'lowed as how a baby in the neighborhood would be a wonderful thing. He and his wife had never had children so he wanted to be a part of this event.

There were enough fieldstones up behind the barn in the pasture that could be used for a foundation. They would only need to buy a few pieces of lumber and some roofing to make a lean-to room on the west side of the house. Emily loved the idea and mentioned that she could help by driving the horse and wagon. She wanted a window in the west wall so she could look out and see the sun set. The men argued that she didn't need such a fancy room, however, she held out for a window to let in the sunshine for warmth in the winter as well as light.

Once he had made up his mind, Papa wasn't one to wait. Thus construction began on the room before the garden crops came in but after the tobacco had been planted. True to her word, Emily drove the horse and wagon to the site where the men loaded the fieldstones. While they unloaded the stones, she would fix dinner for them, then go back to the high ridge, and get another load of stones until the foundation was completely laid. They found a large flat rock that she liked and she urged them to bring it to be used as a step out the door they were putting in the west wall. She had asked for the door so she would be closer to the outhouse. Papa had agreed to do this just for her. She knew he would put up a screen door for her so she could have the door open in the summer and it would make a cross breeze to cool the cabin. She would always have the memory of the slapping of the screen door each time someone went out or came in the entrance. It would be nearly the end of the summer before the room would be done but Emily was in no hurry since she didn't expect to give birth until late November.

The tobacco had already been planted before work began on the room. It was really a hard job. The settings were about five inches tall and each one had to be set in a hole. When Emily started to set the plants she had not envisioned how big a two-acre field was. It seemed that the more she planted the more there was to plant. The weather had been just right for a few days, then there had been a thunderstorm and the planting was delayed for a few days.

While they were waiting for the ground to dry out so the next batch of seedlings could be set out, she discovered the radishes, lettuce, and peas were coming on strong. Also, it was time to hunt for "spring greens" and mushrooms. The fields around Papa's cabin were lush with spring greens. Emily had never known how to pick these greens. She hardly knew a "green" from a poisonous weed, but Papa was eager to show her what to pick and what to leave alone. Many of the greens were simple plants like dandelion, poke, sour doc, lamb's quarter and wild mustard. All of these together made what Papa called a "mess of greens". She would take a large basket each morning and go hunting spring greens to fix for their dinner. If she could find "morrels"; a type of mushroom that grew wild in the woods, she would fix those with the greens. Sometimes if she was lucky enough to find a lot of morrells, she would roll them in flour and fry them in the skillet as a substitute for meat. The meat would sometimes run out in the early spring since the only good hunting was in the fall and winter. In the spring the chickens would begin to mature and be a good size for frying. Papa assured her they would have chickens all year and she didn't need to worry about canning them. He 'lowed as how no one in Sandy Fork canned chicken. Emily breathed a sigh of relief at this news.

Chapter 25

Papa and Emily had been attending church regularly at the Landmark Baptist Church. Emily loved hearing the preacher and she loved the music. One Sunday the preacher asked Emily if she would play the piano since their regular pianist was not going to be at church. Emily jumped at the chance to play the piano. She didn't know all the songs they sang, but after hearing a few notes, she could play them with ease. She also began to question the messages the preacher gave. If she understood them correctly, the catechism she had taken when she was in Peterborough did not make her a Christian. If she was not a Christian, then she was not going to go to heaven. As she was leaving the church on Sunday mornings after the service, she began to question the pastor about this subject. He assured her that he would come by to visit her real soon so they could discuss the entire subject. She wanted to become a Christian, yet she didn't want to forsake her faith as a Catholic. Somehow she knew the preacher would make it clearer to her when he stopped in to visit.

One Monday afternoon when she was working in the garden, she saw the preacher coming up the lane in his horse and wagon. She hurried to the house to put on a clean apron. They no longer fastened around her middle like they once did, but she felt cleaner when she had one on to cover the dress. He came into the cabin and laid his Bible on the table as Emily was fixing him some tea. He began to talk to her about her life before she came to Sandy Fork. He questioned her about the times she had attended the Quaker church. Then he proceeded to lay out the plan of Salvation to her. He tried not to destroy her previous beliefs that she had learned as a child, and half apologized for the Quaker pastor who had been so adamant about her not being a Christian at all. He explained to her that the pastor should have been more concerned about what she didn't understand than to condemn her for her previous religious instructions. Brother Whitney, as Papa called him, explained to her that the Bible teaches that Jesus was the Savior of the world. He was sent by his Heavenly Father to be the sacrifice for all mankind so they might have eternal life after death, if they accepted the Biblical teachings of Jesus as this Savior. Emily could hardly comprehend all the information. He explained that she only needed to believe and pray the prayer of sinners to be forgiven of her sins and receive the Salvation that belief in Jesus offered. Emily readily agreed to be "saved" and asked to have a book to study so she could understand more fully what Salvation meant to her and to her future. Brother Whitney simply offered her the Bible and suggested that she study it and make a note of the questions she had. He would visit with her again real soon and they would have a study class until she felt comfortable with what she had learned. He insisted that she learn to pray daily even if they were simple prayers. She should also ask for God's help in all her decisions whether they be for today or next week, or next year. He also noted that he was aware of the impending birth of a child. He wanted her to specifically be praying for the health and welfare of her child. Emily readily agreed to begin immediately praying that way and to begin studying the Bible daily. Brother Whitney rose to leave and asked Emily to join him in a prayer of Salvation. She agreed and with tears in her eyes, she heard the preacher pray a prayer for her and the entire family. Brother Whitney told her that there would be a Baptismal at the creek in the early summer when it got a little warmer and he would want her to be Baptized. She had to think about that and told him she wanted to study what the Bible said first. He left the cabin and the screen door made the familiar slap as he mounted into the wagon to go on his way. Since Papa had been in the tobacco field, he had not noticed that Brother Whitney had been there, but he did wave to him as he left. No doubt Papa knew what the visit was about and thought it was best to let the preacher meet with Emily alone.

Shortly after dinner the mailman came by the house and left two letters addressed to Emily. One was from Eustis, and it was a big envelope. The other letter was from Mrs. Thompson. She could hardly wait to open them. The big envelope intrigued Emily and she literally tore it open. It was a large picture of Eustis in his uniform. She grabbed the picture and went out in the yard under the shade tree and cried. She had been so busy with the chores and her classes with Papa she felt that she had neglected Eustis. She had written to him almost daily, but she was sure her letters did not convey to him how much she missed him. His picture only made her miss him more. She began to cry even harder until she had no tears left. In the envelope with the picture was a letter and as she wiped the tears from her face with her apron, she began to read the letter:

My dearest Emily:

Last week we had our pictures made. I hope you like this one of me in my uniform. It looks strange to me since I have never had such nice clothes.

I got your letter about us having a baby. I can hardly believe I am going to be a father. I wish I could hold you in my arms and tell you how much I love you. I will sometime soon, I promise.

I am sending you my paycheck from the Navy. I kept $5.00 for myself and had the rest sent to you from the Quartermaster. The check will come directly to you in an envelope. I know you will use it wisely to buy things for our new baby.

The food here is good. For breakfast each morning we have eggs, hot cakes, canned milk, and mush. For dinner we had boiled spuds, franks and kraut, canned milk, and macaroni with cheese. And for supper we have chicken, mashed spuds, canned milk, and ice cream. I have never eaten ice cream except what we cranked for ourselves at a church social, but it sure was good.

I must go now; it is time for "lights out" and I am sleepy. I hope to see you soon. I will have a furlough coming up soon.

Your loving husband,

Eustis Carmichael

Emily read the letter several times as she sat under the shade tree and wondered what canned milk would taste like. Then she thought about ice cream that you didn't crank yourself and decided that life was pretty good for Eustis. But, she wanted him to come home soon. She ran to the field to show the picture to Papa. She wanted to set it on the shelf in the kitchen until the new room was finished. "And Papa", she asked, "will the new room be finished before Eustis gets here"? Needless to say Papa went over to

Jasper's house that very afternoon to see if they could speed up the construction on the new room. Eustis was coming home soon!

In the excitement of the moment Emily had almost forgotten the letter from Mrs. Thompson. She reached in her apron pocket and pulled out her letter and quickly began to read through it.

Dear Emily:

I received your letter the other day and was so glad to hear from you. I am also glad that you are teaching your grandfather to read. He will always be thankful that he learned.

I know that you will enjoy playing the piano at church if you ever get the chance. It is a God given talent that you have.

I saw your Aunt Margaret in the hardware store a few days ago. She says that your Uncle Russell is not very well. He has a bad cough and is having a lot of trouble trying to work. However, he is working back in the mine again.

I am so happy that you are going to have a baby. I know that you will be a good mother. Do you know what you would rather have; a boy or a girl? I guess it really doesn't matter as long as it is healthy.

Please write to me again real soon. I love receiving your letters. Remember that I love you as if you were my own daughter.

Your friend,

Mrs. Thompson

Emily folded the letter and put it in her apron pocket. Tears slowly fell on to her dress. She never realized how lonely she was until she got that letter from Mrs. Thompson. Then, she knew how much that dear lady's friendship had meant to her. Living in Sandy Fork had taught her a lot of new lessons about life, but she had not developed any friends whom she could visit other than Mr. Hay and Jasper Baker. She could not share her many questions or interests with them. She wondered just how long it would be before she would have a good friend again. Oh, if only she knew where Charlotte was; she could be her intimate friend.

It just so happened that Papa saw Emily as she was reading Mrs. Thompson's letter. He saw the tears, even though she had quickly tried to wipe them away. He put his arm around her shoulders and attempted to console her. His gesture of sympathy only made a torrent of more tears to come involuntarily. She sobbed into his shoulder as she realized just how much she missed Meadville. When she had finished her cry, Papa wanted to know what he could do to help her. He wasn't accustomed to having someone cry on his shoulder. He had never shown much emotion even to Mama, but Emily seemed so fragile. Besides he really considered her his baby daughter. Emily was barely 20 years old, but he saw her as just a child.

Quickly she blurted out how much she would like to go to visit Aunt Margaret and all the others in Meadville. Would it be something she could do soon? When she got the government check from Eustis she would have the money to pay for a train ticket. She promised to get the garden in good shape before she left, and expected to work extra hard when she got home to catch up with the chores. She was talking so fast trying to get all the information out before Papa might say "no" that he began to laugh. He hugged her shoulders as he told her that he thought it would be wonderful for her to go visit everyone in Meadville. She could go next Monday if it didn't rain. They would go to Huntington to the train depot where he would find out when she would be back. He planned to meet the train when she returned. Realizing that she could catch the train in Sandy Fork on Monday, he thought that they should go into town and find out the schedule of the train from Pikeville into Huntington.

Emily could hardly believe her ears. She had much to do in a short amount of time. She quickly wrote a note to Mrs. Thompson and Aunt Margaret telling them that she would be in Meadville on Tuesday evening. As she sat at the table she also wrote a letter to Eustis.

My dearest Eustis:

I loved your picture. I am so happy to get it; because now I can show everyone what you look like in your uniform. You look so handsome and it makes me lonesome to see you. I hope you can come home on a furlough before long.

I am going to take a trip to Meadville to see Aunt Margaret and Uncle Russell. I will also go to visit your mother when I get there. I will visit Mrs. Thompson, too. I received a letter from her last week. She says that Uncle Russell is not doing well.

I read about the new program that President Roosevelt has come up with called Social Security. It was in the newspaper that Mr. Hays gave to me. I sent it to Uncle Russell. It is a government program that helps people who have not been able to save money for their old age because of the Depression. I hope it is something that Uncle Russell can get since I feel he is nearly unable to work. He is 73 years old and I wonder how much longer he can go down into the mines.

I must go now, I need to get my chores all caught up before I leave to go to Meadville. Please write soon.

Your loving wife,

Emily

Emily hurried to post the letter before the mailman came. She had a number of chores to do before she would be ready to go to Meadville. She remembered that the train from Pikeville ran on Monday, Wednesday, and Thursday. She thought that she could be ready by Wednesday of the next week. She hoped to stay a week in Meadville and come home on Wednesday, thereby riding the train all the way to Sandy Fork. She planned to change trains in Huntington and then ride all the way to Meadville without having to change from one train to another again.

Emily knew that she needed to get a dress or two finished before she left Sandy Fork. The ones she had been wearing were really worn and they hardly fit around her expanding tummy anymore. She did not want Aunt Margaret or Mrs. Thompson to see her in old clothes. She dug around in her closet to find something she could wear, but none of the feed sack dresses she had been wearing seemed to fit. She went to the closet where Papa hung his clothes. Mama's clothes were still hanging there.

Since Mama had been gone nearly three years, she wondered if she dared to ask Papa if she could use the fabric to make something for herself to wear. She did what Brother Whitney said to do; she prayed about how to ask Papa for Mama's old clothes. The next morning as they were eating breakfast before starting to do chores, she mentioned she didn't have much to wear to Meadville. He 'lowed as how Mama's things were still hanging in the closet and maybe they would fit Emily. It would make Mama proud if Emily could use them rather than see them rot to nothing. Emily smiled and thanked the Lord for answering her prayer. She hurriedly milked the cow and pulled weeds in the garden before the sun got too hot. Then she picked the lettuce, the peas, and pulled radishes for dinner and rushed into the house to begin her clothing project. She put on a pot of soup to cook for their dinner and in order that she could sew while it cooked. Papa and Jasper were not going to work on the new room that day so Emily would be able to sew uninterrupted until noon and then again after they had all eaten dinner. Emily was ecstatic about her new wardrobe and her impending trip back to Meadville. She was surprised that she was so excited to return to Aunt Margaret's house, but she felt that Uncle Russell might need her help. Also, she could hardly wait to see Mrs. Thompson. She wanted to talk to her about the baby. She still knew nothing about having a baby and she was sure Mrs. Thompson would fill her in on the details.

Chapter 26

As the local train stopped at the station in Sandy Fork to take on water and coal, there were several people waiting on the platform to board the train going to Huntington. Emily was among them. She had packed herself a large basket of food to take since she remembered the trip when she first came to Sandy Fork. She knew it would be a long ride and that she would get hungry. The check from the government for Eustis' Navy pay had arrived on Monday. She had gone to the bank to cash it. The banker asked if she wanted to open an account, but Emily felt that an account could be opened later. She knew that she needed to take the money with her. The teller gave her a $20.00 bill and a $5.00 bill and told her to be careful with her money. He said that next time she might want to deposit it in an account for safekeeping. Emily hardly knew what that meant, but she was too excited about the trip to give it much thought. As the train finally pulled away, Papa stood on the platform and watched it move away. She thought she saw a tear in his eye as he waved to her.

When the train pulled into the station at Huntington, Emily ran into the station to check on her piano. It was still there. She sat down at the keyboard and played just like she did before and the stationmaster 'lowed as how no one else ever played it. However, as she played a crowd gathered around to listen to her play. She loved the attention and the memories that flooded her mind as she played. She decided that soon she would figure a way to get it to the cabin. There would be room in the new room when it was finished. She realized that it would take several men to help her load the piano onto a wagon. So she dropped the idea from her mind for the moment and concentrated on boarding the train for the trip to Meadville and old friends.

Chapter 27

On the train ride Emily began to reflect on the life she had lived since her early beginning in Peterborough. Her mother had always wanted her to be educated and to become a teacher. She, also, had such a great admiration for Father John at St. Anthony's Catholic Church. All that changed dramatically when she left Peterborough and went to Meadville. Her life had taken a different turn. She had never felt a kinship to Aunt Margaret because of the strictness of her discipline and her rigid rules. However, she adored Uncle Russell. He was so kind to her and to Charlotte. When she thought of Charlotte she always wanted to cry. She had missed her so and she felt she had been stolen from her life. Each time she looked in the mirror, she saw Charlotte in spite of the fact that their hair was a little different in color. She felt she knew exactly what Charlotte might look like today. Then, she remembered Brother Whitney saying that she should pray for what she wanted. Faithfully every morning she had been praying that the Lord would lead her to Charlotte.

When she had left Meadville to go to Sandy Fork as her husband had suggested, she felt that she was leaving a part of her soul behind. Although she had never felt that she had roots there, to go to somewhere so different had left a big hole in her heart. Now, she had grown to love Papa and felt that she was a part of his whole life especially since she had been teaching him to read and write. She felt her efforts had made a big difference in his life. However, she wasn't at all sure that she had been making a life for herself there either.

As she was reflecting on all the past she was forced to look to the future. She and Eustis had hardly come to know each other as man and wife before he left for the service. She knew that it was the best thing to do at the time, but she missed having a kindred soul in her life. Now that she was going to have a baby, she felt a big responsibility to try to be both mother and father to their child. She was anxiously looking forward to the impending birth. Would it be a boy or girl? If it were a boy, she would name him Eustis after his father and if it were a girl she would name her Charlotte Marie. If she never found her twin then at least the name would always be with her.

The train rumbled along the tracks far into the night. She was able to sleep on the train without waking at all. She had eaten part of her food that she brought with her and the train porter brought her milk and lemonade as they traveled along. Even though the train stopped in the big cities along the way, she did not get off the train. She felt more secure when she just stood and walked around inside the train car. She knew that Uncle Russell would meet her at the train station and she began to think about seeing him again. She could hardly wait to see Mrs. Thompson, too.

Just as it was beginning to get daylight, the train pulled into the station at Meadville. The conductor came by her seat and touched her on the arm telling her it was her stop. She quickly awakened and grabbed her bags and walked down the aisle to the steps leading to the platform. She glanced around the crowd looking for Uncle Russell. When she didn't see him, she searched the crowd again for Charlotte as she always did when she saw a crowd of people. Then she saw a man resembling Uncle Russell who was so thin, gaunt, and pallid. She wasn't prepared for this; it brought tears to her eyes. She had last seen him a strong and virile man who stood upright and tall. Now he looked bent with age and somehow he seemed fragile. Nevertheless she ran to him as fast as her cumbersome body would take her. She embraced him in a long touching embrace.

He seemed to be very near tears as he told her how much he had missed her. He held her at arm's length and hugged her again expressing his pride in her maternal condition. She smiled and agreed that she felt good about it too. Suddenly she remembered Aunt Margaret and asked about her. Uncle Russell simply stated that she was at home and would have breakfast waiting for them when they got there. He walked ever so slowly through the station and to a car parked by the station. She was surprised to find that he now had an automobile. It was about three years old, he stated, but it was a wonderful convenience. It seemed that Aunt Margaret had decided the money they paid for the use of a horse and wagon from the livery stable could be applied to a car, therefore she had insisted they buy their own car. Emily loved the car and wondered if she could ever learn to drive one. She remembered trying to learn how to drive the horse and wagon and quickly decided driving a car couldn't be any harder.

As they drove through the streets in the early morning light she remembered them to look the same as they did so long ago when she came to Meadville the first time. The town was not alive yet, so the streets were nearly vacant giving her that same feel she remembered about them so long ago. As they rounded the corner to go home, she saw the library still standing tall and she was reminded that there was no library in Sandy Fork. She wondered how one went about trying to bring a library into town. She had read about Mr. Carnegie who had built a lot of libraries in the country. He had made a huge fortune in the steel business and had donated most of his money to making the country literate by building libraries. She wondered if she could get him to build one in Sandy Fork. Suddenly she saw their house come into view. It looked exactly as it had when she left. The flowers were in bloom, the garden was growing, and with disdain she spied the chicken coop. Standing in the doorway, as Uncle Russell pulled the car into a newly constructed driveway by the house, was Aunt Margaret. She looked the same as she did when Emily had left with only a few more gray hairs. She rushed to Emily's side of the car to help her alight. She casually noted her condition. Emily hugged her and mentioned how glad she was to see her. Inside the kitchen Aunt Margaret had prepared a big breakfast for all of them and the conversation flowed like water in a fountain. There seemed to be so much catching up to do. They all rattled on and on about what had happened in the few months that she had been gone. Emily surprised herself at how happy she was to be back in Meadville. Maybe what she enjoyed the most was to be able to go to the bathroom without having to take a walk out back.

As the day progressed she asked Uncle Russell if he would like to take a walk with her since she had been sitting on the train all night. They walked to the lake nearby and proceeded to talk about a lot of things that had happened. He wanted to ask a lot of questions about the "Social Security Act" that President Roosevelt had signed into law. He was sure it would apply to him, but he wasn't sure how to go about getting it. He stated that he did not want the money if it was welfare. Emily patiently explained that Social Security was not welfare, but a program that allowed people to pay into the plan each week from their paychecks. When those same people could no longer work because of illness or because they were 65 years old, they could draw on what had been paid into the fund. She assured him that she would go with him to the office in Meadville and apply for him to get his share.

It was during their walk that Emily became aware of his continual hacking cough. She had noticed it before, but now it was a real problem. Sometimes he would cough so hard that he would be faint and forced to sit down. She didn't like what she saw in his health, but she needed to be near him for a while until she discovered the problem. They continued talking as they walked about lots of things. She wanted to know about how Aunt Margaret was doing and if she still had to work so hard. Uncle Russell told her that they didn't raise as many chickens as they once did and that the garden was much smaller. She loved their car and asked if she could learn to drive it. Uncle Russell mentioned that if he could learn to drive, anyone could. It was easy to drive he stated. She wondered if they still had Snowball since she had not seen her in the house the night before, but he commented that she had run away shortly after Emily left. He guessed she was lonely and looked for a family with children that would let her sleep with them just as Emily had done. Uncle Russell wanted to hear all about her being "in a family way" and how she was feeling. She couldn't stop talking about the life she was living in Sandy Fork. She related the stories of planting tobacco, teaching Papa to read and write, visiting the schoolhouse where Mr. Hay was the teacher, and even mentioned that her piano was still in the train station.

They had walked a long way from home and he was getting very tired. Emily decided it was nearly time to head back to the house to help Aunt Margaret fix their lunch. As they arrived at the door, Aunt Margaret began to talk about being alone and having to work so hard preparing food for them that Emily began to feel guilty. She immediately went to the kitchen to help. When she and Aunt Margaret were together, she asked about Uncle Russell's health and mentioned the bad cough. Aunt Margaret seemed to think it was nothing to worry about, that he was just getting older and that those things happen, she commented. Emily was not convinced and decided she would try to get him some help.

Shortly after lunch when they had finished cleaning the kitchen, she decided to go to visit Mrs. Thompson. She could hardly wait; she had so much to tell her. As she knocked on the door, she could hear Mrs. Thompson walking with her cane to the door to greet her. When the door opened, Emily burst into the room all bubbly with enthusiasm and Mrs. Thompson hugged her almost as if she didn't want to let her go. They sat near the fireplace in the parlor, and Emily continued to talk incessantly. She talked about all the things she had learned on the farm, and about Papa, and the things she wanted to do before the baby came. Mrs. Thompson listened ever so quietly and let her describe her new experiences. When there was a lull in the conversation, Mrs. Thompson asked her about the coming baby. Did she intend to come to Meadville before the baby was born? Emily had not thought about that. Did she have the layette for the baby ready? Emily replied that she had not had time to prepare anything but she still had about 5 months before the birth to make those preparations. She didn't want to tell Mrs. Thompson that she hadn't had the money to buy the things she needed until Eustis' check came from the government. Of course, Mrs. Thompson was smarter than Emily gave her credit for and she sensed that was the reason. She got up from her chair and with her cane thumped her way across the room to the trunk she kept in her bedroom. She opened the trunk exposing the contents. It was full of baby clothes. Emily knew they were from her little girl, born so many years ago. Mrs. Thompson reached into the trunk and took out the first layer and handed them to Emily. "I want you to have these for your baby" she said. "They will never be used by anyone else again and you should have them. My little girl would want you to use them, since I now consider you my daughter". Emily was overcome. No one had ever been so good to her as Mrs. Thompson. She just didn't know how to say a proper word of thanks. She began to cry as Mrs. Thompson cradled her "new" daughter in her arms. Emily sobbed out the trauma she had experienced since her real mother passed away in 1917. It seemed to be a torrent of pent up emotion that she had harbored for many years. When she was finally able to control herself, she murmured that she had not had a real mother for a long time and if Mrs. Thompson wanted to be her mother, she would welcome her with open arms. They sat together sharing a pot of tea that Mrs. Thompson had prepared and talked about the upcoming birth, of Eustis' training that he was receiving in Illinois, and life at Sandy Fork. She really didn't think she would be able to come back to Meadville for the birth of the baby but as soon as she was able, she promised to visit and bring the baby for Mrs. Thompson to see. After a long afternoon Emily could see that Mrs. Thompson was growing tired. She felt that she needed to get back to Aunt Margaret's house. She told Mrs. Thompson that she would return the next day with boxes to pack the baby clothes in so she could carry them on the train. Mrs. Thompson adamantly replied that the trunk should be strapped for her to take the entire trunk with her. She stated that she had no further need for the trunk or the baby clothes. She wanted her new "grandchild" to have them all. As Emily was leaving, she fought hard to not break into tears again. She turned to Mrs. Thompson and asked, "have you ever heard anything about Charlotte" to which Mrs. Thompson slowly shook her head no.

Emily fairly skipped, in her cumbersome state, all the way back to Aunt Margaret and Uncle Russell's house. She was so happy to have found someone who really loved her for herself. As she rushed into the house the thought occurred to her that she should not mention Mrs. Thompson's gift to her. She would wait until time to leave before she would tell them she had to pick up the trunk to take to Sandy Fork. She pondered the thought that she might have to leave it at the train station too, however her ticket would take her to Sandy Fork so she dismissed that fear from her mind. Aunt Margaret was preparing supper as she came in the door. She couldn't imagine why Emily was so filled with excitement and she immediately asked her to help prepare the food. Uncle Russell was napping in the parlor and didn't hear her return.

As they sat around the table enjoying supper of canned chicken, the mere thought of such a thing sent shivers up her spine. She wondered if this was some of the chicken that she had helped to can last summer and decided it was better than she had expected. The vegetables were great and Aunt Margaret had prepared tomatoes and rice that Emily loved. And she had baked a dried apple pie especially for her since she remembered it was Emily's favorite. Uncle Russell told her there was a play at the theatre in downtown Pittsburgh that he would love to take her to see if she would have the time. It seemed to be a good idea but Emily knew money was short and besides, she wasn't sure he had the energy to go so far from home. She politely stated that she would consider it and maybe they could go later in the week.

Early the next morning after the kitchen had been cleaned, Emily stated that she wanted to go to St. Anthony's church to see Father Paul. She wanted him to know that she was doing fine at Sandy Fork. Uncle Russell asked if he could go with her since it would be a nice time for a walk. As they entered the church, Emily was reminded how pretty it was. It brought back all the memories she had of the days when she was here. She also remembered her wedding at the altar and it made her homesick to see Eustis. Father Paul was surprised to see her and was delighted to know that she was "in a family way". He asked if she was in Meadville to stay. She explained that this was a hurried trip and she needed to get back to Sandy Fork soon because of the work to be done on the farm. As she was leaving the church, she went to the altar and prayed. She prayed for Uncle Russell, Mrs. Thompson, Eustis, and her unborn child. She could hardly hold back the tears as she remembered to pray for Charlotte, wherever she was.

Chapter 28

Shortly after lunch, Uncle Russell and Emily went to the courthouse to check on the possibility of Social Security for him. The lady behind the counter asked him lots of questions. Did he have a birth certificate? If not, was his birth recorded in a family Bible? If he did not have that, then did he have an older sibling who would vouch that he had been born? Emily laughed out loud at that remark, since she was standing by his side. She thought that was enough evidence that he had been born. Since he was born right in Meadville, the lady sent them across the hall to the Recorder's office to look up his birth records. He was very fortunate since his birth was recorded and he obtained a copy of the birth certificate for three cents. They went back to the lady and showed her the certified copy of his birth. She then explained to him that he was old enough to receive his share of Social Security which would be about $200.00 per month. Uncle Russell's jaw dropped. That was more than he had ever made at the mine. Why was he entitled to that amount of money? She explained that President Roosevelt had signed into law a document that stated that those persons older than 65 were entitled to this amount of money to help them when they could no longer work. If he should die, then his widow would receive one half the money until she died. Uncle Russell promptly insisted that if this was "poor relief" he did not want to accept it. She convinced him that this money was based on how many years he had worked and that all future generations would be paying into this fund which would be self-perpetuating. With his head full of information, he signed the papers and asked just when would he receive that amount of money? She explained that the check would come from the government about the 3rd day of the next month. They turned and walked out of the office quietly, but when they reached the street, Uncle Russell let out a shout that could be heard for blocks. He was so excited that he turned to Emily and exclaimed that he was rich; at last!

True to her word, she returned to Mrs. Thompson's house the next day. She had asked her if there were straps to put around the trunk to secure it. Mrs. Thompson directed her to the pantry just off the kitchen and stated there was probably enough straps hanging in the storage closet to wrap around the trunk. While Emily was searching for the leather straps, Mrs. Thompson had brought out all her dresses she had worn when she was pregnant with her daughter. She had laid them out on the bed and asked Emily to put them in the trunk as well. It seemed to Emily that she was taking everything the lady had back to Sandy Fork with her, however, Mrs. Thompson remarked that she was not able to do much or go many places anymore to use these things. She wanted Emily to have these clothes to add to her wardrobe. Emily thought about all the lovely things and wondered just what she would do with them at Sandy Fork. She certainly couldn't wear them in the tobacco patch. Then she realized that maybe she would not always be in Sandy Fork and someday she could wear them to see a play as Uncle Russell had suggested.

Her visit to Meadville had been all too short. It was time to prepare to leave. She had finally mentioned to Aunt Margaret that there was a trunk at Mrs. Thompson that she needed to take back with her. As she was readying her own bags Aunt Margaret came into her room with her arms full of something. She laid her burden out on the bed and displayed for Emily to see; the most beautiful handmade layette she could have imagined. Aunt Margaret had been busy for a long time, she thought. When she asked about the lovely pieces and commented about the finery of the handwork, Aunt Margaret confessed that she had once expected a baby but it had been stillborn. Tears came to Emily's eyes and dropped slowly onto her dress. She had never known this about her. Was that the reason Aunt Margaret was so bitter about children; because she had lost her only one? She hardly knew what to say to her. She walked over to Aunt Margaret and started to hug her as a way of saying thanks, but she backed away, not wanting the familiarity of her gesture of love. Emily could only say thanks verbally and she swiped away the tears. She was never sure if she was crying for the lost baby or the lost opportunity for Aunt Margaret to be loved by someone. She really wanted to love her but there had been no chance.

The trunk was loaded, Emily's carpetbag stuffed to capacity, and a small box carrying what wouldn't fit into her grip, were all put in the car for the trip to the train station. Aunt Margaret had prepared a large lunch for her to take with her for the long trip. Emily had all she could carry in her arms and more than she could carry in her heart. She wanted to ask about Charlotte, but she just couldn't bring up the subject to Aunt Margaret. It seemed that if she knew where she was it was a secret she would carry to her grave. Uncle Russell drove her to the train station and watched as the train rumbled out of the station carrying her back to the mountains and an entirely different world. Emily wasn't sure where she belonged: maybe neither place.

Chapter 29

The trip home was tiring. Emily began to feel that she was getting heavier. Her emotions were at their peak. The slightest little thing made her cry. But then she had experienced a lot in such a short time. She had reason to cry. She was now the keeper of Mrs. Thompson's legacy of baby clothes for her daughter, but she had the beloved dowry that Aunt Margaret had prepared for a baby she never got to see. At the mere thought of Uncle Russell's frail body and hacking cough made her cry even more. She did not want him to die. He had been the best thing in her life and their friendship was like a thread running through the past. She thought if he could just live a while longer, she could tie the thread to her future as well. As the train reverberated along the tracks through day and night, Emily slept intermittently between her thoughts. Someday soon she would sort it all out.

When the train pulled into Huntington, Emily hurried into the station to play her piano. When she looked in the corner by the big stove, it was bare. She was horrified. Where had her piano gone? She ran to the stationmaster, but he was not the one that was always there when she came through. He knew nothing about any piano. He had just started to work at the depot and he had never seen a piano in a train station. She gathered up her bags and stood watch by the trunk until the train to Pikeville came into the station. She made sure her box and trunk were loaded on this train and hurried to her seat but she could hardly keep back the tears. What would she tell Mrs. Thompson had happened to her piano? Who would steal a piano? She hoped a little girl of the man who took it would enjoy her piano as much as she did. Maybe the train company came and took it and chopped it up because it was in the way. She could hardly sit still in her seat she was so agitated. When the train stopped at Sandy Fork she spied Papa at the station. She fairly flew down the steps and right into his face telling him that someone had stolen her piano from the station in Huntington. He 'lowed as how someone wanted it worse than she did. She had completely forgotten about her bounty she had been given in Meadville. And she failed to ask how he had managed without her. She was too distraught about her piano. Their ride home was rather silent.

It was getting dark when they went up the lane to the cabin. In the dusk light she could see the outline of the lean-to on the side of the house. Did that mean it was completed? Papa and Jasper must have worked non-stop to have completed the room in such a short time. She hurried into the house, dropping her bags just inside the doorway and rushed into the new room. There, standing in the middle of the floor, stood her beloved piano.

Emily was sure there were no more tears in her head, but she burst into a flood of new tears as she hugged Papa so tightly he began to cough. "You sure fooled me", she sputtered through her tears. "I was so worried someone had stolen my piano" she announced as she sat down and played nearly every tune she knew. Reality set in and she realized it was time to fix supper for Papa when she turned and saw that he had the table laden with food for them to eat. As they sat around the table in the lamplight, Emily tried to explain the entire visit in one long sentence as she related to Papa what a wonderful time she had in Meadville.

Morning came too soon for Emily. As daybreak began to peep through her new room, she realized it was time to get up and make breakfast. She had to be so careful where she walked because she had merely dumped her treasures onto the floor in the new room. She quickly donned a robe and went to the kitchen to fix something for them to eat. It was beginning to warm up outside and she wondered about cooking on the coal stove in the summer. She would soon find out that you just get accustomed to being hot all the time. If it was unbearable you simply sat outside in the shade 'til the sun went down.

Emily worked all day trying to get her baby's finery in a proper place. She had no dresser to put them in so she simply left them in the trunk. She would get some boxes when they went to town and she could make a dresser by putting box on top of box in stacks to hold all the tiny clothes. When she continued to sort through all the things she had, she was surprised to find that she had clothes for a baby up until it was three or four years old. There were hand knitted sweaters, gowns, dresses, stockings, blankets, and even tiny shoes. She would have the best-dressed baby in the world, certainly Sandy Fork. These clothes were fit for a king or queen. Up until that moment, she had not had any preference in the sex of the baby. Now she really felt she would like to have a boy for Eustis.

While she was working on her new room, Papa came in with the mail of several days. She had three letters from Eustis. When she began to read them, she realized she had been gone a long time.

My darling Emily:

I received your letter today. I am glad you are going to visit your Uncle Russell. I hope he is not too ill to visit with you.

Work here is hard, but I love it. I am learning to do a lot of things that I never had thought about. Everything is measuring and calculating. That was always easy for me when I worked as a carpenter.

I am so happy to hear about our baby. Be sure you take good care of yourself and eat right. I will try to come home when it is time for you to have the baby.

I must close now but remember I love both of you.

Your loving husband,

Eustis.

She laid the other letters aside as she realized it was time for her to check the garden to see what needed to be done. Papa had milked the cow and gathered the eggs. As she went through the kitchen, she spied a big bucket of fresh greens, cucumbers, tomatoes nearly ripe, a mess of green beans, and a few peas. Stuck in a fruit jar filled with water she saw a bouquet of spring flowers in the middle of the table. All this was Papa's way of saying, "welcome home".

Emily set about doing as much as she could get done during the day. She spent her evenings working with Papa on his reading and writing skills. She would play the piano just a little before they went to their rooms to go to bed. She found her energy level was not as good as it once was and she was sure it because of the extra weight she was carrying. The morning sickness had abated and she could get a lot accomplished in the early morning times. The crops were coming on rapidly and required almost all of her time, although Papa would tend the fire in the yard for her to do the canning of the vegetables. Papa would work most of the morning in the tobacco patch and then again in the late afternoon. Jasper Baker had brought them some guineas to put in the tobacco patch. They looked strange to Emily, but Papa explained they were somewhat like a turkey but their favorite meal was tobacco worms. They would wander through the tobacco field and eat virtually all of the worms on the plants. If the guineas didn't eat the worms, the worms would eat the tobacco and ruin the plant. Emily ventured out into the field to see this procedure and was so squeamish about those ugly worms, she decided the guineas were her best friend. If the guinea missed one Papa would pull the worm off and throw it on the ground as hard as he could, causing them to burst open. Emily thought this to be one of the most disgusting exercises she had seen on the farm. But she was sure glad that Papa had not discovered they might be good to eat because she was sure it would have been her job to can them.

Summer was in its fullest bloom and Emily was busy with her schedule of hoeing, harvesting, canning the vegetables while teaching Papa, playing the piano at church and writing to Eustis. It seemed she was on a merry-go-round. She didn't seem to have a moment of her own. She had sorted through and handled all the beautiful baby clothes she had brought from Meadville. She had many lovely lacy items that would transform her baby into a cherub. She had many practical items such as diapers. She counted four dozen diapers from the items that Mrs. Thompson and Aunt Margaret had given her. Surely that would be enough. There were several band type items that she couldn't identify. She asked Papa and he informed her they were "belly bands". You wrapped them around a newborn baby holding the umbilical cord stub in place until it healed and fell off. She had never seen one or even heard of its use, but she decided she would use them because someone thought they were important. She carefully folded all the items and placed them back inside the trunk. She wanted to take another trip to see Mr. Hay, but wondered when she could work it in. If it rained, she wouldn't have to work in the garden, but also, if it rained very hard, the road would wash out, so she just couldn't find a day she could go to town. And in between all these chores, she found a minute or two to play her piano. She wondered just how she could ever take care of a baby and do all these chores too. How did Papa do all this work without her around, she asked herself?

Papa had been busy in the tobacco patch. First he had to pull the suckers off at the bottom of the plant so the good plant could receive more of the fertile ground and moisture. Then he had to de-tassle the top of the plant to keep it from cross-pollinating with other types of tobacco. Because Papa grew the broad leaf variety, he couldn't run the risk that it would pollinate with the Burley variety. Then it would produce a mixture of both and no one would buy that type of tobacco. The guineas had been busy feasting on the tobacco worms. When Emily thought about them, she would shudder.

On Thursday morning, a lady knocked on the door. Emily was busy preparing tomatoes to be canned. She had washed the jars and lids and had them drying on the porch. When the lady knocked, Emily took off her apron to appear as neat as possible and cleared a place on the table in case she needed to serve something cold to drink. She went to the door and greeted a lady in her mid 50's who told her she was a mid-wife for all the area. Emily brought her inside and apologized for the mess still on the table. Mrs. Miller assured her she would only stay a few minutes but she wanted to ask Emily a few questions. She queried her on when she might expect the baby, to which Emily replied the thought it would be sometime around Christmas. She explained that the last menstrual period that she had was in February, in the middle of the month. Mrs. Miller smiled and stated that she wasn't aware of any 11-month babies, and by her calculations it would be born around the middle of October. Emily cringed and stated that would be about the time the tobacco would be cut. She couldn't possibly be down during that time. Mrs. Miller laughed and told her that babies don't wait even if tobacco didn't. Someone else would need to cut the tobacco. She proceeded to tell Emily some of the things she would need for the birthing. Emily proudly showed her the lovely layette that she had received on her trip to Meadville. Mrs. Miller scowled at the finery and muttered something about it being the fanciest dressed baby in Elliott County. She gave her a few words of things not to do. She told her not to let anyone examine her internally or she might die of "childbed fever". In modern terms that means infection because many times the mid-wife did not wear sterile gloves or even wash their hands before attempting an interior examination. She also told Emily not to eat any more Kraut or pickled beans until after the baby was weaned. Emily listened carefully to what she told her to do and she wished later, that she had made a few notes to help her remember. She asked Mrs. Miller how she could reach her once her labor pains started. "Just have Papa come and get me, I am only livin' over on the next ridge", she said. With that information, she rose to leave and wished Emily good luck in her baby's birth and cautioned her to remember that birth would occur around the middle of October.

Emily finished her job of canning this batch of tomatoes. She put some meat on for their supper, and hurried to the table to write a note to Eustis.

My Dearest Eustis:

The midwife was just here and gave me some instructions for birthing our baby. She says the baby will be born about October 15. Could you possibly get a furlough at that time? I can hardly wait to see you. I miss you so.

Papa is busy tending the tobacco and I have been busy canning vegetables for us to eat this winter. I hope you have not been working too hard. Write to me soon.

Your loving wife,

Emily

Emily thought through the things that Mrs. Miller had told her about her unborn baby. She wondered if she had done anything that was harmful to the child because of her ignorance. If only Charlotte was here maybe she would have known what to do and what not to do. She went to the piano and began to play a lullaby. It really got her in the mood to become a mother. Papa came in from the field and heard her playing and soon joined her in singing the only words he knew. Emily loved the feeling of being the instrument of love to the old man. Somehow she felt he had not had much joy in his life and she was glad for any happiness she had been able to bring to his life.

Early the next morning Emily finished her chores then hitched the horse to the wagon and prepared to go to town. She really felt she needed to buy some more items for the baby. She had seen in the hardware store an array of baby powders and oils that she thought she would like to have. She had been saving the money from Eustis but felt she could afford to buy a few things. She also knew that when the baby arrived and she could determine if it was a girl or boy there would be things she might need then, but for now she only wanted the necessities. On her way home, she stopped in at the schoolhouse to see Mr. Hay. She had never mentioned to him that she was going to have a baby. This time when she went inside the building it was obvious. He came to her immediately and congratulated her. He asked her about her husband and when he would be home. Somehow Emily wondered if he thought she didn't have one but she quickly put that thought out of her mind. She exchanged the books she had borrowed for other books and asked for any novels that he had been able to get from the library in Newfoundland. He had brought her the Bridge of San Luis Rey by Thornton Wilder. It was a small book so she thought she might have time to read it. She told him she would miss the month of October because that was when the baby was due, but she still had September when she would come back to visit. As she left the school, Mr. Hay stood in the doorway and wondered how such a fine young lady ended up in this "God forsaken county". He almost mourned for her status. It was so obvious to him that she was of a finer breed and he didn't want her to be damaged by the dire circumstances that she was experiencing. He knew Papa to be a good man, but living in Elliott County would give her no hope for the future for herself or her child. He stepped back inside the classroom and said a prayer for her safety and well being. Now he knew why the Lord had sent her to him; to give him the courage and ability to continue to teach those whose life was within his grasp, that there was a better world out there.

Chapter 30

Summer was winding down in a blaze of heat and humidity. Emily was cumbersome and awkward in her movements. She was unsteady on her feet when she was on uneven ground. She was so careful not to fall; she was sure that if she fell on her face she would not be able to get up. Sometimes she felt like a turtle on its back. She was glad that Eustis did not see her in this overgrown condition and she wondered how soon it would all end. She had the baby's layette all complete. She found an old cradle in the loft of the barn and she had scrubbed it clean. It was an effort to make it useable since it appeared the chickens had been using it as a nest for the last few years. She was sure it was the one that Eustis' mother had been rocked in when she was a baby, but it was the best Emily could do right now. Papa brought in an old rocker from the same storage space and she went to work on cleaning it also. It needed a new bottom in it since the last person who used it appeared to have been bigger than the chair. Emily knew that couldn't have been Papa because he was so frail, but since she never knew Mama, she decided it had to have been her who broke the webbing. Jasper Baker took it with him one morning and told Emily not to worry, for a person who was as small as she, it wouldn't take much to make it like new. He informed her that all mothers had to rock their babies and she would need this chair.

Emily had gathered all the root crops she could and stored them in the root cellar that Papa had prepared near the barn. She had pulled the turnips and dug the sweet potatoes and the white potatoes. The tomatoes were about all gone, but she gathered the green ones and made pickle relish for them to eat in the winter. She had canned everything the garden had to offer and she was sure they could feed all of Elloitt County if a famine set in. However, the biggest problem was the tobacco. Who would help Papa cut the tobacco? She worried about that dilemma for several days. She remembered the mid-wife telling her that someone other than Emily would have to do that chore. Emily felt she did not have much time left before delivery. The baby had been kicking fiercely for several weeks. She thought for a while it would kick its way out of its cocoon but she seemed to have survived its stalwart efforts. No one told her that she should expect all this movement from the baby within her. When the baby first began to move around, she was afraid something was wrong. She just waited to see what happened. Then, she realized it was the baby showing signs of life. She loved the feeling even when the movement was so strong that it seemed to take her breath away. She was sure the child would be nearly full grown by the time she gave birth.

Emily was in the garden pulling the last remnants of the vegetables that she could find when she heard Mr. Baker coming up the lane to the cabin. He seemed to have someone riding with him. Perhaps he was returning the rocker, she thought. She waddled to the front of the house to welcome him and she could see the person seemed to have on a strange set of clothing. Suddenly she realized the person was in uniform!!! It was Eustis. She could hardly walk, and impossible to run, however, she hurried to the side of the wagon as fast as she could make her body go. He came down from the wagon and swept her off her feet. She began to cry uncontrollably. All her emotions that she had held back for months came running in a torrent of tears. Why didn't he tell her he was coming? How did he get here? How long could he stay? So many questions and she gave him no time to answer. They hurried to the house to sit down to talk all at once. Jasper brought the rocker into her room and placed it by the cradle. "Now you are all set", he said, "that baby can come anytime now that daddy is here".. He turned and left without staying for lemonade. Papa had been in the tobacco patch but came to the house in time to see Eustis get down off the wagon. Emily was still overcome with emotion as she kept gazing at Eustis. He was so handsome, she thought, and the uniform made him look like a real gentleman. She had prayed for days for the Lord to send someone to help cut the tobacco patch. He had answered her prayer.

Emily and Eustis had so much to talk about that there didn't seem to be time enough to say it all. He looked at her over and over and told her how radiant she looked. He didn't mind her big belly. He looked at her face. He stroked her hair that she had let grow and had curled it with the curling iron that she heated in the lamp chimney. He looked at all the baby things that she had so carefully placed in neat piles on the top of her piano. And without much coaxing, she played the piano for him. The lullabies that she had been playing now sounded so real since Eustis was here. They were a family now and soon they would have a new baby all their own. As they crawled into bed and held each other, it seemed like time had not passed and that it was just yesterday since he had said goodbye. There was one thing between them; Emily's big tummy that housed their baby. Emily could hardly believe he was with her again and would be here for the birth of their child.

Morning came and they were all back in the field taking care of all the crops they could before the frost. The weather was turning cooler each day and the daylight hours seem to be speeding away. Even though the almanac said the daylight would only fade about 7 minutes per day, those who were using it to see by would argue that it was more like 20 minutes. Cold weather comes early in the mountains and seems to stay longer. Emily had to get out the woolen things she had from last winter. Her sweaters didn't quite meet around her but they kept her shoulders warm. She brought out the heavy blankets from the trunk so she could wrap the baby in warm clothing. Papa and Eustis cut more wood to be used in the cook stove since it was the only source of heat for the cabin. Tomorrow they would begin cutting tobacco, Papa told them. He had already prepared the racks to place the plants on for the smoking and drying. They would begin early and work as long as they possibly could before dark. Emily would cook for them and feed them, but she was unable to do much more.

In the early morning hour around 2:00 A.M. Emily awakened Eustis. She told him she was having a lot of pain and she was sure it was labor pains. She had been awake for nearly an hour and the pains were coming closer together. He should get dressed and go get Phoebe Miller, the mid-wife. Eustis didn't know where she lived, but he hurried to get Papa. They were both so excited they could hardly get their clothes on. Emily just walked the floor and tried not to give in to the pain. Mrs. Miller had told her to put a knife under her pillow and it would cut the pain. She didn't believe that for a minute, but she placed it there anyway. Her thoughts were that it wouldn't help, but it sure couldn't hurt unless, of course, she ran her hand under the pillow. Emily stoked up the fire and made some coffee for everyone in between her pains that seemed to be coming almost non-stop. She wandered back to her room and thought she would lie down in the bed, but that didn't seem to help much. She got back on her feet and got the rags ready and the pan for the hot water so Mrs. Miller would have everything she needed. Then she stopped by the door and prayed for Eustis to come back soon and for God to let the baby wait until he did. As she was finishing her prayer, she heard the old hound dog barking so she knew someone was on their way. Eustis burst through the door to see if she was still ok, and Papa was right behind him. Mrs. Miller could hardly get in the door for the two men. She calmly put Emily to bed, gave her some tea which she had brought with her in a fruit jar, handed her some towels rolled up and told her to squeeze them when she had a pain. She then tied an old blanket to each side of the head of the bed and told her to pull as hard as she could and push with all the muscles in her stomach. Emily could not understand any of what she told her, but she didn't have the breath or energy to ask for an explanation. It was nearly daybreak when Emily finally was ready to give birth to this child. She was near exhaustion, but everything seemed to be going along fine, according to the mid-wife. Eustis was nearly as exhausted as Emily from hearing her screams and moans in the next room. He had a difficult time handling the pain she was enduring although he had seen his mother give birth several times. Somehow it was different when it is your own wife, he told Papa. Suddenly he heard the noise that he had been waiting for; he heard his baby cry. He rushed to the doorway and asked to come in, however Mrs. Miller asked him to wait a few minutes. She was still tending to the birth. Eustis was sure those few minutes were the longest he had ever endured. When she came to the door, she handed him his newborn son and congratulated him on such a fine specimen. He carefully took the baby, smiling from ear to ear, and went to Emily's bedside. What a beautiful baby, he thought, and it was theirs! Emily was wet with sweat, her beautiful hair was plastered to her head, and she looked as if she would rather sleep than talk about it. She looked at the baby that Eustis had placed in her arms and she cried as she thought about what a beautiful event this really had been. The horror of the pain was gone, and the new life was just beginning for both of them – no all three of them! With that thought, she drifted off to sleep.

Mrs. Miller tended to the clean-up of the birthing room and went to the kitchen to enjoy a cup of that coffee. She glanced at the clock and wrote down that it was now 6:14 A.M. on Wednesday, October 8, 1933. "A fine time to be born", she said.

Eustis and Papa had survived the birthing since both of them had been through the experience before; however, Eustis was as giddy as a kid when he talked about the boy in the bed with Emily. He could hardly believe that this child was his. However, his frivolity was short lived when Papa brought him back to the present and told him that they had tobacco to cut. Mrs. Miller told them she would stay most of the day if Emily got along as she expected. She would have to go home in the evening but would return the next morning to help Emily learn to bathe and feed the baby. The men went to the field and Mrs. Miller returned to Emily's room. The baby was waking and would want to eat. Emily was awake and cuddling the little one in her arms as if he was still an unbelievable miracle to her. The mid-wife showed Emily how to clean her nipples with warm water and help the baby learn to suckle. It would be painful, at first, but it would get easier as time went on. Emily's breasts were full. She felt like they would burst, and when the baby tried to nurse, it was such a warm comfortable feeling until he had been trying for a few minutes with no success, then it became quite painful. He was hungry and he didn't seem to get the hang of trying to suckle enough to be satisfied. Mrs. Miller came to his rescue by getting the milk started for him and then it was easy for the baby to figure the whole process out. He was a hungry little rascal and seemed to enjoy being held so tightly by his adoring mother. Emily was astounded at the entire event. First she endured the pain, then the joy of the birth, then the love flowing from the baby through her. What a blessing, she thought as she closed her eyes to pray a prayer of thanksgiving. God had answered her prayers for a healthy baby and a loving husband. All at once she wondered what Charlotte would think of her new little nephew. Where was Charlotte? She knew she was alive, somewhere. As she drifted off to sleep, she vowed she would find her someday, somehow.

Chapter 31

The men spent most of the day, from sun-up to sundown cutting and hanging the tobacco. It was hard work and they would have another week, maybe two, to go before they were finished. Emily could see them from her window as she rocked the baby each time she fed him. She had not been able to do much just yet. Mrs. Miller assured her that it would be a week before she would have the strength to do much. She told Emily that she would need to register the baby's birth at the courthouse as soon as they decided on a name.

The two of them had to decide on a name. Emily wanted him named Eustis but Eustis wasn't so sure. Why not name him after her father whom she could barely remember or maybe name him for Uncle Russell whom she adored? Emily smiled and suggested they could name him Eustis Guy Russell Percy Carmichael and that would cover everyone. Eustis laughed a big laugh at that suggestion when he saw the humor in trying to please everyone. The boy would be named Eustis Carmichael, Jr. and he would be called Buddy. They both agreed on the name and the nickname and that argument was settled once and for all time.

Eustis' furlough was for 30 days. There would be plenty of time for them to get the tobacco in and maybe enjoy a hunting trip with Papa. He loved spending each evening holding Buddy and singing while Emily played the piano. When Buddy was two weeks old they wrapped him in warm blankets and went for a walk with him. Emily walked up to the back of the farm and back down the hill. That exercise seemed to take most of her energy. She knew her gardening days were over for the current year; nevertheless, she still had plenty to do. Now that winter was upon them, she would do some of the sewing she had laid aside. She would also make new curtains for the cabin since she had been saving the feed sacks all summer and was sure she had enough to cover most of the windows. She was also anxious to get back to the classes with Papa since he had progressed so nicely with his arithmetic. She hoped to take Eustis up to the schoolhouse to meet Mr. Hay while he was still home. She just wanted to get back to normal again, but she wondered if "normal" wasn't an ever changing condition. Emily knew that things would never be the same for her.

She went to the table and wrote to Mrs. Thompson.

Dear Mrs. Thompson:

My baby was born on October 8. He is a fine baby boy. We named him Eustis, Jr., but will call him Buddy. The mid-wife estimated his weight to be about 8 pounds. He is just beautiful. Eustis came home on a furlough and surprised me. He was here for the birth of the baby. I am feeling fine and doing well. Our baby looks just wonderful in all the clothes you gave us. Thank you, again for your generosity. I will try to see you next spring and will write as often as I can.

The tobacco has almost all been cut and hung in the barn to dry. Eustis has been here to help. I am very glad because I was not able to help at all.

The weather is turning cold in the mountains, as I am sure it is in Meadville. I hope you are warm this winter. I play my piano and sing lullabies to Buddy every day. I must close for now. As usual Buddy seems to be hungry all the time.

Your other daughter

Emily

As soon as the baby had nursed and was put in the cradle for a nap, Emily took out the pen and wrote to Aunt Margaret and Uncle Russell.

Dear folks:

Our baby was born on October 8. He is a fine healthy boy. The mid-wife estimated his weight at about 8 pounds. He is handsome and looks like Eustis. His name is Eustis Carmichael, Jr., but we will call him Buddy. I am feeling fine and will gradually get all my strength back. Eustis came home on a furlough and surprised me.

He was here for the birth of Buddy. It was wonderful to have him at home and he loves the baby so much that he hardly lays him in his cradle.

I will write again soon.

Love,

Emily

Chapter 32

The men had been gone since before sun-up. Breakfast was a lonely time without them. They had gone deer hunting. If Papa got a deer he would cure it for meat for the winter's use. If they didn't get a deer, maybe they would see wild turkeys or badgers. Most of the meat from the year before was gone so it would be important for them to bring home some kind of game. When they came in the back door, each of them was carrying something. They had Mallard ducks, wild turkeys, and some pheasants. It seemed that the deer were hiding from them, but the fowl had been unaware that they were in danger. Papa went to the back yard and dressed their bounty. He placed them in cold water and put the pan in the window box until the next day. He would not try to smoke them until he had more of them. He didn't want to waste his green firewood for smoking unless he had a lot of meat to do at one time. However, the men would go every day until they had a large amount of meat on hand to smoke.

Emily was continuously busy learning how to be a good mother. She loved her baby more than anything. She didn't want him to cry, but the mid-wife had told her not to rock him every time he cried or she would spoil him. She wondered what was wrong with spoiling her baby. He would be all that she would have to hold on to when Eustis went back to camp.

Emily had put her classes with Papa on hold as long as she had her husband at home. She wanted to spend her time with him as much as she could. At night when it was quiet in the house and they had gone to bed, they put little Buddy in the bed with them and held him close to them. They cuddled together and talked about what life would be like when they finally had a home of their own. Eustis vowed to make her a good home when he got through his time in the service.

She thought that she wanted to leave Sandy Fork, but she wasn't sure how to tell him. He seemed so at home with Papa, and she didn't want to be selfish. She sometimes felt that she was just hired help for Papa. She cooked, cleaned, washed, ironed, preserved his garden that she had made, and he rarely expressed any appreciation. Actually, she wanted to do all those things, but for Eustis and Buddy. It was beautiful in the mountains, but it was so lonesome. Had it not been for Mr. Hay, she wondered how she would have managed to make it through the summer. He had been such a breath of fresh air for her, and she appreciated his lending her books; both to teach Papa and for her to read, too. She was sure that Papa had no idea how she felt, and she didn't want to complain. She simply wanted to do something for her own family. Besides her piano and Buddy, she felt that she had nothing in Sandy Fork except Papa and he was starting to really show his age.

Brother Whitney came by the cabin one afternoon in November. He wanted to see the baby, and he also had good news for Emily. He held the baby and rocked him in his arms while singing a hymn in his ears. Buddy responded by smiling a big smile and then promptly filled his diaper. The preacher laughed and told Emily he was honored that Buddy felt that comfortable being held by a stranger. Emily was embarrassed but quickly took the baby and changed him to a fresh diaper and returned him to Brother Whitney.

The preacher asked her about her spiritual life and if she was doing her daily Bible studies and prayer time. She assured him she was not as faithful as she should be, but that she wasn't negligent either. She told him that she knew that God had answered her prayer about what she needed for the baby and for getting her piano to the cabin. He smiled and told her that she should continue her prayer life and Bible study. Because it was wintertime, the church would not want to baptize her during the cold season, but when summer came they would schedule a Sunday when she could be baptized and become a full member of the congregation at the Landmark Baptist Church. He also wanted her to know that the lady who had been playing the piano for the services had decided she was unable to continue the schedule of playing for the church. He wondered if Emily would like to assume that role of pianist. He also mentioned that someone in the congregation would tend to Buddy while she was playing the piano so she would not need to concern herself about that's being a problem. Emily was so excited she promptly went to the piano and played the Old Rugged Cross while the preacher stood singing. Buddy had become bored with them all and had fallen fast asleep.

Eustis had continued hunting with Papa every day and had brought home enough meat to feed most of Sandy Fork, or so Emily thought. It was all hanging in the smokehouse being smoked. They also had finished cutting all the tobacco several days earlier and the two of them, along with Mr. Baker, had taken their crop into the auction barn to be sold. Papa didn't say exactly what they got for the tobacco. He simply stated that he would take his money to the bank for safe keeping and there would be enough to last all winter. Emily wondered just what "enough to last all winter" meant, since he had never given her a penny for anything.

It would soon be Thanksgiving and Eustis would have to report back to the Great Lakes training center. He was scheduled to be in Illinois for another eight weeks before being sent somewhere else. He did not have any idea where it might be, but it would be somewhere where there was water. Emily quickly prayed it would not be in California but somewhere on the East Coast. Since Eustis would need to leave before Thanksgiving, Emily wondered what Papa would do for the holiday. When she had lived in Meadville, Aunt Margaret would plan a big dinner and invite her pastor to dinner. Emily wasn't sure she should be so bold as to mention this celebration memory to Papa. He had never invited anyone to his house since she had lived there. Mr. Baker never came in when he stopped by except when he helped move the piano inside. He always stayed on the porch. Emily wondered if Papa was antisocial or just unaccustomed to having company. And what had they done when Mama was alive. Well, she intended to find out and soon.

The day of Eustis' departure arrived. Emily had gathered all of the clothes that Eustis had brought home and repacked his suitcase. He donned his uniform for his trip back to the base. He was allowed to travel on the train free if he was wearing his uniform. To Emily he looked so handsome in his complete outfit that she was filled with pride and reduced to tears when she saw him. She wasn't sure she was crying because he was leaving or crying tears of pride; nevertheless, they seemed to come unwillingly. Emily decided not to accompany Papa and Eustis to the train station. He was going to take the Pikeville train to Lexington. She thought it was too cold to take the baby out because of the uncertainty of the weather. She stood in the doorway holding onto Eustis as long as she could. He bent down and kissed her and promised to see her again as soon as he could. He told her he loved her more than anything in the world and that he loved their baby beyond all measure. He quickly turned and got into the wagon for the trip to the train station. She stood in the doorway until the wagon was out of sight. Then Buddy let her know that she was neglecting him so she turned to the cradle and picked him up to feed him. As she sat in her rocker, feeding the baby, she could already feel loneliness coming on. But she had work to do, and she decided that work would help to solve her loneliness. Besides she had already realized that she had no choice but to make the best of a bad situation. It certainly would not last forever, she thought.

Thanksgiving week was ushered in with a wintry blast. Emily had hoped to invite someone in for the feast, but the snow had hit the mountains with a vengeance. It had blown hard against the house. The coal stove had to be tended during the night just to keep the cabin warm enough for the baby. The snowdrifts were nearly as high as the rooftop and Papa had to tunnel a path to tend to the cow and horses. He gathered the eggs three times a day to keep them from freezing. He was also still tending the slow burning fire in the smokehouse where the meat was hanging; because he 'lowed if it was cold enough to freeze the meat before it was properly smoked and cured, it would spoil as soon as it thawed. Papa had to continue to feed the fire while keeping the embers at a low temperature. He talked a lot about other severe winters that he had experienced, and he was sure that this was going to be another one. The three of them were virtually marooned at the house. The horse and wagon could not get out to go anywhere. Emily gave up on the idea of having a guest for Thanksgiving dinner. She was not even able to get to church on that Sunday because of the blizzard.

It was nine days after Thanksgiving before the wind let up its ferocity. The snow had continued and the temperature had remained at a low point. Papa had an old thermometer hanging on the barn, and he told Emily it had registered at minus 4 degrees. She had endured these cold temperatures when she lived in Peterborough. She remembered that the lake would freeze over, and she and Charlotte would skate on the lake. However, those temperatures were endured in a house that had a stove or fireplace in several of the rooms. The windows fit and so did the door. She just couldn't believe that Papa had lived all these years in this cabin and endured the winters without making some changes in the windows and doors. She finally decided he didn't see the need since he would put on his "long-johns" and two pair of overalls, heavy woolen socks, and his boots. On top of all that he had a "mackinaw" coat that he wore and all this made him look like he was three times his size, but he swore that he never got cold. She could hardly believe he wasn't cold, because she had on almost everything she owned and she had felt like she would freeze. She kept a roaring fire in the cook stove, moved the baby's cradle into the kitchen by the stove, and bundled him up knowing that he, too, could suffer frostbite. She prayed the bad weather wouldn't last long.

Chapter 33

The Christmas season came to the mountains around Sandy Fork with very little ceremony. The weather was so crisp and so cold that most folks stayed inside. The church was planning a Christmas pageant for which Emily would be playing all the music. She had been practicing when she had free time, which wasn't very often. Emily also wondered just what kind of a celebration, if any, would be held at their house. Would they have a Christmas tree? Even Aunt Margaret celebrated Christmas. Usually their gifts had been of the "necessity" type such as socks, or a new set of underwear.

In her childhood before she had left Peterborough, Emily's mother had always given both girls a doll and doll clothes for Christmas. She now wondered just what she should do for Papa. Maybe she could make him a new shirt. Buddy was small so his gifts would be of the "necessity" type too, but she did wonder if she might find a teddy bear for him. He could play with it in the summer when he got a little older. Suddenly she found herself remembering the Christmas cards that Charlotte had made for the family. She had drawn those beautiful animals with soft, appealing eyes that seemed to talk to you, on each of the cards and had given them to each member of the family including the preacher at the Friends Church. Emily ran to her room and pulled out a box to find the one that had been given to her. Just looking at the card produced a flood of tears. Emily continued to miss her sister so very much. Slowly she placed the card back into the box and decided that she needed to concentrate on things in Sandy Fork. She wanted to do a good job at the church so she went to the piano and played those songs again.

As they were eating dinner that evening Emily asked Papa if he would find a nice Christmas tree that they could put in the window. He grumbled that such a celebration was just a nuisance and a waste of time. He said that Christmas was just another day in his life. Nonetheless she urged him to soften a little bit and bring her a tree that she could decorate. He left the table and put on all his winter clothing and stomped out of the house as if he was upset at such a frivolous request. Emily cleaned the table and went about doing the chores she needed to get done. Buddy demanded a lot of time and so did Papa. She had lots of mending to do on Papa's clothing as well as her own. In about an hour Papa came through the cabin door dragging the biggest tree that Emily had ever seen. It nearly touched the ceiling and smelled of a wonderful mixture of pine and snow and wet wood. She loved the fragrance and suddenly she wondered just how she would decorate this monster of a tree. She was never short on ideas but this one had her stymied. She would have to sleep on it, she thought.

The next morning, after her chores were done, she went to her sewing machine and the box of scraps she had been saving. It took most of the morning, but she managed to find some trims left over from her dresses, buttons which she strung in a long garland, scraps of fabric which she cut into smaller pieces and strung them on a large cord and vowed she would buy popcorn on the next trip to town so she could string popcorn on the tree as well. The more she planned on putting on the tree, the more she came up with ideas. She found an old "Sears" catalog and tore the pages from it, rolling them into a cone shape, glued them, and strung them on the tree. When she had finished, the tree was a work of art. Papa 'lowed as how it was the most beautiful tree he had ever seen and since she had worked so hard on it, maybe he could get into the Christmas spirit too.

On Sunday when they went to church for the Christmas program, Emily dressed Buddy in his new outfit. She didn't have time to make herself a new one, but she put a scarf and new buttons on an old dress so that she felt like it really was new. She played the piano while Buddy slept on a church pew. The little children acted out the Nativity story on the stage. Many of the children had memorized speeches of varying lengths, which they stood in the center of the stage and recited. Some were spiritual in nature and some dealt with humorous stories of the life of a child. When the program was complete, Santa burst through the back door carrying a big bag with him. He handed out a treat to each of the children. This treat consisted of an apple, an orange, a few peanuts in the shell, two chocolate drops and two orange slice candies, all housed in a brown paper bag. For many of the children this would be all that they would receive for Christmas. For some of the others, it was all the candy that they would see for a year until next Christmas came around. As Santa was leaving the church the children all stood and sang Silent Night. Emily was so overtaken with emotion she could hardly play the piano through her tears. She smiled as she looked at the treat Santa had left for Buddy as he lay sleeping on the seat. She wanted to always remember that it was his first Christmas and that it was as good as she could ever give him.

When the mail came on the day before Christmas, there was a package from the Great Lakes Training Center for Emily and Buddy. Emily could hardly wait to unwrap the outer wrap. When she got to the inside of the box she found another package wrapped in Christmas wrap of holly leaves with red berries. She quickly tore open the wrap and peeked inside the box. There were two tiny boxes inside the bigger one. In the first one was a baby ring for Buddy and inside the other one was a ring for Emily. Attached to the box was a note from Eustis saying he had never had the money for a wedding ring for her and this was his gift to her for their first family Christmas. Emily was so overcome with emotion she sat in the rocker and cried until she thought her heart would burst. How could she ever have found someone else who loved her so much?

Chapter 34

True to form, the winter winds and snow left the mountains as abruptly as they had arrived. By February, most of the snow had all melted and the skies were blue and clear. Emily knew that winter wasn't over, but she could see a ray of hope in every new day. The crocus had popped through the frozen ground and some of the wild hyacinths were blooming. She knew it wouldn't be long before spring would come. It was wonderful for her to see the evidence that summer would not be far behind. Admittedly she didn't look forward to summer because of all the work that had to be done.

Buddy was beginning to sit up and trying to crawl. He had outgrown his cradle and Emily had placed him in bed with her. She could snuggle with him as he slept which added to a sense of bonding with him. She knew he would always be her baby son no matter how old he became. Before the spring chores began, she felt that she had time to work on a new wardrobe for him. He had outgrown most of the things that Mrs. Thompson and Aunt Margaret had given her earlier. Her checks from the government for Eustis pay had been coming regularly and she had some money in the bank. She needed to go to town to look for some fabric to make Buddy's clothes but the roads had been so bad that the horse and wagon couldn't make it onto the main road. There had not been any mail for more than a month because of the mud roads. She was sure there were letters for her in town. She had not been able to see Mr. Hay since he had come to visit them at Christmas time. She was anxious to get more books to read. Suddenly she realized what it felt like to be house bound. Maybe she just needed to get out of the house for awhile.

Early the next morning she arose and checked the weather. Was it a fair day? As she gazed out the back window she could see the sun was peeping over the ridge to the East. She felt the window glass to judge the temperature. It didn't seem to be as frigid as it had been, but she was sure the road was still frozen so the horse could maneuver safely on the road. She hurriedly fixed breakfast, cleaned the kitchen, bathed Buddy, fed him, then dressed him in the winter woolens from Mrs. Thompson, and wrapped him tightly in a heavy blanket. As she went to the barn to hitch up the horse to the wagon, she encountered Papa. He asked about where she was planning to go; and as she explained her plan, he 'lowed as how he needed some stuff at the feed store. She was elated and disappointed at the same time. She wanted to get away, but she wasn't sure how she could handle the baby and the horses too.

They took the regular trip to town but ever so slowly. Papa went to the feed store, and Emily went to the general store that the townspeople called the hardware store. She shopped for fabric, buttons, and thread to make Buddy some more clothes. She also looked over the magazines in the store for clothing styles for herself. She had a few extra dollars that she could use to buy some things for herself. She even looked at bonnets for spring. She loved the flowers and ribbons on the bonnets and saw similar ones in the magazines. She was sure she could do that with some of the old hats that she had at the cabin. She just needed the ideas. She bought the new Ladies Home Journal magazine for ten cents and knowing that she could get many ideas from it. She found the fabric that she wanted for Buddy. Then she spied some new fabric for ladies clothes. She fondled the material; it was soft and "lady-like" to the touch. She decided she would buy enough to make a new dress for spring. She left the store with more packages than she could carry with the baby in her arms. She was excited at the prospect of having a new dress for spring. She and Buddy would both have spring outfits if she could get them made before time to begin the planting.

Meanwhile, Papa had gone to the Post Office to get the mail and discovered he needed a box to put it in. There were letters from everyone they knew. There was also a letter from the government for Papa. He had opened the letter, but could not comprehend some of the big words. He read what he could and asked Emily to finish reading it. While the horse waited at the curb, Emily read the letter to Papa. The letter explained that Papa was old enough to draw Social Security. President Roosevelt had signed the bill into law and everyone over the age of 65 could now draw Social Security. It would amount to about $200.00 per month. Emily had helped Uncle Russell get Social Security, but

Papa had never worked outside of the farm, so she didn't understand that he was eligible, too. They would have to go to the CourtHouse in order for him to sign up for this money. Since the CourtHouse was right in front of them, they would be able to sign up while they were here.

Papa insisted that he did not want any "Poor Relief". He was not poor, and he had enough to live on. Emily tried to tell him that this was not Poor Relief, but a law that the Government had enacted so the folks who had never been employed did not have to live without means of support. He accompanied her into the CourtHouse, but he wasn't listening to Emily. They went into the Social Security Office that had hastily been set up in this county so Papa and others like him could apply. The clerk asked him some questions about a birth certificate and how old he was. He replied that he had no birth certificate and his age was his business. He wasn't telling anyone. The clerk tried to reason with him over some of the legal papers that were necessary to be completed before he could be granted the money. Papa refused to cooperate. He 'lowed as how he didn't need their help; he never had needed it, and he never would need it. President Roosevelt just hadn't looked around at "mountain folk" cause they didn't need his handout. With that remark, he stomped out of the CourtHouse and went straight to the bank.

He walked up to the counter, and told the clerk he wanted to see his money. The clerk opened up the ledger and showed him that he had $12,483.21 in the bank. Seeing the ledger sheet was not satisfactory for Papa. He insisted that he see his money. It was his and he wanted to see it for himself. The clerk, having encountered this old man before, calmly went to the back of the bank, took out a large container of tens and twenties and came to the front to show him and even counted out the 21 cents so Papa would be convinced. He thanked him very much for his time, turned and left the bank, stepped up into the wagon and headed for home without looking back.

On their way home from town, Emily went to see Mr. Hay. As they went up the lane to the schoolhouse, she could see that all the children had to be inside. She climbed down out of the wagon, carrying Buddy, as she wanted to show him off. She opened the door and went inside, but the building was cold. There were no children in the room and it didn't look like there had been for several days. Emily went to the desk where Mr. Hay sat and she glanced across the paper work he had been working on. There didn't seem to be anything amiss, but she was puzzled. On one corner of his desk was one volume of Don Quixote with a note on it for Emily. She was sure he had borrowed it from the Newfoundland Library for her. But, she wondered where he was. She prayed "Lord, let him be ok", as she slowly closed the door and climbed up into the wagon. She turned to Papa and told him what she found. He told her that sometimes the roads were too bad for the kids to come to school and so the teacher didn't come either. She certainly hoped that to be the case and she vowed to return soon to find out for herself.

They hurried into the cabin when they got home. Buddy decided he needed his lunch first, then she and Papa could eat. She fed him then changed his diaper and put him down for his nap. She quickly fixed some dinner for them since neither one of them had eaten. They ate quickly and Emily began to read the mail. There were letters from Eustis, Aunt Margaret, and Mrs. Thompson. Eustis' letter stated that he had loved his visit and that he was back to work. Aunt Margaret stated that Uncle Russell was still coughing badly and not feeling too well some days. He had also received his first check from the government. He had bought them both a new pair of shoes with his newfound wealth. Mrs. Thompson's letter touched her the most.

My dear daughter Emily:

I was so glad to hear from you telling me all about your new son. I think you named him properly since all first born sons should carry their fathers' name. Buddy is a fitting nickname since Jr. is overused by a lot of people. Buddy sounds more individual than anything else. I am sure he is a real delight for you, and you will be a wonderful mother.

It is cold here and I do not venture out. I have enough things on hand to feed me so I sit by the fire most of the day. I read a lot and I am studying the Bible again. I am glad you have been involved in your church. Playing the piano for them will be a wonderful experience for you and for the congregation.

I hope you will come back to visit again soon. I hear that your Uncle Russell is not doing very well. I miss you very much and want to see my new "grandson" before he grows too big. I think he needs a grandmother to love him.

Your adopted Mother,

Mrs. Vivian Thompson

Emily cried as she reread the letter. A letter from Mrs. Thompson really warmed her heart. Not since she left Peterborough had she enjoyed such loving terms from a woman. She stopped to thank God for sending her this beautiful lady to be her surrogate mother.

Buddy snapped her consciousness back to the present when he began to fuss. Surely it wasn't feeding time yet but when she glanced at the clock she realized she had been reading mail for almost an hour. She hadn't cleaned up the dinner table yet and now she would be behind the rest of the day. The baby was beginning to eat a few things from the table. She mashed the potatoes and carrots together making a paste. He didn't much like this concoction, but Emily continued to try to get him to eat it. She had some apples that she had canned and she mashed some of them for him. He liked the apples but not the potatoes. She tried mixing the apples and potatoes hoping to fool him, but he spit it out every time. Well, she thought, this kid better learn to like potatoes. In time, she would discover that he never did accept potatoes as something he wanted to eat.

Chapter 35

Emily had many projects to occupy her time. She had clothes to make for herself and for Buddy. She also wanted to make curtains for her room before the hot summer sun started beaming in the window. Lessons also had been resumed for Papa, and he was learning arithmetic quite rapidly. He seemed to have an uncanny sense about math. His reading also was coming along nicely, and he was beginning to read and understand the Bible. However he was still having problems with writing. Emily was sure that it was her teaching that was causing the difficulty, but Papa tried to tell her it was just that the English language was so messed up. He had a distinct mountain accent that he could not transfer into writing. Emily was convinced that he should learn to do it right, but Papa was just as confident that what he wrote was good enough for his kin.

In due time Emily had finished two new outfits for the baby before she started on her own clothes. She wanted him to look his best for another trip that she was planning to the schoolhouse in order to see Mr. Hay. If he was not there this time, she planned to ask around town where he might be. Before she went to the school, she got another letter from Eustis. She hurriedly tore it open and began to read.

My darling wife:

I am writing you to tell you that the base is going to have an open house type of event during the first week in April. I hope that is before planting begins at the farm. I would like for you to come to the Training Center to visit me during that time. Buddy will be big enough to travel, and I hope he will not be too big for you to carry. Maybe you can get a perambulator for him to ride in. You can take the train out of Sandy Fork as I did when I came back to the base. You will stop in Lexington, Kentucky and then on to Chicago. I will meet you at the train station, and we can take a taxi to the base. You can bring

Papa if you want to, and he could help you with Buddy. Please write to me soon and let me know if you can be here.

I love you more each day.

Your loving husband

Eustis.

Emily could hardly believe what she had read. Eustis wanted her to come to the Training Center to visit with him. It was a wonderful idea, and she could hardly wait. She would need to continue getting her clothes ready and also finish some more things for Buddy. She envisioned having a wonderful time in the big city. Not since she was a little girl had she been able to go to any city. As she was anticipating the event, Uncle Russell came to mind. She remembered when he used to take her and Charlotte by the hand after he had taken them to Pittsburgh to see the ballet. It had been a long trip and Aunt Margaret did not like to go so they usually went alone. Uncle Russell would tell them that he wasn't sure about men jumping around on a stage, but he loved to see the girls enjoy themselves. She went to the table at that very moment and wrote to Uncle Russell and Aunt Margaret.

Dear Uncle Russell and Aunt Margaret:

I was thinking about you this morning and I wondered if the weather was as pretty there as it is here. The sun is shining and the flowers are beginning to bloom.

Buddy and I are doing fine. He is growing so much that I can hardly keep him in clothes. He is sitting up by himself now and eating almost everything I put in front of him. He does not eat potatoes. I wonder why he does not like them?

I hope the two of you are doing fine. I will try to come visit again in the early fall. Summers are just too busy here for me to get away. Write me and tell me how you are doing.

We're going to be able to visit Eustis, soon. Of course, that will be fun for all of us.

Love,

Emily

Emily ran to find Papa, who was out in the barn tending to his tobacco seedlings. She rattled on about the invitation that she had received from Eustis about a visit to the Great Lakes Training Center. She was so excited she hadn't thought through the plan, and it made very little sense to Papa. She finally sat down on a bale of hay and slowly painted the picture. She wanted to go to Chicago on the train with Buddy to visit Eustis. They would stay only a few days and then come back in time for the spring planting. Papa could go with them if he wanted to, but if not, she would go alone. She would have to go to the train station to see about when a train would leave and what it would cost. She had saved almost all the money that Eustis had sent home. After Buddy had been born, she began receiving another $11.00 per month. She now had enough money in the bank to go on the trip without spending all of it. If they were going to go to Chicago, she dreamed of visiting some of the sights in the area. She loved museums and art galleries. She also wanted to shop for some clothing for Buddy that she was unable to buy in Sandy Fork.

While her head was reeling with the excitement of the trip, Papa was pondering his involvement in the adventure. He had never been to a big city like Chicago, and he thought he might like to look around at the big buildings. If he could get Jasper to take care of the farm for him while he was gone, maybe he would go. Emily having finally awakened to reality, discovered that it was time to check on Buddy, but Papa broke her line of concentration when he told her he wanted to go, too. Emily was elated. She quickly ran into the house and while Buddy was still sleeping wrote a note to Eustis.

My dearest husband:

I am so excited about coming to visit you. Papa has decided that he will come with us. He wants to see the sights of a big city. We can come the second week in April, if that is ok with you. We can stay a week if you can make the arrangements for a hotel during that time.

Please write to me as soon as possible.

Your loving wife and son.

Emily and Buddy

She hurried to the mailbox and posted the letter. Then she ran to the sewing machine to see what else she could do before fixing dinner. She had so much to do.

Early the next morning she finished breakfast, helped with the milking, bathed the baby and was ready to go into town before 9 o'clock. She wanted to be sure she had the right things to wear in a big city. She needed a new hat to go with her new clothes. She could remake some of the things she already had if she could find the right fabrics to add accents to them. She gathered her ideas in her head, and with the baby in her arms, was ready to go to town when Papa brought the wagon around to the door. He 'lowed as how he would need to get a few things in town too. She quickly grabbed her book of Don Quixote that Mr. Hay had loaned her and planned to stop by there on the way home.

They made the usual rounds of the shops in town. Emily was still curious about the Café, but decided this was not the time to explore. She had too many other things on her plate at the moment to consider something else. Papa was coming out of the bank when she went in to get some travel money. Then she went to the train station to get the information on the departure and arrival of the various trains that she would need to take to go to Chicago. The fare would be only $4.00 for a round trip ticket. Buddy would be allowed to travel free. They would be able to leave on Monday morning, go to Lexington, and then catch another train to Chicago. It would be early evening when she arrived there and Eustis could hopefully meet them then. It all sounded so wonderful that she could hardly contain her enthusiasm.

They all loaded into the wagon and started up the ridge to the schoolhouse. There still was no horse hitched to the tree and no children in sight. Emily wondered where Mr. Hay had gone. Today was not the time to concern herself about his where abouts. She had to get back to the cabin before noon, but she planned to ask questions about what might have happened at the school when she had the opportunity to talk to Mr. Baker or Brother Whitney.

Chapter 36

Emily had all of the laundry to do before they left on their trip, but the weather cooperated with Emily completely. She had to scrub Papa's overalls and clean all the heavy "long johns" plus all his work shirts. They would have to be starched and ironed. He didn't have very many sets so it would necessarily be a last minute event. Since the weather was so nice, she would be able to heat the water on a fire outside and hang the things out to dry in the spring breeze. She would also have to get Buddy's clothes ready as well as her own. He didn't have many diapers, so she decided she would use some of the feed sacks she had been saving for curtains to make him some more. They were a bit rough but if she boiled them and bleached them they would soften a bit. She would have them to use in an emergency, she thought. She was sure that she would not be able to do laundry in a hotel even if time permitted.

Papa had ridden the horse over to Mr. Baker's house to see if he would tend to the animals while they were gone. He took the Bakers a big deer roast and a wild turkey as a gift for his tending the farm. Mr. Baker didn't do as much hunting as Papa did, and he would be very appreciative of a gift of meat. While he was gone, Papa also went into town to run a personal errand. Emily had wanted Mr. Baker to come to the cabin in order to inquire about Mr. Hay, but Papa told her he had already taken care of all the details for the trip. When the mail came, there was a letter from Eustis.

My darling wife and son:

The second week in April will be fine for your visit. I have made arrangements at a hotel in Chicago for you and Buddy to stay. If Papa wants a room there too, he can make those arrangements when he gets there. I am so glad you had the money saved to buy your ticket. I know you are very careful with your spending but there must be lots of things you will need before the trip. Please use our money to buy what you need. You will also have to bring some cash to be used while you are here since I send most of mine to mother for the children.

I can hardly wait to see all of you. I will inquire as to when the train will arrive as soon as I hear what day you are leaving. I can hardly wait.

Your loving husband,

Eustis.

After reading his letter, Emily knew she would need to make another trip to town to buy their tickets and draw down money to pay for their trip. She wanted to be sure that she would have enough to feed all of them in a café and to buy things for Buddy as he needed. She planned to fix a lunch to carry on the train in order to save a little money as they traveled. She wondered what Papa's plans were, but she decided not to inquire at this time. He already had said that he would buy his own ticket and pay for his own room and board. Emily went into town the very next morning and made her arrangements at the train station. She then went to the bank and drew down $80.00. Her bank balance was now $83.00. She was sure she would be able to save more when she returned from the trip. She told Papa that she had her tickets, and he would need to get his. They planned to leave the very next Monday.

When they got home from church on Sunday, Emily was hurriedly fixing their dinner. She needed to get more of her preparations for the trip completed. Before they could sit down to eat, they heard the dogs barking. That always meant a stranger was coming up the path. Emily straightened her dress a little and brushed back her hair in preparation for meeting this stranger. She always wanted to look her best. When she opened the door, there stood Mr. Hay. As she invited him in they all noticed that he was walking with a distinct limp. He told them that he was still recovering from a fall.

Emily told him that she had been to the school to see him on two separate occasions but he had not been there. Naturally, they were concerned. She had left the books that he had loaned her and had thanked him in a note, but continued to wonder about his absence. Mr. Hay smiled and told her he had come by to explain why he had not been at school. It seems his horse had slipped on the slippery mud road on the way to his home one evening and had fallen. He had fallen off the horse, and broken one of his legs in two places. Mr. Hay had been laid up for sometime and unable to walk. The Trustee couldn't find another teacher, so they had closed the school for a while. He had found the books that she had returned and wanted her to know that he would be back at school on Monday if she wanted to come by for a new supply. He had been able to bring additional books from the library in Newfoundland, especially for her. As he was telling her about what he had brought for her, he heard a baby cry. She quickly ran into the bedroom and returned with Buddy. Mr. Hay was shocked to see him. He then asked if he could hold the baby in his arms. Although he had no children of his own he had become a teacher, in part, so he could be around children. Emily admired his ability and interest in children. She had similar feelings herself. Buddy seemed to have made her a whole person albeit a busier one. Emily began to tell Mr. Hay about her pending trip to Chicago. She babbled about how she wanted to see everything she could while she was there. She remembered the story she had heard from Mrs. Thompson about the fire that was started when a cow kicked over a lantern that had burned the city down. She wondered if there was still evidence of this horrendous fire that she might see there. Mr. Hay told her he, too, had been to Chicago when he was very young. He didn't see any such evidence so he didn't want her to be disappointed if she didn't find the embers or ashes.

As he was leaving, she told him it would be a few weeks before she would be able to visit the school again, but that she would be there as soon as possible. She admonished him about riding horses on slippery roads, and they both laughed as he left. He was such a nice man, she thought, and what a "breath of fresh air" to this community. It was ironic that he had thought the same thing about her a few short years ago.

Chapter 37

On Monday morning they boarded the train in Sandy Fork for the short trip to Morehead. They journeyed on to Lexington and then to Louisville. Emily was fascinated at what she saw out the window. There were big factories all along the train tracks. There were big houses and small houses. She wondered what it would be like to live in one of those big houses. When the train pulled into the station at Louisville, she decided to step down and walk into the station. Buddy was big enough to enjoy the sights. It was such a beautiful station that she was awestruck. She perused the area looking for Charlotte. She never stopped looking for her twin sister. She also bought a cookie for Buddy and a cup of coffee for herself, spending 5 cents. Papa never left the train and kept their seat. Since leaving Sandy Fork he had never ceased clutching his tackle box in his lap. Perhaps he was planning to go fishing in Lake Michigan, she thought.

The train pulled out of the station at Louisville and headed straight for Indianapolis; from there they would go on to Chicago. They had already eaten part of the lunch she had prepared while they were leaving Louisville. She kept the rest to for their supper. Buddy was still nursing part of the time, so she excused herself and went to the bathroom on the train to nurse him. She sat on the commode while he was nursing because there was no bench in the bathroom. Papa had gone to the bathroom but quickly came back out. He 'lowed as how it was too strange for him. He would just wait 'til they got to Chicago. Emily wondered if he thought there would be an outhouse for him to use in the hotel in Chicago.

It was late at night when the train finally pulled into the station in Chicago. Buddy was sound asleep and had been for several hours. Emily took all the things she could carry and hurried down the steps to find Eustis. He was waiting for her and immediately took the baby from her arms. Papa was right behind her carrying his bag and tackle box. They gathered up their bags, the baby and Papa and boarded a taxi to go to the hotel. Papa had never ridden in a "horseless carriage" before, and he was reluctant to get in the vehicle, but Eustis assured him that he would have to sleep in the train station if he didn't ride in the automobile. They got to the hotel in a few minutes and as they were leaving the taxi, Emily looked up to see the most beautiful building she had ever seen in her life.

They went into the lobby of the hotel. It had a marble floor. The lights along the wall were not candles but beautiful electric sconces. There was a huge chandelier hanging in the center of a gigantic room. The room had chairs and sofas all around the wall and in the center of the room too. There were real flowers in huge vases on small tables called "coffee tables" which Eustis explained as they walked toward the elevator. She wondered how they could have real flowers this early in the spring. They walked down a long hallway that was covered in beautiful floral carpets. The wall had more of the electric sconces on them that lighted their way. When they approached the elevator, Emily was completely befuddled. She had no idea they could get inside this little room and ride to the floor where their room was. There was a man in uniform who had escorted them down the hall. He explained to them that their room was on the third floor. They could ride the elevator up to that floor and then go to their room. Emily cautiously stepped into the small "room", glancing at Eustis for his guidance. He stepped inside with her and the uniformed man closed the door, leaving Papa on the outside. Papa refused to get on this contraption and the man in uniform pointed to the stairway where he could walk up to the third floor if he chose to. When they alighted from the elevator the man unlocked a door to a room that had a beautiful high back bed and a dresser in it. There was more floral carpet on the floor and more lighted sconces on the wall. Emily was in awe of the entire scene. She wondered about how she could sleep with all these designs and colors racing through her head. As they all stood inside the room, Eustis reached into his pocket for a tip that he gave to the uniformed man. He later explained to Emily that he was a "bellboy" and he had to "tip" him.

Papa had not opened his mouth since they got out of the taxi. He was completely mystified. Eustis told him he would have to get his own room, since there was not room for them all in this one. Papa looked as if he were a bit disappointed, but Eustis went back down the stairs with him to the front desk to get his own room taken care of. After Papa paid $1.50 for the room, he 'lowed as how that was robbery. However, his room was next to theirs so Eustis told him that he would check in on him in the morning so they could eat breakfast together.

While Eustis was taking care of Papa, Emily was taking care of Buddy. Since he was still sleeping, she quietly laid him on the bed. She then went to the dresser, opened up the bottom drawer and placed the baby in it. The drawer served very well as a cradle. After all it would just be one week. The drawer was deep enough to keep Budding from getting out and near enough to the floor that he wouldn't be hurt if he did manage to fall out. He had already begun sitting up, so she would have to watch him closely. She unpacked her bag and hung her clothes in the armoire that was in the room. She then went to the window to look out at the view. It was spectacular. She could see tall buildings and streetcars and other automobiles that seemed to be driven by dapper men dressed in business clothes. Not since she left Peterborough had she been so captivated by the sights in the big city.

Eustis returned to their room and for the first time since they arrived, he embraced her in his arms. He was so glad to see her that he nearly squeezed the wind out of her, and she held him ever so tightly as if to keep him from ever leaving her again. They could hardly talk because their emotions were so near to bubbling over. Eustis led her to the bed to tell her his news. He had completed his training and would soon be transferred to a permanent duty station. He felt certain that he would be sent to the port on Lake Erie very near Erie, Pennsylvania. They were going to build a new port there for the landing of transport ships. He would probably be stationed there for four or five years.

Emily contemplated this move. Would this mean that she could go there to live and be with him? Would she be able to leave Sandy Fork and move back to Pennsylvania? How far would that be from Mrs. Thompson, her new mother, and Aunt Margaret and Uncle Russell? She had so many questions that she needed answered. And what would happen to Papa? He would again be alone in Sandy Fork. Eustis got out a well-worn map that he had been scanning since he got his orders. They unfolded it on the bed and began to study it. Erie, Pennsylvania was very near to Meadville where the family lived. If she moved back there, most likely Eustis would probably be able to come home nearly every weekend. She could get a place to live there in order to look after her own extended family, and she could visit him when she had time or he could come home to visit.

Emily began to cry. Though she often fantasized leaving, now she wasn't so sure that she wanted to leave Sandy Fork. She had grown to love the place in spite of its backwardness. Papa would be all by himself with no one to help him. Eustis quickly assured her that Papa would do just fine. He had managed all those years without them, and he had not changed one bit since Mama had died. He was still plodding through life as he always had with same old habits, some bad, that Eustis remembered from his childhood. Besides, Emily would be able to go visit there anytime she wanted. As they lay together in the bed in the stillness of the night, she held him as tightly as she could, and she began to pray that God would make them a family again. She wanted her family near by and it appeared that he and Buddy were all the immediate family she had. Oh, where was Charlotte?

Emily again felt her age-old loss of Charlotte, now gone for some fifteen years. What a joy it would have been to share her life and her family with her twin. She never had had another person in her life, not even Eustis, who could share her joys and sorrows and problems as Charlotte had. Just maybe, a return to Pennsylvania would also include a longed-for reunion with her sister.

Emily determined to enjoy their stay in Chicago without anticipating a return to Meadville too much in advance.

Chapter 38

Morning in Chicago came early. Emily listened to hear the bell on the streetcar and the chug-chug of the automobiles on the street. As she opened the blinds, she realized the sun was already up. She also wondered where Papa was. Soon she heard a knock on the door, and as she was gathering a robe to put on, Eustis opened the door to Papa. He wanted to know where breakfast was and how was Emily going to cook; there was no stove in his room. He was glad that he didn't have to build a fire because his room was good and warm. How did they heat this place if there were no stoves in the rooms? Eustis explained that the hotel had a huge boiler system in the basement and the hot water was piped through the "radiators" that stood in each room heated them. Papa went to the radiator that Eustis was pointing to and felt the heat coming through it. He 'lowed as how it wasn't hot enough to cook on but it was too hot to sit on. He figured the whole place would burn down soon, so they had better leave while they could. Emily stepped back into the room to hide her laughter. Papa just couldn't grasp modern technology into his mountain way of thinking.

She quickly dressed, put Buddy's new clothes on him, and they all went together to the dining room to have breakfast. Papa ordered from the menu and Emily smiled with satisfaction that he was able to read most of the words. He ordered "French toast" and bacon and eggs. She and Eustis simply ordered pancakes and a scrambled egg for Buddy. When they brought the meal, Papa quickly told the waitress that he did not get "French toast". She assured him that was what it was. He told her he didn't want all that sugar on it and he rose from his chair and went to the kitchen. He told the chef who was donned in a tall white hat how to make "French toast" mountain style. You just put butter or lard in the skillet and put the bread in it. When one side was brown you turned it over and browned the other side. He didn't want any sweet syrup on it either. The chef courteously prepared what he wanted then told him that in Chicago, they called that fried bread. Papa took his plate and returned to the table to eat his breakfast in silence. Emily noted that he brought his tackle box to breakfast with him and she figured that he thought they would be going on a fishing trip that day.

As soon as they had finished eating their breakfast and got the things they thought they might need for the day, they all piled into a taxi to go sightseeing in the city of Chicago. The driver took them all around downtown and showed them things they had never seen before. He also showed them the remnants of the disastrous fire that had leveled most of the city. They saw factories that manufactured everything from shoes to automobile tires. When they passed the shoe factory, Emily remembered that her own father had once worked in a shoe factory in Peterborough. For lunch they found a little café where they could get a sandwich as they sat on a stool by a counter. Emily thought about the café in Sandy Fork that Papa had said she couldn't enter. It didn't appear any different than this one and she wondered if he just told her that because he didn't want her to find out that she could buy a sandwich for a nickel.

In the afternoon they took a bus to the United States Naval Training Center. They were able to go right up to the door of the building where Eustis had been living. All the buildings looked the same. All of them were painted a strange gray. Eustis told her that the color was "battleship gray" and that it was the color the Navy used on everything. The many buildings all in a row were barracks where the men lived. They ate in a dining room called a "mess hall", a strange name thought Emily. There were also a few large two-story buildings that were used as training buildings. Those buildings housed the classrooms used in training the men. He also showed her the chapel where they held services each Sunday. He assured her that he had been faithful in his attendance.

He went to the port area and showed her where the sailors had to stand guard over the ships in the port. She didn't understand why they stood guard, but he explained that part of their training was to make sure that the men were ready if they ever did have to go to war. She could barely remember the First World War and she certainly hoped that America would never have to do that again.

By the end of the day, all four of them were worn to a frazzle. Papa was still carrying his tackle box, but he had not mentioned going fishing. Eustis decided not to mention it; because it was too late now. They returned to the hotel and rested a bit before going to dinner in the dining room. Buddy had to take a nap. He had been very restless all day; because he was unaccustomed to being carried all day. Emily really wanted to buy a perambulator for him but there were none in Sandy Fork. Maybe tomorrow she could find one in a shop in Chicago. While they were eating dinner in the dining room, the waiter served them coffee in a silver coffeepot. Emily was very impressed. She loved the feel of this elegant style of dining. Papa was able to order by himself again and not only was Emily proud of him, but it was evident that he was proud of himself for having taken the time to learn to read. Strangely enough, he brought his tackle box to dinner with him.

Wednesday morning was a lot like the day before, except that Emily insisted on shopping at the lovely nearby shops. They could walk to many of them and she wanted to enjoy the shops one at a time. After about three of the shops, her feet began to hurt. She wasn't accustomed to wearing dress shoes all day, so she just took them off and carried them with her. Eustis was carrying Buddy, and he was wearing down too. At the very next shop, Emily spied a perambulator in the window. She hurried inside to inquire of the price. The clerk looked at her standing in her bare feet and smiled, telling her the price was only $1.98. Emily thought that to be a bargain so she promptly laid out her money. The clerk then questioned her as to whether or not she would like a comfortable pair of shoes to wear. Emily blushed when she realized she was still barefoot. The clerk brought out a pair of "brogans" and Emily tried them on. Oh, they felt so good, she thought. Eustis reached in his pocket to pay the $1.25 the clerk asked for, but Emily would not let him pay for them. Since she was the one who had been foolish in her choice of shoes for the day, she felt that she should pay for the new ones. Anyway, the new ones would be good to wear in Sandy Fork, she thought.

They found another café where they could eat lunch. This time they all ordered a Chicago Hot Dog. None of them were familiar with that term, but they soon found out what it was and they loved it. Even Buddy enjoyed the bite or two that he got. Since he didn't like potatoes, Emily asked for a boiled egg, which they were glad to serve. As they left the café, Papa was still clutching his tackle box, Eustis told him that it was still early in the day, if he wanted to go fishing. He told Papa that they could find a place to go, but it probably would not be a good time to catch fish since Lake Michigan was so cold. It was known more for swimming and boating than as a fishing hole. Papa agreed with Eustis' observation and assured them that he didn't want to go fishing anyway.

As it turned out Emily, Eustis, Buddy, and Papa spent the rest of the week just touring around Chicago. They saw so many things that none of them had ever seen before. Emily loved the Museum of Fine Art. There were some very famous paintings hanging in there that she had only read about. She never dreamed that she would be able to see them herself.

As they were leaving the building, Emily noticed an art exhibit on the far side of the building. The usher that had been their guide explained that it was a gallery showing of local artists. Emily wanted to see those paintings, too. As she wandered into this room, she was taken aback by the talent of some of these artists. Some of the landscapes were so real that you could almost hear the birds singing. Some of the still life paintings were so realistic that the apples looked good enough to eat. There were some black and white etchings and sketches of the fire area. Emily studied them for a long time trying to understand how tragic that must have been. As she was leaving this area, she spied a few colored paintings of animals. It brought back memories of when Charlotte would sit by the window and draw the cat or the neighbor's dog. Her drawings were almost alive because of the eyes she had been able to draw. Looking at one of her pictures had made you see life in the eyes of the subject. As she glanced around the exhibit her eyes stopped on a painting of a tiger that was nearly life-size. The eyes of the tiger followed you around the room as you moved. It was in a walking position and you knew it was watching you as though you were its next prey. Emily rushed to the picture to see the artist name. It was signed Sister Mary Victor. Emily was so disappointed since she could not even imagine anyone painting just like Charlotte. Apparently this lady could.

The rest of the week was spent in doing the things that they could do with little or no money since their money was getting scarce. It would be another month before Eustis would get paid, so he didn't have extra money to spend. Emily had brought $80.00. She had spent almost $60.00, and she still needed to buy food on the way home. On Sunday morning they all went to the Chapel on the base for the church service. It was a small building that was full of sailors. The service they attended was a Catholic service, but Eustis explained that they had a lot of different services for other religions as well.

As they walked out of the chapel, they noticed that Papa was still carrying his tackle box. Eustis told him that today would be his last chance to go fishing but Papa assured him that it was not a good time for that. During the afternoon they took a walk in the park. They saw many people with their babies walking along the pathway through the trees. The spring flowers were beginning to bloom. It actually made Emily homesick for Sandy Fork. They stopped to rest on a park bench and when they did, Papa dropped his tackle box. The lock sprang open and out popped bundles of money. He quickly scooped up the money and fastened the lock. Much to the surprise of Eustis and Emily, they realized he had been carrying his money with him everywhere they went. Eustis asked him why he was carrying a box full of money. Papa told them that he didn't want to leave it at the bank in Sandy Fork because someone just might take it while he was gone. Emily and Eustis had a good laugh and tried to explain that no one could have taken the money from him. They didn't feel that they had convinced him that there really was no risk of theft while his money was in the bank.

As the week's vacation came to an end, Emily reviewed their time together. Emily's trip to the Training Center had been a great experience, but now her time with Eustis was running out. She was elated by the good news about his being transferred to Erie, and that she possibly could join him. But, for now, she wanted to spend as much time with him as she possibly could. Buddy had been so good on the trip and during their stay. He loved his new vehicle of transportation that relieved them from having to carry him as they continued sightseeing. She wondered if she would be able to maneuver it on the streets of Sandy Fork and if it would roll down the mud paths at the farm.

As she and Eustis lay in the bed on their final night together, she snuggled in his arms and held him as tightly as she could. He assured her they would soon be together again for a long time. He wanted her to write to Aunt Margaret and inquire if maybe she could return there until she could find a place to live in Erie. Emily nestled even closer to Eustis as he fell asleep. Sleep alluded her for most of the night. She thought about their future, the move back to Pennsylvania, but most of all, she thought about that painting in the exhibit on the wall in the Museum that had been done by Sister Mary Victor. Those tiger-eyes continued to haunt her. She knew that Charlotte had painted such a cat. Was that it?

As morning dawned and the light streamed through the window, Emily was still busy planning her own future. Since she was expecting mail from Meadville she would wait to hear from Mrs. Thompson and Aunt Margaret before she shared the news of Eustis' transfer with Papa. She wasn't sure how he would take the prospect of her moving back to Pennsylvania. And, she also wondered about Mr. Hay. She would certainly miss his friendship.

The train ride back to Sandy Fork seemed farther than the one that took them to Chicago. She still had a little bit of money, but she had to buy all their food along the way because she had been unable to prepare any lunches for them. Buddy had to be fed on a regular basis. She insisted that Papa pay for his own food. She could exist on very little herself, but she had to feed the baby. He was no longer nursing very often, but she nursed him more than usual because they weren't always where she could buy food for him, and he had not learned to drink from a cup very well. She wondered why the return trip was more of a problem than the first trip.

When they arrived at the train station, Jasper was there with his wagon to take them home. Emily thought to herself that Mr. Baker was the best friend Papa could have. She wondered if Papa ever did any favors for him. When she got to the house, her flowers were all in bloom and the grass was high. They would need to stake the cow in the front so she could eat the grass before it got too high. If the grass was short, the snakes didn't come around as often. And Emily was not fond of snakes since there were many that were poisonous or so Papa had told her.

Emily hurried into the house to put the baby to bed. It was already dark, but Jasper had built a little fire in the kitchen so the house was not cold. He had set the coffeepot on the back of the stove for it to warm, and his wife had sent a pot of soup over for them to eat for supper. Emily immediately had pangs of guilt when she realized that she had never done anything that nice for Mrs. Baker. She made a mental note to bake a pie for them real soon.

Early Tuesday morning, after Emily had finally put away all of their traveling clothes and finished the laundry, the mailman came by with mail for her. She could hardly wait to read the stack of mail from Meadville. The first letter was from Uncle Russell. Emily thought it strange that he should write to her so she frantically tore the envelope open and read it:

My dearest Emily:

I am writing to tell you that your Aunt Margaret is gravely ill. She started feeling poorly around Christmas time, and she has not been able to get any better. I am sure she would love to see you if you can take the time to come and visit.

I hope you and Buddy are doing fine.

Love,

Uncle Russell

Emily pondered the letter and then laid it aside. She opened the one from Mrs. Thompson next.

My dearest daughter:

I received your letter with the exciting news about going to visit Eustis. I have been to Chicago many times and I know that you will love your visit there.

When I was in the general store last week, I spoke with one of the neighbors about your Aunt Margaret. It seems that she is not doing very well. She took sick at Christmas time and has not been able to get her strength back yet. I don't know if you will be able to come to see her but if you can, I think that it would be wise.

Write and tell me about your trip to Chicago.

Your "other" mother,

Vivian Thompson

Emily leaned against the kitchen door as she thought through the news from Meadville. She wondered just what she should do. She had just returned from a trip. She didn't have much money in the bank. She had no one to ask about the situation in Meadville, and it might take too long to get a letter back from Eustis if she wrote to him for guidance. She would just have to decide on her own. She thought about what Brother Whitney had told her. She should just pray about it. As she went inside the house to check on the baby, she prayed for a sign as to what her decision should be. She personally felt that she should go see Aunt Margaret but she had so many obligations on the farm. And, she was the only person in the world who knew where Charlotte had gone. What should she do? Would Aunt Margaret ever tell Emily what had really happened?

It was time for dinner. Emily went to the kitchen and started to fix their meal. When they sat down to eat, Emily could hold it all in no longer. She began to rattle off the story of Aunt Margaret and how she might die before Emily could get there. She didn't have the funds to go and it would be two more weeks before another check from Eustis would come. She knew that there was work to be done on the farm and she needed to be working here. Who would plant the garden and take care of all the chores if she went to Meadville? She hardly stopped for a breath as she outlined all her troubles to Papa. She was visibly panic-stricken. She had never before burdened him with her problems. Now she suddenly seemed to be dumping all of her unanswered questions on him. He stood up and walked to her side, putting his arm around her, trying to calm her with his caring voice. He reached into his bib overalls and pulled out a $20.00 bill and placed it in her hand. Take this, he told her, and go to your Aunt Margaret as soon as possible. He 'lowed as how he ran the farm before she came and he could do it again. Emily stood to embrace him but instead she burst into tears and cried uncontrollably. She had not realized how much she had grown to love the old man. He was so cold and gruff on the outside, but now she realized that he had a softer side on the inside. She dried her tears on her apron and then hugged him again. She would need to go to town to find out about a train to Meadville immediately. She would leave tomorrow, if possible.

Emily hurriedly put together the same carpetbag she had just unpacked. Since she had finished the washing she would need to stay up most of the night doing the ironing. She would have to get Buddy's clothes ready as well as her own. As she was getting all the work done she continued to pray that Aunt Margaret would hold on until she got there. She prepared some food to put in the window box for Papa to have while she was gone. She also packed a lunch for her and Buddy to eat on the train. It was a long way and she knew it was important that she keep her money for any unexpected expenses. She didn't know how long she would stay and she knew the money from Eustis would come to the farm so she wouldn't have it until she got back. Her train was not scheduled to leave Sandy Fork until about 10:30 AM so she would be able to go to the bank and draw out some of her savings to have for the trip. When her check came she would be able to put it back in the bank for next month's expenses.

The train trip would take most of Wednesday and all night. She would arrive at Meadville in the early evening on Thursday. She would probably need to get a cab from the station to Uncle Russell's house since she had not had time to write to him that she was coming.

It was well after midnight when Emily finally crawled into bed. She was exhausted. She had just returned from one trip, and now she was going on another one. She wondered if she would ever be able to think clearly without listening to a train whistle as they went from town to town.

Emily arose very early and tried to help with the farm chores, but Papa was already finished doing everything that needed to be done. She fixed breakfast for both of them and fed the baby. She scrambled an extra egg and packed it in a small jar for lunch for Buddy. She fixed a sandwich for herself and took some cookies that they both could share. She had also baked a pie for Papa. She wondered if she could possibly get some pie into a container so that she could take a piece with her, but she gave up. She just bypassed that idea and went on with the other chores she needed to get done. She put the clothes she had ironed the night before into her bags, grabbed Buddy's perambulator and a quilt to wrap around him and loaded them on the wagon. Papa was waiting to take her to the train station whenever she was ready. She informed him that she needed to go to the bank in order to get her money. He really couldn't understand why the $20.00 was not enough. She explained that if she had to stay very long, she would need to buy more food for Buddy. He reached into his bib overalls and brought out another $20.00 telling her that he would not let her take all her money from the bank. Emily had never seen him part with a penny of his money and now he had given her a significant amount of money on two different occasions. She just couldn't imagine what had inspired him to be so generous. Perhaps she had misjudged him by mistaking his frugality for miserliness. She was almost awe struck as she said a tearful "thank you".

The train was on time and they were quickly on their way to Meadville. Emily settled back into the seat hoping to take a nap. It did not happen. Buddy was restless and didn't want to nap until after he had eaten his lunch. She played with him and showed him the sights out the window. The trees flying by the window seemed to fascinate him. When they pulled in the station at Huntington, she knew that she would need to change trains. In the rush of things it seemed like she had hardly got her seat warm when they had to disembark and board yet another train. She went inside the station to thank the stationmaster for having been so patient with her for leaving her piano there for so long. When she went up to the ticket window he looked at her and smiled, telling her that he was sure glad she finally had her piano at home. Then he noticed Buddy and asked about him. She explained that the child was about 8 months old and was quite a handful. She then told him that her husband was in the Navy, but would be home again real soon.

She turned and boarded the train to go on to Charleston, West Virginia and from there on to Morgantown. They would not arrive in Pittsburgh until in the early morning hours, but she was sure that she could sleep some since she had been awake for nearly 18 hours. As she settled back into her seat, she began to reflect on what was really happening to her. She had not been home to Meadville for nearly a year. Neither had she visited with Mrs. Thompson in that time, but she had continued to write to her.

During the Chicago vacation and now on this latest trip, Emily scanned every crowd for the face of Charlotte. She was sure that someday she would find her, but tonight she just needed to fall asleep while Buddy was sleeping. The search for Charlotte would have to wait a little longer.

The train pulled into Pittsburgh and the clock on the station wall said 4:45 A.M. Emily awakened and saw that Buddy was still sleeping soundly. The man across the aisle from her rose to leave the train. He turned to her and asked if she would like a cup of coffee. It was such a wonderful suggestion, and she wouldn't have to leave her seat or awaken Buddy. She searched in her purse for the coins to pay for it, but he refused her offer. When he returned with a hot cup of coffee, she thought how nice it was for him to bring it to her and how badly she had wanted this treat. She continued on to the next part of the journey and into Meadville without stopping again. It was beginning to be daylight as the sun peeped through the morning clouds. The sky was blue and it looked like a beautiful spring day. She was anxiously awaited the visit with her family. She had never had much family. All she really had was Aunt Margaret and Uncle Russell even though Mrs. Thompson had become her surrogate mother. As she thought about family, she realized that she could only vaguely remember her own mother and father. She could remember Grammy Mamie because she had loved to visit her house and hear her tell stories about the trains and the great Chicago fire. Her life in Meadville had been the only life she had ever known until she went to Sandy Fork. Somehow she felt lost in a sea of events and happenings over which she had no control. She had never really discussed her true feelings about not having a family with Eustis. He had such a big family that he might think it strange; at least that is how she felt. At that point she grabbed Buddy and hugged him to herself in almost a death grip vowing to herself that he WAS her family and it would always be that way. She knew, at that moment, that she wanted to have more children so they, too, would have a real family of their own.

Chapter 39

As the train pulled into Meadville it was early afternoon. She and Buddy had eaten the lunch that she had purchased in Pittsburgh and he had fallen asleep. Emily was too anxious to relax as she looked for any signs that she could remember about Meadville. Although it had not been that long since she left, she was sure that there were many changes in the town. She first noticed that the old jail on the corner of the square had burned to the ground. She wondered how that happened. Then she noticed that the big tree on the court house lawn had been cut down; or maybe a storm had taken it down.

As the train stopped with a jolt, it brought her back to her senses. She gathered up her things and went to look for a cab. The cab driver recognized her since he had been in school with her. He was more than willing to help her get her belongings from the baggage car. As she walked toward the cab, he asked her about Eustis. She quickly went into a long dissertation about his being in the Navy and being stationed in Chicago until recently.

The ride to the house was a short one. She paid the driver the fare, he helped her to the door. Uncle Russell came to the door and was surprised to see her, although it was a welcome surprise. He took Buddy in his arms and tried to hug both of them at the same time. Emily was sure she saw a tear roll down his cheek as he embraced her. She was here to help him, she told him. And was Aunt Margaret any better? He told her that Aunt Margaret was sometimes almost incoherent when she talked and sometimes she just slept all day. The doctor had told him that there wasn't much else that could be done for her. It seemed that she had just not been able to fight off the "bad spell" she had in December. Emily put her bags down, put Buddy in his perambulator, and went to Aunt Margaret's bedside. She leaned over her and whispered in her ear that Emily was here to see her. Aunt Margaret opened her eyes to see for herself, grasped Emily's hand and squeezed it with a weak grip. She smiled faintly as an acknowledgement that she understood that Emily was home. Emily stayed by her bedside until her aunt had fallen asleep. She promptly went to the kitchen and decided that she would try to make soup to feed her. Emily was convinced that she needed some hearty soup. She laughed at herself since that is exactly what the mountain folk would have said and now it all was making more sense to her, personally. Aunt Margaret slept through the night giving Emily an opportunity to get her things unpacked and to arrange for Buddy's comfort.

Uncle Russell had not felt like talking with her very much when she arrived, but had gone to bed early. He was showing signs that he was weary of taking care of Margaret ever since December. Emily was up early feeding the baby and getting something for all of them to eat on the table. When she had left Meadville, a year and a half earlier, she hardly knew how to boil water without scorching it, but after nearly a year in the mountains, she had learned a lot about being a housewife. Aunt Margaret awakened briefly and Emily had some oatmeal ready for her to eat. She had made coffee, mountain style, but Uncle Russell enjoyed it even if it was a wee bit strong. Emily laughed at that remark since Papa always thought her coffee was too weak. She stayed by the bedside of Aunt Margaret coaxing her to eat as much as she could. Margaret spoke a few words to Emily and asked about the baby. Emily brought Buddy to the sick bed in his perambulator long enough for Aunt Margaret to see him. She remarked about what a pretty boy he was. She hoped that he would grow up to look like Emily. With that remark, she drifted off to sleep again and seemed to be resting quietly.

Emily told Uncle Russell that she would like to run over to see Mrs. Thompson while Aunt Margaret was sleeping and that she would be back in about an hour. She bundled up the baby and off they went to see her "other mother". Imagine the surprise when Mrs. Thompson answered the door and found Emily and the baby waiting to enter. She was so overjoyed at seeing them that she could hardly speak. She brought them inside and offered tea. She wanted to hold the baby but he was such a robust little boy that Emily wondered if he would be too much for her to handle. Mrs. Thompson sat in one of the big chairs and Emily placed Buddy in her lap. She cuddled him in her arms as the tears rolled down her cheeks. She loved him so very much. She assured Emily that this was indeed her grandchild. Emily felt that, in time, Buddy would love to know that he was so loved by everyone. They visited for just a short time, all the while Emily was rattling on and on about Eustis being transferred to Erie and that she, quite possibly, would be coming back to Meadville. She had not shared this news with Uncle Russell or Aunt Margaret. Then she told Mrs. Thompson that she must return to her house to tend to the patient. She promised to return as soon as possible with more of the news of Sandy Fork.

She hurried back to the house and found Uncle Russell pacing the floor. He felt sure that Aunt Margaret was "having another spell". She had been having them regularly and the doctor didn't seem to have anything else that would help her to improve. Emily rushed to the bedside and grasped her aunt's hand, speaking quietly to her. Aunt Margaret roused for a few moments and asked about the baby. She, then, asked Emily to look after Uncle Russell. Emily did not want her to die just yet. She held her hand firmly and whispered to her the hard question; "Aunt Margaret, please tell me where to find Charlotte?" Aunt Margaret frowned, tightened her grip on Emily's hand, and shook her head as if to say "no". Emily saw a tear in her eye as she drifted off to sleep, never to awaken again. She carried the secret of Charlotte's whereabouts to her grave.

Uncle Russell went to his room in order to shed his tears of grief in private. Emily tried to comfort him as best she could; however, he preferred solitude. In a short time, he emerged from the room and went to Emily. He wanted to tell her how much he loved her, but the words wouldn't come. Emily knew she should be grief stricken but she only felt sadness and the betrayal of half a lifetime. The only person in the world who could solve her life long mystery had just gone on without revealing anything to her. Although Emily wanted to comfort Uncle Russell, she was at a loss for words. She just didn't know what to say. As they sat around the table drinking the remnants of the morning coffee, he began to talk. He told Emily that they had been married for such a long time. He mentioned that she had once been "in a family way" but had lost the baby. She had never quite gotten over the bitterness of the loss. He had tried to love her for all these years, but his love was rejected. He had been so lonely for so long and now all that he could feel was emptiness. Emily knew this was not the time for the unanswered question to be brought to the surface again.

A memorial service was held at the Friends Church for Aunt Margaret. She was laid to rest in the church cemetery. Emily and Uncle Russell returned to the house as soon as the burial was over. He seemed a little distraught at the fact that not many persons attended the service. They had always been faithful to the church where Margaret had always been available to help those in need. He admitted that she had not been a very friendly person. She had seemed aloof when in the company of a lot of people. He just expected more people might have paid their respects.

Uncle Russell and Emily sat at the table drinking a cup of tea together just trying to collect their thoughts when a knock came to the back door. A group of ladies from the church were standing with their arms laden, waiting for an invitation. Emily hurriedly invited them to come in and they spread their bounty for them to enjoy. There were cakes, pies, fried chicken, and all sorts of vegetable dishes. They wanted to make sure that Uncle Russell was well cared for in his time of bereavement. Emily was overwhelmed at their generosity and benevolence. She thanked them profusely and stated that she was there to care for him for a while.

After the ladies left, the two of them returned to the table and prepared to eat their evening meal. Emily needed to feed Buddy and she wanted Uncle Russell to get better acquainted with him. Uncle Russell brought him into the room in his arms. "Grampy" is here for you, he stated, and Emily nearly burst with pride to think that Uncle Russell wanted to be his grandfather. As they sat around the table eating, everything seemed to be much more relaxed than Emily had ever experienced before.

When the evening meal was completed they went to the parlor to enjoy the evening. Uncle Russell built a fire in the coal grate just to knock off the chill of the evening. Emily perceived him to be released from a heavy burden. After she had put Buddy to bed, just the two of them sat around the fireplace by the light of the lamps and Uncle Russell started to talk to her. He told her that things had not been very good in his life for many years. Since Aunt Margaret had lost their baby several years earlier she had never really adjusted to their life together. She seemed to shut him out of her life. When the girls came, he thought she would change and become a loving mother, but their coming had the reverse affect on her. She seemed to resent the fact that they were not hers. He tried hard to please her and make her life better, but when the mines finally laid him off, and he had little or no income, the tension between them only got worse. He explained to her that he had overcompensated for his own loneliness by having doted on the girls. He didn't really have much else in his life. Margaret had made his life miserable if she perceived that he had spent too much time with them and not her. Yet, she didn't want him around either. He simply didn't know how to make her happy. He had tried to take care of her when she became ill, but even then she seemed to resent the fact that he was well and she wasn't. Emily listened to him talk but her heart was breaking. She always had felt victimized. Now she realized that Uncle Russell had also become the victim of another person's misery. She wanted to love him even more because he seemed almost childlike. She envisioned holding him in her arms as she would Buddy, but she knew that would not be the right avenue to take because he would consider her gesture as pity. He didn't want pity, just understanding.

She asked him what his plans were now. He shrugged his shoulders and stated that he hardly knew. He knew that he could take care of himself, but he wondered if the loneliness would kill him. Even though life was not pleasant, there had always been someone in the house with a light on when he came home. He would miss that part of their life together.

The fire died down and the room began to chill. She glanced over at "Grampy" and he suddenly seemed to have a glow about him. She knew he had found peace at last. She thought it so sad to be old and alone but she knew he was not burdened with the inability to make Aunt Margaret happy, which had been his lot in life for so long. She could see that he was getting tired and so was she. They said their "goodnights" and both went to their rooms. As she lay in bed she began to pray for him that he might find some happiness in his last years.

Emily arose early the next morning because the baby had awakened. She took him to the kitchen and planned to give him a bath while she was preparing breakfast for all of them. Grampy was already up and had coffee on the stove. He took the baby and decided that he would bathe him. He drew a tub of water, bent over the tub, and played with the wet child while Emily cooked. It was a sight to see. Buddy loved the tub of water and Grampy loved playing with him. He took him from the tub and dressed him to receive visiting friends. No scrubby clothes for his grandson, he stated, and Emily wondered just what these clothes would look like after Buddy had eaten breakfast. She tied a big towel around his neck and hoped for the best.

While Emily was cleaning the kitchen, Grampy and his new grandson went for a walk around the lake. Emily could hardly believe what she was seeing. An old man with a renewed spirit had been born at a funeral the day before. And her baby boy had acquired a grandfather that he probably would never have had without the death of Aunt Margaret. She cried tears of joy and of sadness at the same time. She wondered if she could have made a difference in Aunt Margaret's life if she had tried harder, but she decided that guilt was not in order.

When they returned from their walk, Emily wanted to go visit Mrs. Thompson. Grampy told her to go ahead. He was prepared to manage the baby. Since Emily knew that Mrs. Thompson would want to see the baby, she invited Grampy to go with her. He quickly accepted and offered to take them in the car even though it was only a few blocks. However, he had just walked a long way so Emily was sure the car was a good idea. They all got inside the car when she realized that aside from the cab ride, Buddy had never ridden in a car. She mentioned that to Grampy and he said that he was about to change that situation. He promised to take Buddy riding in the morning, in the afternoon, and after supper, too. Emily laughed to herself and wondered what she would do with this spoiled baby when she went back to Sandy Fork.

Mrs. Thompson was delighted to see them and welcomed Uncle Russell in her home. She hobbled to the kitchen to make tea for them while Emily was babbling about the trip from Sandy Fork. She had to relate the story that she had kept from Mrs. Thompson for so long about her piano and how it was in the train station for so long. Mrs. Thompson laughed and told her she often wondered how she got it home knowing how bad the roads were in the winter in that part of the country. Mrs. Thompson expressed her sorrow about the loss of Aunt Margaret, both to Uncle Russell and to Emily. They were grateful for her expression of condolences, but they both stated that things would get better soon. Suddenly Mrs. Thompson and Uncle Russell began talking politics and Emily felt like an outsider. She smiled at the turn of events in all of their lives in only 48 hours.

Chapter 40

The visit to Meadville was short but sweet. Her "goodbye" with Uncle Russell had been emotional but encouraging. Emily had had so many new experiences that she was filing away in her "memory bank". She was delighted that Uncle Russell had become Grampy. She thought about his revelation to her about his life with Aunt Margaret and felt so much grief for him. But, she thought it through and felt that he was "free at last". She prayed he would find someone with whom he could develop a friendship in his later years. Loneliness is a miserable experience, she thought. She also remembered her last words with Aunt Margaret when she asked where to find Charlotte. She had a clear picture of her closing her eyes, shaking her head negatively and then leaving the question unanswered as she slowly slipped away. When she thought about it, she was angry at Aunt Margaret's secrecy and cruelty. Why would it have mattered if she had given her the information as to where she might start to look for her sister? Would she ever find her? Suddenly the thought came to her! She would find her before she died if it took every penny she had and every bit of breath she could muster. She would not be defeated. As the train rolled on through the cities and towns, her thoughts ran rampant through her head as if they were on a track. Buddy had slept most of the way, except when he had to be fed. It was a good interruption from her intense reverie.

The train arrived in Sandy Fork shortly after noon. Papa was at the station. He had received her letter telling him that she would be home on Thursday. He was so proud of himself because he could read and understand what she had written to him. He 'lowed as how nothing had gone on at the cabin since she left except the garden was in full production. She winced when she realized her work would be never ending once she entered the door. She would have to finish her "files" in the memory bank because there would be no time until after the tobacco was cut in October. Suddenly she felt tired just thinking about the whole process.

Chapter 41

Emily had lots of mail waiting for her in the kitchen when she arrived. Most of it was from Eustis. She wanted to read them immediately, but Buddy gently informed her it was time to eat. She quickly fixed dinner for them. Having fed the baby, cleared the table, and went to her room to unpack. When she took the time to read the letters from Eustis she found this news.

My darling Emily:

I will not be getting my transfer as I had told you. There is a project here in Chicago that we must complete at this time. The plan to work in Erie has been put on hold for the moment and I will be staying here for a while. Maybe in the future, you and Buddy could come to Chicago and live. We could find an apartment here for the two of you to live in. We will write about it later.

I must go now, I have guard duty and I must report there immediately.

Your loving husband,

Eustis.

Emily sat down as she read his letter again. She was very disappointed that they would not be moving to Erie since it was so near "Grampy". She felt a little sorry for herself but especially for Buddy and Grampy. It would have been good for both of them to be together. She quietly prayed that God would send them another plan soon.

Chapter 42

Time seemed to pass very slowly for the next several years. Emily was consumed with planting, harvesting, tending the stock, raising Buddy, and spending what little time she could manage, doing for herself. She had continued to play the piano in the evenings for anyone who would listen. Buddy had learned to walk before he was one year old and was talking a "blue-streak" by the time he was two. She was busy trying to keep him in clothes since he was growing like a weed. It appeared that he was going to be tall like his father. She had also been teaching him his ABC's and his numbers.

She had also paid regular visits to see Mr. Hay at the schoolhouse. He continued to bring her books to read and encouraged her to go to a nearby college to learn to be a teacher. She entertained the idea, but just couldn't figure out how she could manage one more chore to do. She knew that she would want to be a good student, but she didn't see how she would have the time. Eustis had been home for a visit when Buddy turned two years old. He, too, was surprised at how much she could accomplish in a day, and he wondered when she ever had time to do anything for herself. She was an accomplished seamstress but she hardly ever sewed anything for herself. She kept Papa and Buddy in new shirts and pants, but she wore the same dresses she had always had. Eustis knew that he wanted to take her away from the country as soon as possible in order to give her time to make a life for just the three of them.

Chapter 43

In the spring of 1937, Eustis came home for a visit with all of them. He was going to be sent to a permanent duty station for the next four years. He had been told that he would be going to Erie, Pennsylvania earlier. This, of course, was the same story that Emily had heard before. She wasn't sure that she could believe it this time. He assured her that it was true and, in fact, he would be reporting for duty this time at the base of operations. He expected to take her and Buddy with him when he went to Erie. They would have to find an apartment in Erie and be able to live together again as man and wife. This was something they had not done for nearly 5 years.

Emily's mind went in a whirl. She could barely comprehend what this meant. She would have to pack up all their belongings. What would she be able to do about the piano. Papa 'lowed as how she could leave it there until she found a place to live in Erie. Eustis had 30 days of furlough before he had to report for duty, so they had plenty of time to prepare for the move. Emily had saved nearly all the money she had been receiving from the government that was in the bank. As she and Eustis lay in their bed at night they discussed what household items they planned to move. They certainly weren't sure about the cost of rent for an apartment and they didn't have any furniture of their own. Even if Papa decided to give her the old bed she had no way of getting it to Erie. She planned to take the trunk that Mrs. Thompson had given her because it was really Buddy's. He had been sleeping with Emily all the time that Eustis was gone. Now he was big enough to have his own bed. As they thought about all these things, Emily considered a totally new life ahead of her. An old thought also occurred to her: how many more times must I start over? She fell asleep in the arms of Eustis with the idea that this change in lifestyle would be the last. Little did she know what really would happen!

Chapter 44

No thirty-day period in her life had ever gone so fast. She made many trips into Sandy Forks to get things that they might need to live on. They had no dishes or pots and pans. Papa told her to go through the kitchen and take what she wanted, but he really didn't have "an over-supply" of anything. While they were trying to get their plans made, Eustis suggested that they go into Huntington and maybe buy a car. It was cheap to ride the train, but they would need a car eventually to get around in Erie. Emily loved the idea and reminded Eustis that Buddy would like the idea, too! He and Papa left after breakfast in the wagon. They were home before dark with a new 1937 Model A. Ford car. It had cost them $295.00 and Papa nearly had heart palpitations when he heard the cost, but Eustis felt it was a family necessity. Emily smiled in disbelief and pondered the thought that she would learn to drive it without telling anyone. She always had managed to meet all challenges put before her and she usually accomplished each task without the prying eyes of an audience.

Eustis had to be at the base in Erie on a Monday morning. So they left Sandy Fork on Tuesday the week before he had to report. They wanted to look for an apartment and get settled before he had to go to work. They packed up enough canned vegetables and smoked meat to last them forever, she thought. Papa gave her an old iron skillet to cook in so she could fry bread for Eustis, he told her. She took blankets, dish towels, and unused feed sacks she could use later. Papa also wanted her to have Mama's sewing machine since he told her that it had never cooled down since she arrived. In addition, Papa gave Eustis hoes, shovels, rakes, and other hand tools that he thought he would need now that he was going to be a landowner. Papa never understood that they probably would have an apartment not a house. They had the car loaded to the top with things to take with them. Emily stood by the side of the car and watched in amazement that the men could get that much stuff into one vehicle. There was barely enough room for Buddy and her in the front seat. They left Buddy's perambulator and the piano at Papa's with the promise that they would return for them as soon as possible.

As they were leaving the mountains, Emily asked if she could go to the school one more time in order to say goodbye to her friend, Mr. Hay. Eustis drove up the narrow lane that was intended for horses and wagons. The car tipped from side to side as they tried to navigate the ruts and ditches. When the children heard the motor, the teacher let them out to see this new fangled invention. For some of them it was the first time they had ever seen a motor vehicle.

Emily quickly ran inside the building (with Buddy hot on her heels) to tell Mr. Hay goodbye. He put his arm around her shoulders and told her how much he had valued their friendship. He wished her the best wherever she went and hoped she would heed his advice about becoming a teacher. She told him that she would always remember his kindness and that she would see him again. She turned and left the building to hide the tears that were forming in her eyes. Although he never dreamed what the future would hold for Emily or for himself as they pulled away he felt a pang of loneliness deep in his heart.

Chapter 45

Erie, Pennsylvania, here we come!

If Emily thought the train ride to Meadville was a long one, she had no concept of how long it would take to get to Erie by car. Just as the train stopped to take on water and coal, a car had to take on gasoline and water. It had taken the most of two days to go to Meadville on the train. It would take about three days to get to Erie in the car. It would only go about 35 miles per hour. Fortunately, the weather was good and they made pretty good time. They decided, as they were leaving Pittsburgh on the third day, that they would stop in Meadville to visit Grampy and Mrs. Thompson. Buddy was certainly in favor of that stop because he was really tired of being cooped up in the front seat so long. Like all children, he wanted to run and play not to continue riding. He promised them that he would never take a long trip again, but Eustis assured him that he would recover soon from this trip and would be anxious to see Papa again soon.

They pulled up in the driveway of Grampy's house, but the car was gone. Emily went inside but no one was home. She thought he had probably gone to town for something so she got back in the car and decided to visit Mrs. Thompson while they waited for him to come home. As they arrived in front of her house, there was Grampy's car. He was visiting Mrs. Thompson. She went to the door and before she could knock Buddy had already burst through the door yelling for Grampy and Grammy. The two of them laughed at his greeting and Grampy swooped him up in his arms to give his "Grampy hug". Buddy wiggled free and informed him that he was now a little man, and he was too big to be held like a baby. Grampy leaned against the door and laughed out loud to be corrected by a child. Mrs. Thompson had hugged Emily and put on the teakettle almost in the same movement. They gathered around the table and told the stories of their trip thus far. Eustis quickly took Grampy and Buddy to show off his new car while Emily and Mrs. Thompson caught up on all the news. Emily told her how glad she was to be leaving the mountains, but wondered how Papa would do without her. Mrs. Thompson assured her he would do fine although she was sure he would miss her terribly. Emily wanted to know more about the visits from Grampy to Mrs. Thompson although she didn't want to pry.

They went into the parlor to visit, and Mrs. Thompson proceeded to tell Emily that he had been a regular suitor for several months. He seemed so lonely and had no one else to talk to. She understood because she, too, was in the same situation. He was not attending the Friends Church any longer and had been going to the Catholic Church with her. He had started picking her up on Sundays to take her to mass. Afterwards they had lunch together and then they would go for a drive in the afternoon. She sometimes fixed a picnic lunch for them when the weather was fine. They also enjoyed going to the library together and sometimes they went into Pittsburgh for a play but it was often too far for their energy level. Emily smiled to think that Grampy had found happiness at last. She commented to Mrs. Thompson that she thought Grampy looked better than he had in years and he didn't seem to be so stooped as he had been three or four years ago. Emily had to believe that the relationship as well as the food Mrs. Thompson had been cooking for Uncle Russell had made him feel better. As Eustis and Grampy returned with Buddy in tow, they all laughed that a 5-year-old was leading them since he had more energy than all of them put together.

Emily and Eustis agreed to spend the night with Grampy and start the last leg of their journey early in the morning. They said their "good-byes" to Mrs. Thompson and told her they would visit often since they would be very near once they were settled in Erie. When their car pulled in behind Grampy's at the house, Emily noticed that the old chicken coop was gone. She smiled with pride to think that she had outlived that contraption and was glad that she would never need to can another chicken.

Morning came all too soon for Emily. She, like Buddy, was tired of riding in a car. She dreaded the thought of getting back in the crowded vehicle to continue their trip, but at the same time she was anxious to get to their destination. She was apprehensive as to what to expect but she knew that they would find someplace to stay and she would begin a new life for herself and her family. She really sensed that many things were in store for her family in the not too distant future.

Chapter 46

They arrived in Erie in the early afternoon on a Sunday. Eustis found a hotel where they would be able to stay until they could find an apartment. The hotel cost $3.00 per night, so they would need to find an apartment as soon as possible. Eustis was scheduled to report for duty on Monday so the job of hunting an apartment was Emily's.

She went to the corner drug store while Eustis was carrying in their carpetbags. They had decided not to unpack the car until they could find someplace to live. While she was at the drugstore, she found a daily newspaper. She scanned it for information about a place for them to rent. The front page of the paper also contained several articles about the unrest in the European countries. She decided that she would read all that later; for now, she needed a place to live. She returned to the hotel and found Buddy and Eustis asleep on the bed. She leaned back in the chair and joined them in a much-needed nap.

Early Monday morning Eustis reported to the base for duty. He told Emily that he would be home early in the evening allowing them time to look for an apartment. Emily kissed him goodbye and wished him a good day. As soon as she and Buddy could get ready, she took him by the hand and they started walking the neighborhood to look for an apartment. After walking up and down the streets for several blocks, she was nearly exhausted but determined not to give up. At that point she spied a small house near the downtown area that appeared to be empty. She inquired of a neighbor who owned the vacant house. The man next door told her that it was his house. His mother had owned it but she gave it to him before she passed away. Emily was ecstatic that she had found a house instead of an apartment. The man told her that the rent would be $35.00 per month and they would have to furnish their own heat. He also wanted them to sign a paper that they would stay a year. Emily could hardly remember all the details, but told him she would be back as soon as Eustis came home in the evening. She hurried home to feed Buddy, but made a wrong turn and found herself totally lost in the streets of Erie. She wandered into a small store that sold dry goods items and asked them how to find the hotel where they were staying. The man in the store was very cordial and was interested in any new families that might be moving into the neighborhood. He gladly directed her to the hotel, and she went merrily on her way thinking about how she could make the little house their home.

When Eustis came home that evening, Emily was all bubbly and full of information about the little house that she had found. She wasn't sure she could find it again, but if they would walk the same way she had walked earlier she could locate it again. They quickly ate the meal that she had brought back from the café across the street and took off on the new adventure of finding the house. Emily knew that she could find the house again, but it might not be the shortest route. As they wandered the streets in search of the house, they also discovered a park, a Catholic Church, a library, and the dry goods store. Already she had fallen in love with her new neighborhood. Eustis loved the house and yard. They paid the owner the rent and promised to move in the next day. Suddenly Emily's thought turned to Charlotte. Maybe she would be able to find her in Pennsylvania.

Emily packed their belongings in the trunk and a box that she had picked up at dry goods store. She had to wait for Eustis to come home in order to move all their things in the car. She couldn't possibly walk and move everything they owned. She remembered how the car was loaded to the top with the things they brought from the farm, and she was sure they would have to pack it the same way this time. However, when Eustis came home, he decided they would just make two trips. Emily, Buddy, and Eustis loaded into the car for the first load. While Eustis had gone for the second load, Emily began to put things away. There was no bed, so she made a pallet on the floor for them to sleep on. They didn't have a table and chairs so she rigged a cardboard box with a tablecloth to be used for a table, but they had to sit on the floor. Eustis held her in his arms and laughed at her ingenuity. They would have to unload the car to get dishes to eat from but the makeshift table would do until they could buy something better. Emily was so excited that she could hardly sleep during their first night in their new home.

During their first week in Erie, Emily went to the bank on the corner from their new home and opened a bank account with some of her money that was left over from their trip. Eustis would soon get his check and she would get hers from the government. They would put it in the bank until they could get settled. She wanted to learn all about her new neighborhood, but that would be for another day. She also planned to take Buddy to the park and library as soon as she had a little time of her own.

One day during the early morning hours when she was unable to sleep, she crept into their kitchen and wrote a note to Papa.

Dear Papa:

We arrived here on Sunday evening.

We found a house to live in near the park. Buddy is so happy in his new home. Eustis went to reported for duty on Monday. I am working on our new home.

I hope everything is fine with you.

Our new address is on the envelope. Please write to us.

Your granddaughter,

Emily

As she crept back into bed, she looked over at Eustis who was snoring very loudly and she realized that he had not even known she had left their bed. She smiled and thanked God for such an understanding husband. Now that they had a home of their own, they would be able to function as man and wife for what seemed to be the first time a very long time. She loved this man lying next to her, but she hardly knew him. He was a wonderful father to their son although he had not had the opportunity to spend much time with him. She had lots of plans for their future, and she could hardly wait to put them into action. Nevertheless, time would soon set a different time schedule for Emily Carmichael.

It was not far to the Post Office and the weather was lovely. As soon as they had cleared the lunch dishes, they would walk to the Post Office to mail Papa's letter. Buddy was a great help to his mother. He loved to help her clear the table and do the dishes. He had a stool that he could stand on to help dry the dishes. Emily would talk to him and tell him stories that she could remember from her own childhood. As they walked hand in hand she admired all the flowers along the way and wondered if her flowers in Sandy Fork were blooming. She wondered if Papa had planted the garden? And what of his tobacco plants; would he have them ready to plant? She even wondered about the chickens; would they soon be big enough to fry for dinner? Buddy was skipping along throwing pebbles into the street. She smiled at having such a wonderful child.

Emily's reverie was broken by a car that was coming down the road as they were walking along. Buddy had just stepped into the street to get another handful of pebbles to toss. While Emily was smiling at him, she realized the car was too close to them. She screamed and tried to grab him out of harm's way but she was too late. The car hit him in the side. He flew into the air as if he were a rubber ball and came down on the road with a thud! She ran to his side and gathered him up in her arms. The driver stopped the car and ran to help her. She was so distraught she could hardly stop her hysterical screaming. They loaded him into the car and rushed to the hospital that was on the far side of town.

By the time he was loaded in the car, Buddy was crying in pain. She knew he had not been hit in the head. It looked to her as if he had a broken leg and maybe his arm might be broken, too. She cradled him in her arms in an effort to comfort him on the way to the hospital. She wondered how to find Eustis? She wondered what doctor they should call? Maybe there would be a doctor at the hospital. As they pulled into the back of the hospital to the Emergency Room, she realized it had only been a few minutes since the accident but it had seemed like hours. She gathered him up in her arms not realizing how big he had gotten and that he was a young boy not a baby. They laid him on a stretcher and rolled him into a big room with bright lights that shown on the white linens that surrounded the child. A young man came into the room and identified himself as a Dr. Daniels and that he would be looking after her son. She was so confused and upset that she only wanted him to stop her child's pain. He tried to comfort her and asked about her husband. She rattled off something about his being stationed at the Navy Yards in Erie and that she didn't know how to reach him. Dr. Daniels comforted her a little when he told her that the Emergency Room Nurse would attempt to find her husband and allow Emily to tell him of the accident. Emily thanked the doctor but was admittedly trying to get a grip on herself emotionally as well as mentally.

The Emergency Room Staff recognized that Emily was under great stress as a result of Buddy's accident. In keeping with their normal hospital practice, they sent upstairs for a nun to come and assist in comforting this distraught mother, Emily Carmichael. Shortly, a nun, Sister Mary Victor, came into the E.R. waiting room to minister to Emily. Sister placed her arm around Emily's shoulders and spoke comforting words to her.

As the sister helped Emily wipe her tears away, she could not help but notice how familiar Emily looked. At the same time Emily began to stare at the nun. She told Sister Mary Victor that her soothing words reminded her of her lost sister Charlotte.

Needless to say, they looked at each other and dared to say "Emily"? "Charlotte"? As they recognized each other, chaos erupted in the E.R. section. The desk clerk was calling Mrs. Carmichael to the telephone. Dr. Daniels was trying to tell them both that he had successfully set Buddy's broken leg and broken arm. Emily and Sister Mary Victor (Charlotte) were in shock as they realized that they had finally found each other after 20 years of separation.

Needless to say, it was a long night at the Emergency Room that night. Eustis talked to Emily, briefly, and satisfied himself that Buddy was not in mortal danger, just pain. Buddy, himself, was sleeping from a sedative that Dr. Daniels had given him. And Emily and Charlotte?? Well the first hour of reunion was spent with tears, hugs, and kisses repeatedly. Then, they exchanged addresses and phone numbers and committed themselves to spending every waking hour together for the next month to try catching up on what had gone on in twenty years and what was going on presently.

Emily began to realize as they looked in on Buddy – fast asleep, that once more in her life, a traumatic experience was leading toward a happy ending. Charlotte, too, was equally awe struck at their good fortune. Once more, as the Bible taught, Our Lord has found the sheep who had gone astray.

Meanwhile Charlotte explained to Emily that she had to return to her duty station and that she would come by the house before work the very next morning. Since she would have to report to work shortly after noon at 1:00 PM, she would come see her at 9:00 AM. She quietly left the room with many things running through her mind. She had searched for many years for her sister and now, her search was over. She had found her in her own back yard.

Chapter 47

It was usually quiet at night in the Lake Erie Community Hospital Emergency Room. Sister Mary Victor had been working there for about four years. She disliked working the night shift in the Emergency Room. She was sure the accident rate would be a heavy one again. Sister didn't really believe in those old wives tales about the moon having control over some people but she couldn't deny that the workload always seemed to be heavier during the full moon. Statistics are just statistics.

Prior to working in Erie, she had worked at a hospital in Pittsburgh, but returned to Erie when the hospital was in such a need for nurses. Since the Navy Yard had transferred a vast number of sailors to this area, the Erie hospital needed a bigger staff to handle the workload.

Charlotte had gone to work as soon as she had graduated from nursing school. She had entered the convent and studied to become a nun shortly after graduation from the Academy for Women at the Benedictine Order in Pittsburgh. Her studies at the Benedictine school in Pittsburgh had been rigorous and strict. It was a discipline she had not been accustomed to. Her adoptive parents had not prepared her for the type of life she would be leading in the convent. They had raised her to be a good Catholic, but had not been disciplinarians.

She had never been told anything about her past. She remembered vividly when the lady came to the door to get her. The woman told her that they would go get ice cream and that she would have a new place to live. Charlotte remembered how stunned she was when they took her to a house far from Meadville. When she realized that she was never going back she went into long term of depression. Because she was so young, she had no knowledge of how to cope with the absence of her sister and a stable environment. She had cried for days and her new parents hardly knew how to cope with a crying unhappy child. She begged to go home, but there seemed to be no consideration for her wishes. Her adoptive parents enrolled her in a Parochial School. Later on she realized that she was in Pittsburgh. She tried to run away on several occasions, and find her way to Meadville, but she had always been brought back to the house. She finally turned all her attention to her artwork. She had completed many paintings and her adoptive parents sold them to people in town. Some of them were eventually displayed in Museums. She was acknowledged in the Art Community as quite an accomplished artist

Meanwhile, Buddy was being well cared for in the hospital and Charlotte could hardly get all the facts straight about the lives of the Carmichaels for so many years. And it would be many more years before the ending of their stories would be written.

PART TWO

Chapter 1

Emily and Charlotte had a lot of catching up to do. It had been more than 20 years since they had seen each other. The memory of the long black car that had pulled to the curb of their home in Meadville and whisked Charlotte away was still very vivid in each of their minds. Both of them thought it had been unfair and cruel to separate them from each other. However, the full story had never been told to either of them. Thus the past needed to be revisited.

As Emily had discovered from talking to Uncle Russell, the reality of their adoption of the girls, in part, was because of Aunt Margaret's inability to have another child after the loss of her unborn baby. As in many cases, adoptions occur after the loss of a baby as a means of healing. Aunt Margaret surely had felt that adopting would help her forget the tragedy of her own loss. However, taking on two nine year olds had not been the healing she sought. In fact, it only enhanced her heartfelt loss. She had not had the opportunity to raise them through the formative years, and when they arrived they were not what she had envisioned them to be. Although they were well bred with impeccable manners, she had seen them as snobbish and spoiled. The girls had suffered dramatically from the sudden loss of their parents to such an insidious disease and the effect of being uprooted from a stable environment.

Their adjustment period to a totally new surrounding had been interrupted by new discipline rules and near ridicule of their past. Emily had tended to adjust more readily than did Charlotte. Emily had found a new freedom in her piano that became her escape from the bonds of Aunt Margaret. Charlotte, on the other hand, had had a more difficult time making the adjustment. She was a moody child and any ridicule became a personal vendetta to her. She would lose herself in her artwork, but that only enhanced her moodiness since it had always been hard to think about something else when drawing. Her every waking moment had been filled with the memories of her parents. Aunt Margaret's constant criticism and unfair treatment of Emily only intimidated her and she had not handled the situation well in her frail mind. On the other hand, Charlotte wanted to be loved and cuddled as her mother had done, but Aunt Margaret seemed unable to grasp this desire or perhaps she chose not to give of herself in this way. As Uncle Russell attempted to compensate for the lack of warmth and attention, it only created more animosity from his wife. The atmosphere had become so electrified it had almost been unbearable. Without his knowledge, Aunt Margaret had made the arrangements to give one of the girls to the County Orphanage with the promise that the child would be cared for and placed in a good environment. The County had assured her that they would find a good home for Charlotte and she would be loved and raised in a good Christian home.

Unfortunately, placing children in homes had become routine for the bureaucracy and very little thought went into the placement of the children in their care. Babies were easily placed because most families realized they could train them in their own family atmosphere. Placing a twelve-year old girl with what appeared to be a personality problem had been more difficult. Finally, when a middle-aged couple had applied for a child, they were introduced to Charlotte. She was a sweet child and although her lovely long curls had been sheared, she still was a cute little girl with a longing in her eyes.

When the Bradleys came to the orphanage to apply for a child they were in their late 40's. They had felt a baby would be too much of a burden on them at their age. The charming little girl with the soulful eyes had won their hearts immediately. They knew she was the one that could bring them internal happiness. They had never been able to have children and yet their hearts had always yearned for the love of a child and a child for them to love. Charlotte had reluctantly nestled into their life. She had been scarred by her tragic past and she had seemed unwilling to risk her emotions fearing another trauma. They had taken her home with them on a weekly basis to see if they could mutually adjust to each other over time.

The Bradley's were lower middle class people. Mr. Bradley worked in the steel mills in Pittsburgh and made a good living. Mrs. Bradley had never worked outside the home but was an expert seamstress and homemaker. She occasionally sewed clothing and costumes for other people in the neighborhood. She had made several wedding dresses as well as suits for some of the women who worked in the business district of Pittsburgh. This earned her a little money that she had carefully saved. She was an excellent manager and with the money that Mr. Bradley made she was able to save enough for them to buy a small house near the downtown area of Pittsburgh. The Bradley's lived comfortably but lacked the one thing they wanted most, a child. Charlotte had seemed to be the answer to their dream of having a child of their own.

Charlotte moved into their home for the trial visit and never left. They gave her the attention she had never been able to receive since she had left Peterborough. Mrs. Bradley doted on her every move. She quickly made her a wardrobe of clothing that enhanced her sparkling eyes. She even had new shoes for many of her outfits and bonnets to match. Because the Bradley's were Catholic, they enrolled her in a Parochial School near their home. They had made trips to the museums and to the shops each weekend. They were not far from the park and Mr. Bradley had walked with her there nearly every evening after work. Charlotte had never experienced this kind of a life even though it had remained incomplete. She had lost Emily. She had frequently asked about her sister but the Bradleys had no knowledge of the situation and were unable to answer any of her questions. At times they assumed that Emily was an imaginary playmate and a figment of her imagination. Because Charlotte became content with her life, she only pined for Emily in the privacy of her own room. When she was alone she drew images of Emily as she remembered her but the drawings also resembled Charlotte so the Bradleys had never made any connection to any real person. Charlotte had continued to draw animals with those haunting eyes that had become her trademark.

School had always come easy for Charlotte and she was a good student. Because she had been confirmed as a Catholic in Peterborough from birth, she felt at home in the Church in Pittsburgh. The Bradleys attended mass each week and were devout Catholics.

As she grew older, Charlotte had continued to wonder about Emily privately and she knew that she should pray for her and she believed that she would be well cared for. She could remember, vividly, Aunt Margaret's harsh punishment to or toward both of them and she prayed for Emily's safety.

Eventually Charlotte was old enough to go to high school; the Parochial School had an Academy for Girls. She was enrolled there for her secondary education. She had been able to take more Art Classes in high school so her ability as an artist seemed to soar. Soon she was becoming recognized in the entire region. She had displayed some of her work at the local art galleries and had won a few prizes during those years. The Bradleys had been so thrilled with her ability that they encouraged her to work even harder with the hope that she might be able to study art in the University. However, Charlotte had other ideas. Because of her intense studies in Catholicism, she was beginning to feel she should become a nun. After all, her faith was the one thing in her life that had never failed her.

Upon graduation from the Academy for Women in Pittsburgh, Charlotte had gone to Erie, Pennsylvania in order to become a novice at the Benedictine Convent, the beginning of a life long work.

As fate would have it, Emily had traveled through Pittsburgh several times in the past 20 years, but she had not had the faintest idea that her beloved Charlotte was so close. And Charlotte, too, had assumed that Emily was still in Meadville living with Aunt Margaret and Uncle Russell. The Bradleys had advised her that they no longer wished to see her or be a part of her life. That is the story the adoption agency had given them and they were bound to abide by it.

Chapter 2

Finally, after many weeks, Emily and Charlotte had spent ample time together telling each other of their experiences since their separation. It was time to settle down to making a life with each other. Eustis was still in the Navy and was frequently sent to other bases leaving Emily and Buddy alone in Erie. One day Eustis announced to Emily that he intended to transfer to the Seabees, a separate branch of the Navy. He realized that he would be assigned to another duty station, but he would be learning the building trades. He had been in the Navy for eight years and was really interested in making the military service a career. He simply wanted the opportunity to learn more about construction. He felt that this training would benefit him whenever he became eligible for retirement from the Navy and could re-enter civilian life.

Meanwhile the War was raging in Europe. Hitler had dominated the small European countries and was making noises that he wanted to conquer England. President Roosevelt was convinced that if he overtook the United Kingdom it would only be a matter of time until he would attempt to conquer the United States. The Japanese had invaded Manchuria and then China. They overran Chiang Kai Shek's empire moving southward and conquering many small ruling parties in their path. They appeared to be a big threat to the United States as well. Many United States servicemen were already stationed in the islands near Japan, and the stories of the Japanese occupation alarmed both Emily and Charlotte. Eustis did not seem to be overly anxious about the eminent war fronts but was excited about learning more of his chosen career.

In 1938 Hitler overran Austria and annexed the entire country into Germany. In the fall of 1939 he invaded Poland. This was startling news for the Carmichael family as well as the entire nation. However, the President did not seem to think it was necessary for us to enter the European theatre of war even though many of our country's citizens were greatly disturbed by this ruthless dictator. Most of the nation huddled around the radio in the evening trying to catch every bit of news coming from the war front. While Emily was engrossed in this activity, Charlotte was a sensitive caregiver. She was greatly concerned about the loss of human lives at the hands of the enemy.

On a bright Sunday morning in December 1941, the Carmichaels and Charlotte traveled together to the Catholic Church for the early mass. Charlotte needed to be at work by 3 PM but Eustis had the day off. After they came out of the church and entered the car to go home for a quick lunch the car radio gave them the news of the bombing of Pearl Harbor. All navy personnel were ordered to return to their post immediately. Eustis quickly drove to the base, kissed his wife and son goodbye and assured them he would be home soon. It was not to be.

Chapter 3

Eustis' unit quickly made ready for deployment to the Indian Ocean and the South Pacific. There had been many sailors killed in the senseless bombing of the naval base at Pearl Harbor and all of the men in the Navy that were not at strategic bases were needed to assist in the efforts at the bombing sight. President Roosevelt immediately asked Congress to declare war on the Japanese and stated that December 7, 1941 was a date that "would live on in infamy" for the United States.

Eustis boarded a ship bound for the South Pacific, taking with him all the required government gear and a locket that had belonged to Emily with the pictures of her and Buddy. She was allowed to come to the dock to tell him a final goodbye, hoping that he would return soon. She went back to their house and tried to settle in to a life of being alone one more time. Buddy was now nine years old and understood that his daddy had gone off to war. Buddy soon gathered together all the information that he could about the ship that his daddy was on and about the war effort in the Far East. Over night he became an expert on the subject. He placed a map of the Orient on the wall in his bedroom and proceeded, as the radio commentators reported, to track the ships and planes as they valiantly fought a war with an enemy that he knew little about. However, his efforts did provide guidance for his mother and his wonderful Aunt Charlotte in dealing with the loneliness that was beginning to become a reality.

Emily settled in to the pattern of making a life for herself and for Buddy. She did not feel abandoned, just left out and alone. It seemed to her that for most of her life she had been constantly in a state of adjustment to some trauma. It appeared that this time in her life would be no different. She wondered if she would ever find long term peace and contentment.

Emily searched for Buddy, who had gone to his room to ponder his position in this newest dilemma. When she entered his room she intended to ease her perceived feeling of his being abandoned. When she opened the door, he ran to her and threw his arms around her sobbing; she joined him in the release of their emotions. She sat beside him on his bed and attempted to calm his spirit and make some sense of the situation they were in. After a few moments she decided that it was a good time to make a trip to see Grampy and Mrs. Thompson.

Early the next morning they left for Meadville to enjoy a few days with the family. Charlotte had been able to get the next three days off from the hospital and joined them in their little jaunt. It would be a time of rest for her as well as a reunion. She hardly knew Mrs. Thompson, having only vague memories of her from childhood. Uncle Russell or "Grampy" as they now called him, was the one person in the world she had trusted as a child. In the last two years she had the occasion to visit him and Mrs. Thompson a few times thus, she looked forward to this visit to renew their friendship. Emily, Charlotte, and Buddy headed down the highway with enthusiasm and excitement. Always, it seemed that a trip home seemed to renew their spirits.

Chapter 4

When they arrived at Mrs. Thompson's house, they saw Grampy's car in her drive. This scene had become familiar to them since "Grampy" had been courting Mrs. Thompson for quite some time. They seemed to enjoy each other's company very much, and it was a good arrangement for everyone. Emily did not worry about either of them because they seemed to take care of each other. When they entered the parlor, both of them seemed delighted to see everyone. Buddy zoomed past the women and headed straight for Grampy. He was his hero. Grampy considered this boy to be the greatest child in the world and didn't hesitate to tell everyone he met about him. He was a typical Grandfather even though he was really an Uncle. No one questioned the status of their relationship since Buddy had always called him Grampy.

Mrs. Thompson and Grampy had good news for the twins. They were planning a wedding, their own. They already had most of the plans made and were delighted to share them with the girls. The wedding would be held in the Catholic Church and officiated by Father Paul. Emily remembered that it had been a long time since she had been inside that church and she was very anxious to go again. Charlotte stated that she had never been inside the church since they had been expected to attend the Quaker church when she lived in Meadville. The wedding would take place at the end of the summer and the twins were certainly expected to come. Grampy wanted Buddy to be his best man and Emily was to be Mrs. Thompson's maid of honor. This event would be quite an experience for both of them. They had planned to call Emily on their new telephone, but the twins had arrived before they had had the opportunity.

After the excitement of the plans for the impending wedding was over, Emily began to tell them about Eustis' being sent to the war front. She was not sure when she would hear from him, but she explained that he had left the day before for a part of the Pacific that he had not been allowed to discuss with her. She explained to them that he had wanted to transfer to the Seabees, a branch of the Navy, but had not been able to do so before the bombing of Pearl Harbor. She continued to explain the Seabees to them. The name actually stood for C.B. or Construction Battalion. This branch of the Navy was responsible for building roads, landing strips, barracks, or other buildings and usually preceded the other Armed Forces into a battle scene. Civilian workers had previously done this work but since they were not a part of the military service, there had been no restrictions as to the time that they must stay on any job. Since the Seabees had become a part of the Navy, many of the older sailors transferred to the Seabees. It would be a good place for Eustis since he had previously had experience in building barns and had also worked for the County maintaining streets in Meadville one full summer before he and Emily had married.

Emily and Charlotte explained that the reason for their visit was to take a vacation before Emily settled down into a life of waiting for Eustis to return. Little did she know what new surprises were in store for her in the future? She was still adjusting to her renewed life with Charlotte, what other surprises could there possibly be?

Chapter 5

Winter that year went out with a blast. Erie, Pennsylvania had the worst winter storm they had experienced in years during the last weekend in April. The wind off the lake seemed to be stronger and colder than any of the long-term residents could remember. It cut like a knife if you were outside in the weather. A trip to the mailbox required heavy clothing, hat and gloves. The snow was deep and each day seemed to bring a new flurry of storms. Everyone stayed inside unless it was an absolute necessity to venture out. Charlotte stayed at the hospital working double shifts because of the vast number of patients who had experienced frostbite and exposure. Emily and Buddy hovered around the stove to keep warm when the temperature outside dropped to a minus 20.

Just as quickly as it came upon them, the sun came out on the first of May and seemed to bathe the entire city in a dazzling light. Along with the sun came a rise in temperature to above freezing and the snow began to melt. Although everyone was glad to see the change in the weather, the streets became a slushy mess. Since the snow was melting rapidly, Emily knew that the flowers would peep their sleepy heads above the earth very soon and spring would have arrived. Spring also meant that school would soon be out for the summer

Emily knew that she would need to focus her energies on the up-coming wedding. She decided that she would make a new wardrobe for herself. She had been so busy previously that she had not realized that her clothes were slowly fading from style. "Rosie the Riveter", an icon of the war effort, was currently being seen in pants. Emily had really never expected to wear pants, but the style piqued her interest, and she proceeded to make herself a pair. She looked at herself in the long mirror and decided that she liked what she saw. She called Buddy into her room to get a "gentleman's" opinion. He, too, was surprised at her deviation from her usual wardrobe but passed judgment on the entire outfit as "snappy". Emily decided that his comment was as near a compliment as she was going to get. She continued on for several days making several new outfits for herself and even finished a dress that she expected to wear to the wedding. She was working diligently at trying to pass the time while Eustis was gone. It was very hard not knowing where he was or how well he was doing.

Charlotte usually joined Emily and Buddy for Sunday dinner each week. Normally, after the kitchen was cleaned up, they went to the park. They all enjoyed the park near Lake Erie, and it was a time for Buddy to expel some energy since he was housebound most of the week. However, in the spring and summer, Emily always insisted that they raise a garden and have a flowerbed. This kept the two of them busy. Emily had coached Buddy in raising roses, and he had become quite a horticulturist. He spent hours pruning, feeding, mulching, and watering his rose garden. His greatest satisfaction was when he could present one of the blooming ones to his Mother. He was aware of her loneliness, and he worked hard at trying to fill in the gaps even though he was still a child. He knew that she missed her piano (that was still in Sandy Fork) and he wondered if they would ever be able to get it home. He vowed to himself that when he got older, he would buy her one of the smaller ones on the market called Spinets. He knew that one of those would probably fit in their small living room better than the big Baby Grand that his Grammy Thompson had given her. He knew that she was very attached to the one left at the farm, but he also was aware that she wanted one she could play right now to help ease her loneliness. He missed his daddy, too, and he kept accurate records of the war effort, but he could hear his mother talking to Eustis at night even though she didn't know for sure where he was. His mother had had the Telephone Company install a telephone in their house so his daddy could call them if he ever got to a base that was not under fire from the Japanese. She could also call Grampy and Grammy and talk to them during the daytime.

Early one Sunday morning, while they were dressing for church, the phone rang and Emily rushed to answer it. It was Eustis. He was stationed at a base in the South Pacific. He had been to Pearl Harbor and had seen the damage. He tried to describe it to her, but she was too excited to understand all that he told her. He told her that the Japanese were everywhere around their base and that they could not go out of their quarters after dark. His ship was stationed in the harbor and one of the sailors had to watch all night long for the "Kamikaze" planes. He explained that a Kamikaze was one who would crash his plane into an American target even though it meant he was committing suicide at the same time. Emily shuddered at the thought. She was so alarmed for the safety of her husband. Eustis talked to Buddy and told him all about that part of the war that he had seen. Buddy loved hearing all about the news from the battlefront.

When the phone conversation ended, Emily and Buddy went to the bedroom and knelt by the bed to pray for Eustis and all the other men in the war. She also remembered that the preacher in Sandy Fork had told her about praying for the things that she needed and she needed Eustis to be safe. She also wanted Buddy to understand that he should pray for them as well. She realized what a blessing the telephone had already become. When she talked to Eustis it was like he was in the next room. She, also, called Grampy and Grammy and told them about the call that they had received from Eustis. She could already see that she was going to love this phone, even though she was unable to call Eustis. She would just have to be patient and let him call her as he was able.

Chapter 6

Emily learned to go about her daily routine without Eustis. It was a severe winter and the weather was extremely cold. Buddy went to school about six blocks away, but because of the cold weather, she had been taking him to school in the morning. Some mornings she was unable to get the car started. On those mornings, Buddy would bundle up even more than usual and trudge off through the snow on his own. He didn't seem to mind the snow since he played in it after school. There was an automobile repair garage a few blocks away that Emily would call when she needed them to come see what the problem was with her car. She had tried to learn some of the tricks of how to make the stubborn machine start. Most of the time mechanical problems baffled her. She just couldn't seem to grasp what to do next. The garage mechanic told her it was because it was a Ford. Emily knew nothing about any other kind of car so she just dismissed his opinion, thinking that if Eustis were here he would know what to do. Well, he wasn't here and she would have to do the best she could.

One afternoon in late April, the phone rang. Emily thought it strange for Eustis to call at that hour. His calls had always come in the early morning. When she answered the phone there was a stranger's voice at the other end of the line. He identified himself as an attorney named Scales; John Scales. He was calling from Sandy Fork, Kentucky. He asked her if her name was Emily Carmichael? When she replied in the affirmative he then asked her if she had a son named Buddy? Again she agreed that she did. He wanted to know if Eustis Carmichael was her husband. She then questioned him. Why was he asking so many questions? And what was going on in Sandy Fork that he needed to know this information? He told her that Papa had passed away and in his will, he had left everything he had to Emily, Eustis, and Buddy Carmichael. Emily had to sit down. It had been several weeks since she had written to Papa and she was sorry that she had not been more diligent in her correspondence with him. She had no idea that he was even sick or she would have made more effort to contact him. Mr. Scales informed her that he had not been sick, but had simply died of old age. Mr. Baker had found him sitting by the stove in the kitchen, and apparently he had been dead for a couple of days. Before Emily could grasp the seriousness of the situation, he asked her if she could come to Sandy Fork to take care of the paper work. She thought for an instant and then replied that she was not going to try to come to the mountains until spring. She could still remember the bad roads and the impassability in the winter. She was not afraid to drive the distance but with Buddy in school she felt she would have to wait until the weather got better. She then thought enough to ask the extent of the will. Mr. Scales only told her that it included the farm, the bank account, and any insurance policies that he might have had. No one had been to the cabin to search through his papers and, at this time, there was not an accurate dollar figure. Emily quickly remembered the cow, the mule and the chickens. She asked who was caring for them. Mr. Scales informed her that Jasper Baker had been taking care of the animals since Papa died which had only been a week ago. The funeral home had taken care of the burial and buried him in the cemetery near the Baptist Church but there was a bill to be paid for the burial expenses. Mr. Scales agreed to have the funeral home send the bill to Emily in order for her to pay it from her savings account with the intention of replacing her money from Papa's estate when it was settled.

When she hung up the phone, she settled back in a chair and pondered the events that had been happening all around her. She was almost overwhelmed. She wondered if there would ever be long term peace in her life. She decided to go for a walk. She donned her heavy winter coat and hat and trudged through the snow to the hospital to see Charlotte. She left a note on the table for Buddy telling him where she had gone and that she would be back soon. Charlotte was working and had only a few minutes to visit with Emily but she listened carefully to the story about Mr. Scales call. Charlotte had never met Papa so she couldn't share in her grief, but she was empathetic to her loss. The real question was what would Emily do with a farm in Sandy Fork, Kentucky? Emily certainly didn't have the answer to that question and she remembered that her beloved piano was still there. While thinking of the farm Emily certainly hoped the winter weather wouldn't harm the piano since there would be no heat in the cabin all winter. And, she also prayed, please Lord, don't let the roof leak. She hugged Charlotte and told her that she would see her Sunday. She needed to hurry home now and break the news to Buddy.

Chapter 7

Buddy had been somewhat younger when they left Sandy Fork for Erie. He remembered Papa as being very kind and playful with him. He loved the garden and the tobacco that Papa had planted so carefully. Now he wondered if anyone had helped him cut the tobacco and taken it to the auction. Of course Mr. Baker's name came to mind and he was sure that the crop was safe. He wondered about the farm animals. Would Mr. Baker take care of them too? Who would gather the eggs since that had been his job when he was a young boy? Buddy just wondered what he and his mother would do with a farm in Sandy Fork, Kentucky. He didn't think he wanted to go back there to live, but maybe they could keep it for a summer place to stay.

Emily and Buddy sat at the kitchen table talking about what their next move should be. They decided that they needed a plan. First she would write to Mr. Baker and tell him he should take the farm animals home with him so he could more easily care for them. She felt he should have the chickens for himself. She hated chickens and giving them to Mr. Baker was not a sacrifice but a blessing to her. She asked him to check the cabin to see if it needed any immediate care. She was willing to pay for any repairs that he felt might be necessary to keep the weather out until she could return in the spring. The thought of returning in the spring brought back memories of the flowers and the lush green countryside. Now was not the time to reminisce; she had to continue to work on a plan.

The next thing that they should do was to contact Mr. Scales and inquire about the next step for them to inherit the farm, legally. Since she could not make a trip to the area before the school term for Buddy had ended for the summer, perhaps some of the legal matters could be settled through the mail.

Before she could do much more, she decided to write to Eustis and tell him their good fortune. He would be sorry to lose Papa but would be delighted that they had inherited his farm. Eustis loved the farm and had always remembered happily spending his summers with Papa when he was no older than Buddy.

It had been a long day for Emily. It seemed that most of her days were long and emotionally draining. With Eustis gone, she was trying to be both mother and father to Buddy. He was a good child, but he still required some guidance and discipline. He loved to read and his books were usually historical which generated many questions. Emily often wondered how she could answer all his inquiries about the Civil War and World War I since she hardly knew the answers herself.

She remembered trying to teach Papa to read and write, but that was easy because she already knew those skills. Trying to teach History to a 10 year old was different. She recalled how Mr. Hay had tried to get her to go to school and become a teacher. Now she realized how much she had missed by not being able to do so. Maybe now she could go to school while Eustis was gone to War. That seemed to be the best idea she had experienced in a while. Maybe she could go to school right here in Erie. There were teachers colleges all around their neighborhood. She could attend classes at the same time Buddy was in school and complete her own studies in the evening while he was doing his homework. The idea seemed like a good one to her and she could hardly wait to share it with Buddy. At the dinner table they discussed her latest idea and tried to determine a plan of action to implement. Emily announced that she would go to the local teachers college and inquire about enrolling in the fall to become a teacher. Buddy listened carefully and added his thoughts that maybe they should investigate the inheritance in Sandy Fork before they made any plans. It could be that they might need to pursue some other idea once they had information about what Papa had left them.

Emily cleaned the kitchen, tucked Buddy in to bed and went to her room. As she lay in her bed, staring at the ceiling, she pondered the brilliance of her ten-year-old son. It seemed he had some insight into the future without having any real facts before him. She wondered what Eustis would say about her plan to go to school and she questioned whether or not Eustis would understand the ingenuity and insightfulness of his own young son.

Chapter 8

Besides having to deal with Buddy in school, Papa's death and legacy, Eustis' on-going absence, Emily had to think about Uncle Russell and Mrs. Thompson's courtship. Emily and Charlotte prepared to attend a wedding in the early summer of 1942. Emily had completed her dress to wear as a bridesmaid for Mrs. Thompson, soon to be Mrs. Garland. She could not call her Vivian because she had always referred to her as Mrs. Thompson. Soon Mrs. Thompson would be her Aunt. She considered "Aunt Vivian" but that didn't appeal to her either, so she settled on Grammy and hoped it would meet with her approval. Naturally, Charlotte would wear her "habit", the usual dress for a nun. Emily had also purchased a new suit, shirt, tie, and shoes for Buddy to wear as the best man for his Grampy. He seemed so grown up and had the mannerisms to match his personality. He looked up to his Grampy for all his adult male companionship, yet at the same time Buddy was a resource to Grampy because of his interest in the war. He kept Grampy abreast of what was happening in all parts of the war in the Far East as well as Europe.

The wedding was scheduled to take place at the small altar in St. Anthony's Catholic Church where the nuptial couple had been attending. Grampy would not need to embrace the Catholic faith since there would be no children from the union. Grammy had a dress made for herself that was of fine ecru lace. It was "princess" style which snuggly fit her slim body and ended with a flounce around the bottom of the hem. She had a large picture hat with a lace bow on the side. The hat framed her face which, while it was aged, contained few wrinkles and was flawless. Her shoes were a fashionable pump that were of silk and dyed to match her dress. Emily was sure that she was the most beautiful bride she had seen in a long time. Grampy beamed from ear to ear at the thought of a new wife, particularly one who loved him and loved his family before she knew he existed. Life for the newly weds was sure to be a happy one albeit a short one since they were both in their late 70's.

The bride and groom had chosen not to have a large reception. Rather, a neighbor woman, who held parties in her home, agreed to host a dinner for the wedding party and the priest. The event was breathtaking and solemn. The dinner featured all the food necessary for a banquet. The wedding cake had a bride and groom atop the double layer and had numerous roses of ecru icing around the top. Charlotte cut the cake and served the punch to all who were in attendance. Buddy, who had been Grampy's best man, could hardly contain himself. It was the first wedding he had ever attended let alone have a place of importance. He was doubly impressed. No one could have loved the bride and groom more than the young man who had no blood relationship with either of them, but had become one of the most vital interests in their life. Soon after the dinner, the newlyweds left for a short trip to Pittsburgh to spend their first night together as man and wife.

Emily stood in the doorway and watched a man and a woman whom she dearly loved leave for a life of happiness and bliss. She could not imagine anyone more fortunate than these two people that had found each other. Buddy interrupted her reverie, and she noticed he was a bit misty-eyed. When she reached out to hug him in an effort to comfort his mood, he wrapped his arms around her and they both cried tears of joy for the newly wedded couple. He calmly stated that he was sure that Grampy and Grammy the happiest couple he had ever seen. He then, commented that he hadn't seen many old people in love. Emily smiled at his perception.

Chapter 9

Emily, Charlotte, and Buddy went back to Erie and continued making plans to go to Sandy Fork. Charlotte would not be able to accompany Emily on this summer trip since there was no indication as to how long they would be gone. She would have to be at the hospital most of the time, and even if she had a vacation coming, she would need to stay nearby in the event that she might be needed.

Emily and Buddy packed the car to the top with everything they thought that they might need during the next month. They weren't sure what their needs might be, but Emily was sure that there would be no food at the cabin. They packed as many staples as they could get in the car. They packed many changes of clothes since Emily could remember that the only method of washing was the old washboard. She shivered when she thought of the primitive methods that Papa had always held onto in the mountains. Her thoughts quickly reminded her of the old "outhouse", and she almost became ill at the thought of it when she remembered the odor. Charlotte had agreed to stay in Emily's house on weekends so that she would be able to handle any problems that might arise while the family was away. Their plan was to leave on Monday morning since Eustis usually called on Sunday evening. When he called this weekend Emily would have much news to tell him.

Chapter 10

Winter went out with a blast. Erie, Pennsylvania had the worst winter storm that they had experienced in years during the last weekend in April. The wind off the lake seemed to be stronger and colder than any of the residents could remember. It cut like a knife if you were outside in the weather. A trip to the mailbox required heavy clothing, hat, and gloves. The snow was deep and each day seemed to bring a new flurry of storms. Everyone stayed inside unless it was an absolute necessity to venture out. Charlotte stayed at the hospital working double shifts because of the vast number of patients experiencing frostbite and exposure. Emily and Buddy hovered around the stove to keep warm when the temperature outside dropped to a minus 20.

Just as quickly as it came upon them, the sun came out on the first of May, and seemed to bathe the entire city in a dazzling light. With the sun came a rise in temperature to above freezing and the snow began to melt. Although everyone was glad to see the change in the weather, the streets became a slushy mess. Since the snow was melting, Emily knew that the flowers would soon peep their sleepy heads above the earth and soon other signs of Spring would show through. That also meant that school would be out for the summer, and she and Buddy would be able to take their trip to the cabin.

Early on June 5, Emily and Buddy loaded up the car to make their journey to the farm. She had mixed emotions about their trip. She wasn't sure what to expect when she got there. She knew Mr. Baker had taken care of everything that needed to be done prior to her visit, but she was still undecided about what she should do with the farm. Eustis had written that he was so sorry to lose Papa, but happy that he thought enough of them to leave them the farm. He could have left it to one of his brothers or sisters, but Papa had loved Emily so very much. He apparently wanted her to have it. Emily was grateful that Papa never knew that she was never in love with country living. She still could remember the first time she visited the outhouse. She also remembered the times that she struggled to get that darn stove to work so she could cook on it. And then there was the time it was so hot in the cabin, but she still had to fire up the stove to cook Papa's "dinner". But there were also good memories of standing around her beloved piano that Papa and Mr. Baker had so carefully moved from the train station to the cabin over nearly impassable roads. And Emily would never forget the birth of her wonderful son, Buddy, in the room that Papa had built for her. As they drove along the road to Kentucky, Emily pondered these thoughts and wondered about their future.

Chapter 11

It was springtime in the mountains. The trees were in full bloom; the grass was green; and the wildflowers were waving their sleepy heads as if to say hello. Emily was coming back to see them. As they jostled down the old road to the cabin, Emily smiled to herself, thinking that nothing had changed in the years she had been gone. The roads were still barely recognizable as roads. The rains had washed away most of them and the "road-graders" had not been through the area yet to fill the ruts with dirt as they always did. The cabins along the way were no different than what she remembered. The gardens were planted and many of the women had their "wash" hung on the lines strung from the trees to the porch. The old hound dogs were still lazily sleeping under the porches; cows were still staked out in back of the barns; and the chickens roosted on the porches if not in the kitchens of some of the cabins. Housewives were still working in the fields, tending to too many babies, and trying to eke out a living from this god-forsaken countryside. Emily wondered how she should express her views to Buddy if and when he ever asked what she thought about Papa's gift to them.

As they traveled along, Buddy suddenly glanced at his mother and asked why these people didn't have nicer houses. A child sometimes sees things with a present realistic point of view. Emily hardly knew how to answer. The lifestyle of the mountain folk had not changed in hundreds of years. For many of them, it would be an impossibility for them to leave the area because of financial status, but for many others, it was a matter of choice. Suddenly she realized that she had given Buddy a lifestyle of affluence without even realizing that he would quickly recognize the difference in the way others lived.

Arriving at the cabin was a trip into the past. Emily had not been back in about three years. It seemed that since she had found Charlotte, her days were filled to capacity. With a child in school, a newfound sister, a sailor husband, and her community activities, she had about all she could do.

As she drove up the drive in the car Eustis had purchased in this area, she realized that she felt genuinely at home. She rushed in the front door and then checked to see if her piano was still standing in its usual spot. Quickly she ran to the other room, sat on the bench and began to play her beloved instrument. Buddy hurried in the door with his arms loaded with things from the car, but dropped them hastily on the table when he heard his mother playing. He could hardly believe his ears. He had no idea that she played so well and he wondered if there was any of her musical talent in his bones. Oh, well, he thought, we will need to discover that talent at a later date. Today, we must get settled in. He ran outside leaving his mother still playing the piano. He discovered the flowers she had planted were in full bloom, and Papa had planted a few tomato plants that were heavy with small tomatoes. The tobacco patch was idle. There was a little evidence that he had started to prepare the ground, but from all indications, he had not lived long enough or had not been well enough to do much to prepare for a crop. The chicken coops were empty. After Buddy heard his mother talk about her dislike for chickens, he knew that she would be glad. The barn was empty of animals with only a few remnants of hay left from the winter months. He knew that Mr. Baker had taken the livestock to his farm so he wasn't too surprised that they were all gone. The yard needed to be mowed and some of the trees also needed trimming. As he explained all these things to his mother she marveled at his understanding of the farm and its operations. She went outside with him, and together, they walked over their inheritance. She wondered just what they would ever do with it and, should they decide to sell it, what might it be worth?

It was not quite evening when they decided to drive into town. The spring rains had not washed out the roads and though they were rough and rutted, the roads were passable. Emily smiled at her ability to drive on all this uneven turf, and wondered what Papa would think of her driving the car that Eustis had bought with him. Not many women drove a car in 1942 but Emily was determined to learn to do what she needed to do in Eustis' absence. As they drove along, Emily explained where the midwife lived who had delivered Buddy. She went to the church where she had played the piano and passed the restaurant that Papa had assured her no woman had ever entered. She vowed to Buddy that they would eat there soon. She could not help herself from also going up the ridge to the one room schoolhouse. She knew that Mr. Hay would not be there, but she wanted to see it again for herself. As the car rambled up the drive, she remembered the day she first came there for the books to teach Papa to read and write. They parked the car and went up the steps through the big doors and directly to Mr. Hay's desk. She paused to leave a note for him. She felt sure he wouldn't be back until fall, but she wanted to repeat her old habit of leaving a note.

Dear Mr. Hay:

My son and I are here at the cabin for a few days. Please stop by to see us soon.

Do you still have books to lend for hungry readers?

Emily Carmichael

She paused to peruse the books on the shelf that she once borrowed from him and found a new Dickens novel. She picked it up and decided to take it with her to read in the evening after their work was completed. She hurried back to his desk and added to the note: *I took The Tale of Two Cities and will return it soon. EC*

She and Buddy quietly left the building, pulling the big doors closed behind them. It was such a special place for Emily that she found it hard to contain her emotions.

The two of them returned to the cabin and completed the unloading of the car. They rummaged around in their boxes to find something to fix for their dinner. Following dinner, she checked to see if there was enough kerosene to light the lamps for a while. Buddy was given the instructions on how to trim the wicks and light the lamps. Emily made sure that he understood the volatility of the kerosene and the necessity of handling it with care. She also explained to him how they would need to build a fire in the old cook stove before there would be breakfast the next morning even though the temperature outside was nearing 90 degrees. Buddy was astounded at the primitive methods that were commonplace in the mountains.

Morning came and the sun beamed through the windows signaling that it was time to get up. Emily went to Papa's room to awaken Buddy but found that the bed was empty. She wandered outside and found him gathering wood to start the fire. He informed her that he had intended to start the fire for her, but she got up too soon. She smiled at how grown up her baby had become since the absence of his father had become a reality. She could see that he was trying to compensate for the lack of a male in the household, and he considered himself the "man of the house".

The old cook stove stepped up to Emily's expectations and easily fired up enough to fix breakfast. She also rummaged around in the pantry for some of the vegetables she had "canned" in the summers that she lived here. She found green beans, carrots, peas, and corn. Quickly she put together a stew that they could have for the noon meal while the fire was still hot. Then she could let the fire go out and not heat the cabin any hotter since the sun needed no help in heating the small building that had very little ventilation.

As soon as they could get the cabin in order, Emily and Buddy went into town again to see what they needed to do in order to settle Papa's estate. She wanted to buy some supplies from the store and to visit the church to inquire about the happenings in the neighborhood.

Their meeting with Mr. Scales, the attorney, had been planned for a long time. The exact date had not been set, but he was aware that Emily would come in the early summer. When she went into his office, she was surprised to see one of the young ladies from the church as his secretary. Mary Harris recognized her immediately. She was able to give her news of the church. The pastor whom she remembered, was still there. From time to time he had asked about Emily. Emily quickly made a mental note that she could eliminate one chore from her list of things to do.

Mr. Scales invited Emily and Buddy into his office and as they entered a room completely lined with books, they were in awe of their surroundings. Mr. Scales explained to them that Papa had left, what was considered a "sizeable" estate for "mountain folks". He had been very thrifty with his money and his savings account had $25,780.81 in it. He had also been concerned about the war effort and had purchased "Savings Bonds". There were 12 of them worth $100.00 each upon maturity. Each of them was in the name of Eustis Carmichael, Jr. Mr. Scales explained that Papa felt the boy should have more education than he had received and this was his way of helping. Emily could not control the tears when she heard this statement. She instantly remembered the nights around the table when she was teaching Papa to read and write. The farm had also been deeded to Eustis and Emily before his death so that the farm was not part of the inheritance, but was a gift from him to them. Although the farm animals and crops were part of the estate, Emily explained that she had given the animals to Mr. Baker when she learned of Papa's death. There were no crops this spring except for a few tomato plants that he had apparently set out before he became fatally ill. If the animals had any monetary value Emily felt that Mr. Baker deserved them for his caring for Papa during Mama's illness and the times he had helped Papa with the farm.

In short order Mr. Scales had the necessary paper work completed and Emily needed only to sign her name before a Notary Public. Mr. Scales informed her that he would file the document with the Court and that the money in the bank was now hers. She would need to change the names on the account at the bank but not until after the document was filed with the Court. Mr. Scales told Emily that the Court approval might take as long as a week but Emily could check back next week.

Emily and Buddy walked out the door of the Attorney's office a wealthy family. Over $25,000.00 was more money than she could imagine, and Papa had earned every dime of it. He had stated in his will that he wanted her to have it since he knew she would be thrifty with it just like he had been. She hoped in her heart that Buddy would inherit those same attributes when he became old enough to know his own mind.

They crossed the street to the feed store/general store to get a few groceries. When she went into the store, the man behind the counter recognized her as the lady who came to town with Papa. They began to talk about the old man and the farm. Mr. Perry asked Emily what she intended to do with the cabin and farm. At this point, Emily's reply was one of indecision. She explained that her husband was in the Navy in the Sea of Japan. She probably couldn't make a decision without his consent. The storekeeper asked if she knew about the Rural Electric Agency that was coming into the mountain area. Many of the homes and stores would soon be getting electricity in their homes. There would soon be electric lights, electric stoves to cook on, even electric washing machines. It was called TVA or Tennessee Valley Authority.. Somehow they had harnessed the power from damming the river to create electricity. It was transported on electrical lines across the mountains and set up with sub-stations all along the way. It was revolutionary in the mountain area. Emily listened carefully, wondering if it might be possible for her to have electricity brought to the cabin. The idea of cooking on an electric stove in the summer sounded wonderful to her. She asked about whom she should contact about this new idea. Mr. Perry told her there was an office set up down in the next block. She could stop in there for more information. She quickly grabbed her groceries and Buddy's hand and off she went.

When she stepped into the REA – Rural Electric Association office, she was instantly impressed with the electric fan blowing the heat away from the doorway. The office was well lit with many lamps and in the window was the newest electric stove. Her kitchen in Erie was modern compared to the cabin, but this room offered the very latest in equipment. Emily asked many questions and even Buddy had a few. He asked about the safety of such a convenience. The lady behind the desk explained that electricity was much safer than gas, which is what they had in Erie. It was explained that Emily needed to find someone who would install the wiring in the cabin. If the lines had been installed on the road where they lived, she could have electricity before winter. Whenever she had the wiring completed, she could also have a gas furnace for heating the whole house during the winter because she could use a fan to blow the heat through the rooms. Of course Emily had a gas furnace in Erie, but it was the last thing she thought would ever be possible for the cabin.

They left the REA office with their heads full of information. As they were pondering their REA experience Emily spied the "Forbidden Café". This would be her chance. She took Buddy by the hand and they entered the small restaurant with the idea that she would learn, at last, why this was forbidden territory for women. They went to a table by the window and sat down. They waitress came to the table and asked if she would like a cup of coffee and would the boy like a Coca-Cola? Emily nodded in the affirmative, and quickly perused the room. It was true that there were no women in there, but the men all looked harmless. She just didn't understand why Papa thought it might be such a den of iniquity. When the waitress returned with a menu, Emily questioned her about the type of people who ate here. She finally had to explain to the waitress that Papa had told her that no decent woman ever ate here. The waitress laughed and told her that most of the women in the community did not have enough money to eat in a restaurant and that the men that she saw were workers that worked at other businesses such as the feed store, or on the railroad work gang. Papa had probably felt that historically they were unsavory characters; however, the waitress assured her that there had never been a brawl or fight in the restaurant. Most of their customers were men who had no wives or lived far away from their work place. Emily and Buddy each ordered a hamburger and enjoyed eating every bite in the "Forbidden Café" and the total price was $1.25 for both of them. The entertainment was free.

The two Carmichael's hurried back to the cabin with their heads full of knowledge and questions. Emily wondered who might be skilled enough to wire the house? How much would it cost? When could it be done? She also needed to get back to Erie, but how could she leave and not have the work completed. If she went home, there would not be enough time before school started for her to return again to Sandy Fork. Buddy also chimed in with his line of questioning. He wondered how hard the job might be, and if they had someone to do it, would he, Buddy, be big enough to help with the job? (Maybe he could stay all summer at the cabin and oversee the job.) Emily smiled to herself at the "would be grown-up" standing by her side who was just shy of 11 years.

When they arrived back at the cabin she noticed a pick-up truck in the driveway and a man on the porch. She stopped and looked closer. Buddy suggested that she not get out of the car until he could establish who this stranger was. When they got nearer the house she saw that it was Mr. Hay. He had evidently been to the school and found her note. She leaped from the car and ran to see him. He explained that he had gone to the school to deliver some supplies and found her note. Since she was on his way home he had decided to stop for a visit. He was about to give up on her when he heard her car coming down the road. Needless to say he was surprised to see that she was the one driving it. She sat down on the porch and rattled off the happenings of the last three years almost non-stop. She explained that Papa had left everything to them and that she had come back to handle the paperwork.

She also shared with him that she was excited about the potential for electricity in the cabin and the whole county. If they had electricity they could also have a pump for the well and have running water as well as other amenities. That would mean that they could also have a bathroom inside the house. Mr. Hay listened patiently and hardly interrupted her. Finally when he could get a chance, he asked her if she had someone in mind to do the work. Of course she did not, but Buddy, who had been standing idly by the sidelines quickly volunteered to be the assistant to anyone who was willing to do the work. Emily commented that some of the men in the "Forbidden Café" might like the extra work. When Mr. Hay questioned the name of the restaurant, Emily had to explain Papa's objection to the eatery. Together they had a big laugh. Mr. Hay explained that the restaurant was as nice a place to eat as anywhere around the area.

Emily questioned Mr. Hay about going to school. She told him that Eustis was in the war, and she would have time to go to school if she could attend during the same hours that Buddy did at his school. Mr. Hay explained that she should inquire at the colleges and Universities in Erie about what they had to offer for a Bachelor's Degree and a teacher's certificate. He felt sure that there would be many schools available for such training. He also encouraged her to do the very thing that she wanted to do for two reasons. Teaching would fulfill her personal goal and it would also help the war effort. There was such a shortage of teachers, especially in the mountain areas.

Emily thought about his insinuation that she might return to the mountain area to teach. When the thought of teaching here crossed her mind, she remembered the trauma she had experienced living on the farm with Papa, the outhouse, the old cook stove, and even the farm animals. But, if the cabin could be modernized to make it livable, maybe, she thought, just maybe, it wouldn't be so bad. She would need to discuss the subject with Eustis the next time he called her. Suddenly she realized that she had not heard from him since she left Erie.

As Mr. Hay rose to leave, he told her that he wanted to make a few inquiries about the possibility of who might do the work on the cabin. He assured her that he would be back in a few days. He asked her how long she planned to stay, and her response was one of indecision. If the work could be started and someone was reliable, she might return to Erie in a few days. If the workers required her supervision on a subject she knew little about, she might need to stay longer. She missed hearing from Eustis and hated to make monstrous decisions without his input. Mr. Hay departed saying he would be back soon.

Buddy and Emily went inside and decided that they would look around at what they thought would improve the cabin to an acceptable standard.

When she went to her room she longingly looked at her piano. Should she take it to Erie or leave it at the farm?

Chapter 12

During their stay at the cabin, Buddy found his mother entranced in a reverie that he had seen often lately. He wanted to be the man of the house in his father's absence, but he really couldn't understand her moods. Youth had its disadvantages, he thought to himself.

He had wandered around in the kitchen and in the bedroom that Papa and Mama had occupied. It had become his room while they were visiting. The closet where he had tried to store his clothes was shallow and the pegs made his shirts and pants hang the wrong way. There was no rod for hanging clothes such as he had in his closet at home. He felt the closet should be changed. The bed and dresser were adequate but the bed mattress was lumpy and hard. He would like to have a good bed to sleep on, if this were to become his room.

He wondered just where they would put the bathroom that his mother wanted. None of the rooms were big enough for a portion to be designated for a bathroom space. He went to the kitchen and looked at all the pantry space. It seemed adequate, but if the old cook stove was to be replaced by a modern electric one then how would they heat the cabin in the winter? If they got rid of the old cot that lined the north wall of the kitchen, then his mother could have cabinets to store her dishes in instead of putting them in the pantry.

When Emily saw her "baby boy" so grown-up and accepting responsibility, she nearly burst with pride. He was such a joy to her.

She listened patiently while Buddy explained to her his plan for changing the bedroom and the kitchen. Together, they wandered the grounds and made assessments about what could be done to make the garden more useable. They noticed that the porch was in bad need of repair. Mr. Hay had said that if they put in water from the well and pumped it to the house for a bathroom, they would need to install a "septic system" with a leach line and a septic tank. Neither of them knew what that even meant, but Mr. Hay had explained the septic system as a large concrete container buried in the ground that held the waste from the bathroom. The leach line would take the run off when the container became full and would filter it off through the field. The lines would also be buried and would snake through the ground like a maze only it would all be buried. Buddy felt sure he understood every word that Mr. Hay had uttered, but Emily wasn't so sure. Finally she just commented that she would have to trust someone in these matters and maybe it was her young son. He obviously had a mind for such things and she was mystified.

They sat together on the rickety old porch in silence gazing off into a purple sunset enjoying the solitude of the country. The night cicadas were chirping and the birds had hushed their singing for the night. Lightning bugs were making their feeble effort to light the evening sky in the absence of the sun. A soft summer breeze kissed their faces as they thought quietly about their situation. What to do and how to do it? Maybe just going back to Erie was the answer for now and leave the rest behind. Such a plan seemed wise. It would give both Emily and Buddy a chance to consider the "whole" picture.

Chapter 13

As he had promised, Mr. Hay arrived at the cabin early the next morning. He had been working on the house plans and getting promises from workers that might do the work for Emily in remodeling the house. Most of them were unemployed neighbors who had little or no income and large families to feed. Since many of the young men had joined the service to fight during the war, these were men with experience as well as some age on them, but were still able to perform heavy work. Mr. Hay laid out his plan to Emily and explained that he thought it might cost $3000.00 to modernize the cabin. He also mentioned that the foundation was made of large rocks that had been unearthed from the hillsides and that the cabin was not too stable. He wondered if she really understood the frailty of the structure. Even though it had stood the ravages of time, there wasn't any assurance it would continue to withstand severe weather and any modifications to the main building. It had been built of rough lumber. Some of it had been green lumber that had warped in some places allowing the wind to come through. Emily had memories of those nights when the wind seemed to come inside whether it was welcome or not! Of course Emily had no idea of the condition of the foundation nor did she understand the complexity or implication of what he was telling her. Her only thought was that if they wanted to come here in the summer, she wanted the cabin to have the modern conveniences that were available to them.

Mr. Hay and Buddy discussed the details with her for quite a while before their conversations turned to the events of the day. Mr. Hay told them about the latest happenings on the war front. It seemed that the Japanese were using suicide bombers to assault Americans in all the islands surrounding Hawaii. The fighting was still intense in Europe as well. Mr. Hay seemed to be disturbed that the war wasn't going well for the United States.

President Roosevelt had been sending more troops to all the war fronts leaving only old men at home. Many of the mothers in the valley had sons who were gone off to war. The custom of hanging a banner in the window indicating the number of sons that were serving in the war had become common place. If the stars on the banner were blue, that meant the boys were fighting, if the stars were gold, that meant their sons had been killed in action. Many of the mothers in Sandy Fork proudly displayed their banners. The newspaper that served Elliott County ran articles in every issue concerning military family members and their whereabouts.

Buddy listened with both ears to the stories that Mr. Hay told and he also listed all the activities on his bulletin board with marks indicating the information he had gathered from him.

As they sat on the porch discussing the war, Emily remembered to mention that she had taken the book from the school. Mr. Hay went to his saddlebags and pulled out another book he thought she might like. It was entitled The Bridge of San Luis Rey by Thornton Wilder. Emily quickly took the book to scan the text. Mr. Hay had also brought books for Buddy, thinking, (rightfully) that he might have inherited his mother's love for reading. Together the three of them went back inside to escape the afternoon heat. Emily served everyone a glass of tea. Since she had no ice, she hoped it would be cold enough for them to enjoy. When Mr. Hay went inside the cabin, he couldn't help but notice the big Baby Grande piano that dwarfed the room around it. He asked about its presence in the cabin. She proudly went to the piano and gave him an impromptu concert of her favorites. She had even learned the Navy Hymn. He was more than suitably impressed.

Mr. Hay excused himself, saying that he had to go to the school to pickup some paperwork. He promised to return the next day in order to discuss the remodeling project with her. Buddy boldly begged to ride the horse to the schoolhouse with him and walk back if his mother would permit it. Emily smiled and cautioned him that he had not been invited to go. Mr. Hay quickly assented by taking Buddy's hand and helping him mount in the saddle, then he mounted behind him and off they rode. As she watched her son and her dear mountain friend ride into the trees, Emily realized how much Buddy had been missing a male image in his life. She was grateful for such a fine schoolteacher whose love for children oozed from every pore.

Chapter 14

The sun seemed to burn, as it were, a hole through the cabin window during the early morning on Thursday, thus bringing Emily to her senses. She had fought the opportunity for sleep all night as she had thought about what to do with the cabin. She repeatedly kept coming back to the fact that trying to improve the old structure wasn't a good idea. Papa would argue that the old house hadn't needed improving and that she shouldn't spend her money on frivolous things. She remembered those many admonitions he had declared every time that she had asked him to save her a place for flowers in the garden. She also remembered that he loved the flowers and would pick them for a bouquet on the table nearly every day. It had been Papa's money and his beloved cabin, but now she wanted to live in it in peace and convenience to suit her own family's needs.

Over the pancakes and eggs at breakfast Emily and Buddy discussed the problem at hand. Buddy finally suggested that they go back to Erie and stop by Grampy's house, and discuss it all with him. Then when they got to Erie, they would wait for his daddy's call in order to get his opinion, too. After all, it was his grandfather's inheritance they were spending. Emily quickly jumped to her feet, kissed him on the forehead brushing back his tousled hair, and thanked him for making their decision. "Get your stuff packed", she said, "and we will leave immediately". She stuffed all her things in her suitcase and set them by the back door for Buddy to load in the car. The groceries that would keep, she left in the pantry. All the perishables, she packed in a bag to take with them. Grabbing a pencil and pad, she quickly scribbled off a note to Mr. Hay.

Dear Mr. Hay:

We have decided to go back to Erie without making a decision about the remodeling. We want to discuss it with Grampy and Charlotte before we decide what to do.

Eustis will call me soon and I will get his opinion on the matter.

Thank you for your help in all the details of the project, but most of all, thank you for being a friend to Buddy.

Emily Carmichael

She stuck the note on the door with tape and jumped in the car to return home to Erie, leaving this life behind again.

Chapter 15

Emily and Buddy rode in silence as they traveled through the mountain areas of Eastern Kentucky up through West Virginia. Neither of them spoke for the fear it would break the spirit that they were feeling about the farm and the cabin. Emily loved the church, the people, the scenery, and the atmosphere of solitude that she found in Sandy Fork even though she disliked the inconvenience. She enjoyed the big city life of Erie with the culture and the opportunities available to her and Buddy, but she disliked the climate. The severe winters completely enclosed her lifestyle. They were captives for two or three months every winter due to the bitter cold coming in off Lake Erie. Buddy did enjoy the times he could go ice-skating and playing in the snow; however, he too, complained about the cold weather with its many restrictions.

After driving nearly a hundred miles, Buddy finally spoke to break the silence with the thought that he was still appreciating the beauty of the mountains. He also questioned Emily about the schools in the mountains. He had been much impressed by Mr. Hay and wondered what school would be like with all eight grades in one room. He thought the horseback ride with Mr. Hay had been wonderful and queried if he could have a horse for the times they would be at the cabin next summer. He asked if Emily knew how to plant tobacco like Papa had and could he learn to do that, too. Emily could see that he really loved the mountains and she wondered if that was an omen for her to consider in the decision making process regarding the farm.

When they finally crossed over into Pennsylvania, they decided to try to find a small café to eat lunch. She was hungry and they had not taken time to pack a lunch for themselves. They saw a big sign that said "Charlotte's Café" and Emily was quickly brought back to the past and the times that she had searched for her sister. She knew if a woman named Charlotte owned the restaurant, the food would be good. They parked the car and went in to eat lunch. As Emily looked around the dining room she discovered that only men were eating there. She wondered if this was another “forbidden café”. A waitress came to their table with a menu and Emily asked if Charlotte was an owner. The girl stated that Charlotte was her mother and she did all the cooking. Emily explained that she had a sister named Charlotte and the title of the eatery had brought them inside. She stated that they were traveling to Erie and needed to eat before they went any farther down the road. They each ordered a hamburger and potato salad with tea to drink.

Back in the car, while traveling through the heat of the day, the two of them discussed their ideas of what to do about the cabin. Buddy’s idea was that they should remodel it to be used as a summer home. They could leave Erie when school was out and spend the summer in the mountains when it was the most beautiful. Winters in Erie were not so bad that they couldn’t endure it. Besides they were close to Grampy and Grammy who just might need their help. Aunt Charlotte also was entrenched in her job and was not likely to have any more time for them than now, which limited her to them only on weekends. Although his mother had searched for her for years, Buddy was aware that Charlotte had developed her own life apart from Emily. They were no longer dependent on each other for survival.

Emily listened patiently as her young son expounded on his ideas. He was certainly level headed for his age. Maybe it was because he had never known a life without her being by his side at all times. Eustis had been gone most of the life of the boy therefore he couldn’t relate to Eustis very well for a father image or for guidance.

Before they got to Pittsburgh, Emily began to express her ideas about the cabin. She explained to Buddy that she really wanted to go to school to be a teacher. Even though Papa had left them money, she felt that she wanted to earn her own money and be self-sufficient. Mr. Hay had encouraged her to become a teacher; because she seemed to have a desire to teach children. She planned to enroll at a state normal college in Erie in the Fall to begin her studies. She would be able to attend classes while Buddy was in school. She would normally be home when he got home, and they would have their evenings to study. Buddy had not heard of her plans before, but he listened carefully to all her ideas. He assured her that he would be home alone for a while if her classes were in session late in the day. "Mother, I am not a baby anymore", he said. The message was well taken by Emily. It was a blessing and a curse. She loved his adult nature, but she missed having a baby who depended on her. Life is full of twists and turns, she thought.

She continued to discuss the cabin with Buddy as they drove along. Emily wondered if the best idea would be to just build a new house. It wouldn't cost very much more to build a new house near the cabin, maybe on the hilltop in back of the cabin. A long lane could lead up to the new house and she would have flowers along each side of the lane. They would have a view of the mountains from every room. In the Spring and in the Fall the view would be breathtaking. Buddy interrupted her to remind her that the present lane that went to the cabin was impassable in the winter. If they were planning a longer one, they would need to park the car at the bottom of the lane and walk when the lane was impassable. Emily laughed at his realism and her lack of foresight.

The rest of the trip was taken up with discussions of little or no consequences. They discussed school, the house in Erie, the roads they were traveling on but nothing was really settled. They left all of these subjects in their thoughts as they sped on toward Meadville. When they left Pittsburgh, Emily turned on the radio in the car thinking that they might get some news of the war effort. Buddy turned his attention to what the commentator was saying. Edward R. Murrow was reporting from the war in Europe and spoke of the battles raging there. Hitler had invaded more of the European countries and was trouncing the smaller empires as he went. The allies were fighting valiantly in an effort to stop his regime'. Many of the Allied soldiers were killed in the Battle of the Bulge, but the army continued to push onward in their efforts to conquer the dictator. The news then switched to another reporter from the Pacific front. The commentator was discussing the bombing raids on some of the islands in the Pacific. They talked about how the Japanese were so ruthless in their fighting. Many of the tropics had the Japs hiding in the underbrush and would fight "hand to hand" against the Americans who were trying to re-take the island for its local rule. Gabriel Heatter was the commentator that broadcast the news from the Pacific Theater and he listed all the details of the fighting that were not classified. The Marines were said to be landing on many islands on runways that were built by the Seabees. Emily's heart jumped in her mouth. She had no idea they would discuss the operations of the Seabees on the radio. She and Buddy listened intently to what he was saying about the roads that had been built by the Seabees for armored vehicles to use as they traveled to the war front. As they were speaking of the airfields that had been built for the planes to land on, to be refueled, she was sure that Eustis was involved in that operation. Mr. Heatter also spoke about the attacks by the Japanese that were brought against the airfields and the fuel storage tanks, she reached up and turned the radio off. "Enough bad news for now", she said. "We need to pray for Eustis and not listen to the devastation occurring all around him".

Chapter 16

Arriving at Meadville was a welcome relief. They went immediately to see the newly-weds. Grammy and Grampy met them on the porch with hugs and greetings. Buddy took Grampy by the hand and led him to the yard to discuss the war effort. Grampy had also heard the news and was more than willing to discuss it with him even though Buddy was still a child. Grampy was also surprised at his adult understanding of the dangers involving his father.

After dinner in the evening, Emily announced that they would like to discuss the whole cabin scenario with them. She laid out their plans and hopes to them about what to do with the farm and cabin. One idea that she had not broached was the possibility that they might sell the farm. Selling the farm didn't seem like the right thing to do; Papa would not want that.

Grampy and Grammy listened carefully to their plans and thoughts concerning the disposition of the property. Remodeling as opposed to building seemed to be the main concern. Grampy voiced his opinion first. He felt that remodeling seemed the proper thing to do. Maybe they could simply add on to the present space preserving the cabin's integrity. The porch in the front sounded enticing. He then mentioned that he was speaking from an old person's viewpoint. He could even see himself sitting on the porch in a rocking chair watching nature's floorshow. Grammy spoke up that all women wanted a new house. She remembered moving into her home with the odor of new wood and varnish to fill her nostrils. Buddy ran to her and promptly hugged her as he quickly caught the vision of her youth. The discussions continued on into the late hours. Finally, Emily decided that they would continue this subject at the breakfast table in the morning.

They all agreed and, one by one, retired to their rooms. Emily and Buddy smiled when they saw the love-light in the eyes of the two of them. Hand in hand they had helped each other to their room. Obviously each one needed the assistance of the other to amble to their beds. "Love knows no age", Buddy said, as he quickly went to his cot where he slept in the living room. Emily went to her bedroom where many of her treasures had rested in the trunk that Mrs. Thompson had given her. It had been filled with the beautiful layette that she used for Buddy. She felt a kinship to the long lost daughter of her now Aunt. How touching!

Chapter 17

As they gathered around the breakfast table, Emily had prepared the meal with bacon, eggs, and pancakes. Buddy loved pancakes so there had to be an ample supply for a growing boy. Grampy stated that he, too, loved pancakes, and that he would fight him for the last one on the plate. Emily and Grammy calmly ate their scrambled eggs, and stated they could have all the pancakes since neither of them cared for the gooey treat.

Having had a night to "sleep on it", the discussion about the disposition of the cabin took on a personality all its own with everyone offering his or her new thoughts of what should be done. The consensus of opinions was that the original cabin should be preserved; therefore, adding onto the existing structure seemed the best plan. For the moment, the only addition really needed was the construction of a bathroom, the wiring for electricity, and the installation of a septic system. All other ideas and plans could be done later since they would only be using the cabin in the summer. Emily agreed to everything except one item. She insisted on the purchase of one of those new kitchen ranges that she had seen in the windows at REA.

Grampy and Grammy quickly gave their blessing to Emily going to school to become a teacher. There were many opportunities for teachers right in Meadville both in the public school system and in the Catholic School. Perhaps when Eustis got out of the Seabees, they would move back to Meadville. They could live in the house where he and Margaret had lived and Emily could even raise chickens, he chuckled. He knew how badly she hated chickens and the whole family enjoyed a laugh. Grammy chimed in that to have Emily and Buddy nearby would a blessing she hadn't anticipated, but welcomed.

Buddy sat idly by with little or no opinion to offer, which was not his usual style. Finally he spoke up and stated that by the time Emily had finished school he would be about 17 years old, and he would be the one who would come to live in Grampy's house while he went to school in Pittsburgh to become an engineer. Such grandiose plans brought more laughter as well as agreement from the group around the table.

Buddy and Emily gathered up their belongings and prepared to head home to Erie. They wanted to be sure that they would receive their usual calls from Eustis. Besides, Emily could hardly wait to discuss her plans with Charlotte. As always, leaving Grammy and Grampy was traumatic. Emily was never sure if it would be the last time that she would see them alive. Time was marching on for all of them and the future was obviously uncertain for the Garlands.

Chapter 18

Arriving in Erie in the early afternoon, Emily first went to the mailbox to retrieve any letters from Eustis. Next she began to anticipate hearing his voice on the phone. She certainly hoped that if he had been calling and not getting an answer, he might break his habit of calling only on Sunday evening and call during the week. Buddy then reminded her they had only been gone 5 days and that the weekend was just coming upon them.

She wandered about the house as if it was her first time there. She seemed to be getting acclimated to her surroundings again. Her thoughts wandered to the many changes that she had experienced in her lifetime. From Peterborough to Meadville to Sandy Fork to Erie with each move requiring a drastic change in her lifestyle. She thought again about her early childhood with Charlotte and all its ups and downs. Her mind then drifted to Sandy Fork and the birth of her beautiful son. She thought about her never-ending search for Charlotte that had finally ended. When she forced herself to think of Aunt Margaret it was only briefly; because that experience only brought her sadness. She often wondered how anyone could have been personally so bitter as to punish a small child. And yet, the bright spots in her memories of earlier days included her friendship with Mrs. Thompson and her beloved piano as well as her strong ties with Uncle Russell – now Grampy.

She was standing in the window looking out over the yard of their house when Buddy interrupted her reverie. He saw the tears in her eyes and wondered how he might help. She gathered her growing son who was nearly as tall as she was in her arms and cried openly. He didn't understand her tears and wondered if he might be the cause. She composed her self and explained that she was simply reminiscing about the past of which he was and was not a part.

They unloaded the car, rummaged through the kitchen for a lunch idea and finally settled on peanut butter and jelly sandwiches.

Emily began to sort through the mail as they sat at the table and found two letters from Eustis. They had come through the whole weekend without a phone call. She felt relieved when she saw the letters. She quickly ripped them open and read them aloud.

My dearest Emily:

We are right in the midst of the fighting. We have been building roads for the Marines to use as they land for the fighting. Last week the Japs blew up a fuel storage dump just down the road from where we are. We continued to build our road anyway. The Marines are fighting their hearts out and many of them are being shot down in their tracks.

Soon we will begin to build an airfield for Navy planes to use when we have finished this strip of road. It is located about three miles from here.

I hope everything is ok with you and Buddy. I will call you soon. I miss both of you very much.

I love you both.

Eustis

His letter struck fear in Emily's heart. She could not imagine the war zone and the fierceness of the fighting. Why does one country have to kill innocent people in war? Buddy explained to her that the battle represented one country's wanting to conquer another for the land value or the industry in that country. Emily shook her head in disbelief. So much slaughter, she thought, for things.

She opened the second letter. It was much the same as the first one except that in this letter his unit had moved to the airstrip previously mentioned. He stated that the pressure was on to build it as fast as they could in order for the Navy to be able to use it to for refueling as they proceeded with bombing raids against the enemy. Emily shuddered and wondered about the imminent danger he was in even though he didn't seem to express any fear. He seemed to be at peace with his mission and wanted her to be convinced that he was doing his job and learning a skill for future use at the same time.

Emily continued her efforts to get their household in order following their past trip. There was still laundry to be done and groceries to get from the store. Buddy had unloaded the car and left it all in the kitchen awaiting further instructions. He had gone to the garage and pulled out the lawnmower and proceeded to do the yard work. The next day would be Sunday and she expected to see Charlotte. She was anxious to discuss with her their recent inheritance, the pending remodeling project at the farm, and the prospect of her going to school to become a teacher. Emily felt so full of experiences and quandaries that she thought she might explode, yet she also felt that she was well blessed with things to occupy her time in Eustis' absence.

She continued to plow through the mountain of laundry and household chores that needed to be done while she lovingly watching Buddy manicuring the lawn that had been neglected for several days. She loved her flowers that Buddy tended for her; because they reminded her of the mountains. Her thoughts rambled back to the cabin and the life of simplicity that mountain people have. She always emotionally struggled with the poverty that she had witnessed. She couldn't get her mind to leave the subject of how she just might make a difference. She loved city life and the benefits it offered, but she also loved the quality of life that she had experienced in the mountains. And, she remembered Mr. Hay, and how he had encouraged her to become a teacher since that seemed to be her calling.

Sunday afternoon was always an exciting event for the family of Emily, Charlotte, and Buddy. Although he was young Buddy was included in all their discussions as if he was an adult. The two women marveled that he could speak with such knowledge and authority and welcomed Buddy's opinions and expressions. When they finally were exhausted from all the conversations about pending decisions, the consensus was that the cabin should be preserved and added to with modern conveniences. They would definitely plan to use the cabin as a vacation home for time away from the big city. In addition Emily was to immediately enroll in school to complete a teaching certificate. All the talk about decision making made them ready for a trip to the park and an ice cream cone, a plan that Buddy enforced as he headed for the door calling behind him for the group to follow.

Chapter 18

Emily soon enrolled at Erie State College for the following two years. She excelled in her classes even though she had to study in the evenings and many of the household chores fell by the wayside. She felt that her education was a priority. Occasionally she remembered from her early days in Canada that her own mother had desired to be a teacher. She also could bring back to her mind the times that she and Charlotte shared the household duties while Camilla had studied far into the night. Now Emily had the same desire as her mother and she could also benefit from the fact that Buddy was her best helper.

She continued to get letters from Eustis in which he talked about the war that continued raging in the Far East. He apparently had moved from island to island building roads and airstrips for the Seabees as part of the Navy. They also constructed huge metal buildings that housed the ammunition necessary for the soldiers and the sailors as well as the planes that landed to refuel. He continued to tell her how much he loved what he was doing, and that he was going to be the best engineer in Erie when he returned.

He spoke of how proud he was of his son who was the man of the house in his absence and of his wife who was preparing herself to become a teacher like her mother before her. Emily wrote to him almost daily even though the news was brief since she and Buddy had little time for frivolity.

On Sunday afternoon August 14, 1944, Emily and Charlotte were enjoying an afternoon of conversation while Buddy was in his room listening to the radio. Gabriel Heatter was giving the latest news about the war in Asia when there was a loud knock on the front door. Emily rose to answer the door, but not before Buddy had rushed to her side. Standing in the door were two uniformed Sailors. They asked if her name was Emily Carmichael. She answered that she was. They asked to come in and sit down. Charlotte had already gone to the living room and the rest joined her there. The two men, both of whom were officers, sat down and ominously announced that Chief Petty Officer Eustis Carmichael Sr. had been killed in action on the island of Corregidor. Emily could hardly believe her ears. Buddy rushed to his mother's side and fell on his knees laying his head in her lap. Charlotte rushed to get handkerchiefs as Emily burst into tears. Like many others before her, she never expected to get such news. Eustis had always been making plans to come home. How could this be? The Captain discussed how vicious the fighting had been on the islands. The Japanese wanted to control all the area for themselves. Allied military personnel, mostly United States Navy were trying to contain the islands for the USA; because they really needed the areas to land and refuel planes. The recaptured islands would also serve the Marines and Allied soldiers as a place to land their amphibious craft. At that point Buddy looked his mother in the eye and told her that he had heard on the news that the fighting on Corregidor was very bad. He said that he sensed earlier in his heart his father was a casualty of war.

A little later on the door closed behind the valiant officers whose job it was to relay the tragic news to war widows. They had carefully explained to Emily that the United States Government would pay her $10,000.00 in life insurance because of the death of her husband plus any back pay. Buddy would also receive a monthly stipend until he reached the age of 18 and that she too would receive a monthly allotment until she remarried. All of the words had fallen on deaf ears as Emily was completely grief-stricken by the news that she was now a widow. She wondered if Eustis had suffered or was his death quick. They had explained it happened in a bombing raid, but she wasn't totally sure what that meant. She thought about the fact that she would never see him again. Little by little as the evening wore on Emily realized that she had seen very little of Eustis in the years since they married. By circumstance, he was almost always gone from her, yet she loved him dearly. Maybe she had only loved the image of him in her life. Oh, well, she thought to herself, she would dwell on all those thoughts later.

She turned to Charlotte and Buddy, pulled herself erect and said, "is it time for a walk in the park". To her astounded family she was not showing proper bereavement, but to Emily she was postponing her grief until she could be alone. She would grieve on her own time in her own way.

Chapter 19

Emily had learned to "begin again" more than once in her life. Now she pieced together the remnants of her life without Eustis. The comfortable amount of money in hand seemed to mean nothing to her. In the last three years she had been introduced to more money than she could have imagined. She felt that she and Buddy could never spend the money they had even if they had tried hard to do so. Her wishes were small and her needs were easily satisfied.

She returned to school in the fall of the year and continued to study toward becoming a teacher. Buddy was now nearly 12 years old and making a lot of life choices concerning his own future. He often had expressed his love for farm life, but felt that he needed to go to school first. Since his father wanted to become an engineer, Buddy had entertained the same idea. When he discussed this possibility with Grampy, the only comment he heard was "not to go to work in the mines". Buddy had already made that decision. He wanted to be educated so he would not need be a "blue collar worker". He certainly had no interest in joining the Navy since he felt they were responsible for his father's death. He considered the war, both in the Pacific and in Europe, a complete waste of human life. He didn't seem to understand the full impact of what the men were fighting for and he was sure that the country's leadership was misguided.

For the remainder of 1944, Emily's days seem to run together with no purpose. She had a difficult time dealing with the routine that she had found so exciting when she first started college. The household routine had also begun to slip and Buddy picked up the slack. He seemed to be doing more than she was, and as they were coming into the Christmas holidays, he suggested they visit Meadville for the season. Emily decided that was a wonderful idea. They had not been down for an extended vacation since Eustis had been killed. Of course the weather was not agreeing with their plans and the usual ice and snow made traveling a hazard.

Buddy had learned to drive the car, and he was anxious to test his newfound skill on the highway. Before they made the trip, he suggested to his mother that they go look at a new car. Emily felt that such a plan was the farthest thing from her mind, but if it pleased him, she wondered why not? They went to the Ford dealer in Erie and looked them all over. There weren't many new models to choose from because all the steel and rubber had been used for the war effort. They scanned the few selections of the few 1945 models that were out. They were sleek and modern looking with rounded fenders and big headlights. Buddy, of course, was ecstatic at the design. Emily let him choose the one he wanted. He settled for a four-door sedan that featured a radio, heater, and windshield wipers. It was green on the outside with corresponding green upholstery inside. When the salesman told Emily it would cost $598.00, Buddy spoke up and stated that he had saved his money and could pay one-half the cost. Emily asked the salesman if they could have the car licensed in both their names. He replied that it was a bit unusual, but he was sure it could be done. As Buddy drove the car from the car lot, Emily certainly thought that she saw a smile of self-satisfaction on his face. How grown up he must feel at this time in his life.

The trip to Meadville was a joyous one. Emily and Buddy enjoyed visiting with Grammy and Grampy although they could see the frailty of the two. Neither of them had any significant illnesses. It was just a matter of aging. They held onto one another for support and their mental faculties were as clear as could be. Buddy insisted that the two of them go for a ride in the new car. The argued with him that it was too cold or they were too frail. Nonetheless, Emily and Buddy bundled them up, helped them into the back seat, and off they went. They were delighted to see the decorations at the town square and at many of the houses in the village.

When they arrived back at the house, Buddy brought in a tree and they all helped in decorating it with the age-old ornaments that seemed to bring back memories. Charlotte had also ridden the bus down to Meadville for the holidays, especially the Christmas Eve services at St. Anthony's. They all returned home to an early morning breakfast following Midnight Mass. They sang the old Christmas Carols that they had sung for generations into the wee hours, and the spirit of Christmas was heavy in the air. For the moment, Emily could forget she was, once more, in turmoil. On December 26, 1944, the three of them rode back together to Erie. The talk was light and filled with laughter.

In January, 1945, Eustis' body had been returned to Erie and they had buried him in the military cemetery there. His parents and three of his brothers and one sister had attended the funeral. Emily placed the flag that the Navy had presented to her on the top shelf of her closet. She could hardly stand to look at it. It just represented too much grief. Neither she nor Buddy could talk much about their loss. They both seemed to be grieving in their own way. Charlotte continued her habit of coming to the house each Sunday after church. Life seemed to resume a normal pattern and they continued to enjoy their time together, especially Sunday afternoons.

Emily had returned to school in September after Eustis' death. She still wanted an education and she was still determined to become a teacher. It had become harder to study since she had difficulty concentrating on her subjects. However, she managed to keep her grades up to standard. Buddy, meanwhile, was breezing right through his first year in high school. He had taken down all the maps and posters that he had kept on his walls indicating where his father probably was at any time. He rolled them up carefully and wrapped them in newspaper to keep them clean. It would seem that he, too, stored his memories on the top shelf of his bedroom closet.

Chapter 20

Emily and Buddy made it through the cold winter in Erie without much time spent discussing Eustis or his death. It was as if neither of them wanted to bring up the subject. When the snow began to melt and the lawn began to green-up, it was like a new day beginning. One evening, as they were eating dinner, Buddy mentioned that it might be time to think about revisiting the cabin. It had been three years since they had been there. He wondered if the spring storm might have blown it away. Emily quickly retorted that she wondered about her piano. The mood suddenly took on a positive air and they began to make plans to do something besides nurse wartime memories.

Emily suggested that she and Buddy plan a trip as soon as school was out for both of them. It would be late May and the roads should be passable. The flowers might be up and ready to bloom, and perhaps the REA would have more of the electric lines installed in Sandy Fork. If so, then they could begin to put electricity in the cabin. Once the electricity was in, they could begin work on adding to the front and installing water in the kitchen and bathroom. "It is settled then", Buddy said. "We will go back the first week after school is out".

Emily only had one more year to go before completing her degree and certificate. She was getting closer to her dream all the time. She was both excited and apprehensive. She didn't know how to look for a job. Job hunting would mean a brand new challenge. Actually, she was looking forward to it. She decided that there would be plenty of time to concern herself with such matters. At the moment she need to make a new wardrobe for herself since she hadn't had anything new in several years. She looked at the calendar and thought 'when will I have time to do that'. On Sunday when Charlotte came they decided that Emily would take a day the following week and go shopping. She could now afford to buy her clothes at the store rather than spend days making them. 'This has to be a luxury', she thought.

Chapter 21

Emily and Buddy headed south to visit the farm as soon as school was out. They agreed to go through Meadville and see Grammy and Grampy to tell them about their plans. They stopped in briefly and discovered them in good spirits. They both wished them well at the farm. Grampy seemed interested in the remodeling job. Emily and Buddy promised to bring back good news about what they were doing as the work progressed. Emily told them that she and Buddy would likely spend most of the summer in Sandy Fork, but she would write to them from there. Since there was no phone at the farm, she couldn't call them like she usually did. If they really needed her, they should leave a message at the church in Sandy Fork. The pastor always knew how to reach her.

As they traveled down the road to Sandy Fork, Buddy seemed happier than he had been all winter. He seemed to have an anticipation about him that made him glow. Emily had been so concerned about her own grief and life adjustment that she had failed to feel his grief. She glanced at her son who was skillfully negotiating the roads in the mountains and remembered what a bright and helpful son he really was. Had she shut him out of her life because of her loss? She paused to wonder how he could have grown so much and became so much more grown up since last summer. Now she realized that he was the same kind of survivor that she was. She had learned to take all traumas in stride. The loss of Eustis was a lot more personal than she had expected, but somehow she now had a new perspective. The times that she had discussed the cabin with him, he had agreed to remodel it and use it as a summer home. He also had expected to be sent all over the world in the Seabees believing that they would be moving a lot. Now all of that was history and Emily wondered what was keeping her in Erie?

They stopped for lunch in a small café in Morgantown, West Virginia. They had eaten lunch in this café so many times that the waitress recognized them immediately. She asked if they were going back to the mountains for the summer. She told them that

that they had returned so often, maybe they should consider moving there. Emily laughed and stated that she had been in school in Erie and had needed to finish before they moved anywhere.

After their rest stop in Morgantown, Emily took her turn driving and the conversation turned to all the things that they had in mind for the cabin. Buddy had already decided that he did not want to plant tobacco, but he would like making a small garden with onions, tomatoes, corn, and maybe some green peppers. He didn't know much about gardening but he thought that Emily did. Since they wouldn't have any livestock any more, maybe Mr. Baker would plow the garden spot in preparation for a garden. If they repaired the porch, maybe they could also get a porch swing. Emily agreed that she would like that.

Arriving at the cabin in the early evening, they went inside to find that the mice had been having fun in their absence. The visiting rodents had been in the pantry and made a shamble of anything made of paper. Cobwebs were everywhere indicating the absence of the owners for three years. The rotten porch was quite naturally in worse condition than ever, and Buddy quickly surmised that it probably wasn't salvageable. There went his porch swing idea. Emily went to the piano and played an old familiar tune. Memories flooded her mind and tears rolled down her cheeks. Even the room itself made her weep. She remembered the birth of Buddy on that bed as well as her last night she shared that same bed with Eustis. She quickly went to the kitchen stating that they needed to get it tidied up before morning. They brought in their groceries from the car and hastily made a peanut butter and jelly sandwich for supper. The rest of the evening was spent trying to make the cabin livable for the night. The following day would be a new beginning. The real clean up would begin then. As Emily held Buddy close, they cried together not knowing fully why the other one was crying. It was a time to cry and be there for one another.

Chapter 22

Morning came in Sandy Fork, Kentucky just like it always did in the mountains in the Spring. The world around them seemed to be clean and sparkling like it had been washed in the lye soap that Papa always kept stored under the cabinet in the pantry. Emily and Buddy knew that they were going to work hard this summer to complete the repairs and additions to the cabin. They wanted it livable for them to use every summer without feeling deprived. She hurriedly fixed breakfast with the supplies they had brought with them hoping to go to the store to get real groceries. Soon, they had eaten their peanut butter and jelly. They wandered outside to survey their "kingdom" once more. As Emily ambled along on the side of the ridge where the cabin stood, she gazed over to each side of the nearby mountain and wondered what was over there. She had never really studied the mountainsides around them. When she lived there, it seemed that there had never been time to visit or understand the environment. She had always worked from sunup to sundown either inside the cabin or outside. The only time off she ever enjoyed, was going to town with Papa or going to the school where Mr. Hay had been so kind to her.

Now here she was back in this atmosphere; only it was 12 long years later. The area had not changed although Emily had changed immensely. When she had lived here she had constantly been surveying the area around her for signs that might allow her to find Charlotte. That traumatic condition of loss was a haunting memory that never seemed to leave her. It was still difficult to cope with the idea of one unkind deed from one embittered woman had caused her twin to be separated from her for 20 years. Emily still shuddered at the cruel memory of it all. She also pondered the cruelty of a war that took a father from a growing boy.

Buddy was busy perusing the yards and garden spots. Since they had no mules to plow the garden, Buddy wondered how he could plant seeds and expect them to grow. The old shed was leaning seriously and it seemed unsafe to even try to find the garden tools, but he was brave and he carefully went inside. There, hanging on the wall, were all the tools he would ever need to plant anything including tobacco. Papa had replaced handles in all of the old hoes, shovels, rakes, and even the axes. The handles were all hand carved from hickory trees and bore the signature mark of Papa's pocketknife and many hours of work. While Emily was dreaming of the past, Buddy was busily planning for the future.

She returned to the kitchen to clean up more of their mess inside and Buddy excused himself for a trip to town. He jumped in the car and took off toward Sandy Fork with the words that he would bring back ice for the ice-box and milk for cereal in the morning. But it was a ruse. He quickly went to the schoolhouse over on the next ridge. He didn't expect to find Mr. Hay there, but he knew that he could leave a note there that Mr. Hay would find. As he pulled up the rutted drive, he noted a horse tied to a tree. It had been three years since he had seen his friend and he had much to tell him. He bolted inside the building and sitting at the desk, grading papers for the school year's end, sat Mr. Hay. Buddy rushed to the desk and Mr. Hay glanced up to see a grown man he hardly recognized. Buddy began to blurt out all the happenings of the past three years in one long sentence. When he had finished discussing the tragedy of the war and the death of his father, Emily's having attended school at the College for three years, and their trip back to the cabin, Mr. Hay closed his notebook, and came around the desk to Buddy's side to ask about his mother. He thought she might be in the car outside. When Buddy told him he was old enough to drive the car, and had been the "man of the house" helping his mother with everything from her homework, to maintaining a household in his father's absence, to learning how to keep their new car running, Mr. Hay marveled at such an astute young man. Buddy invited Mr. Hay to stop by and see them soon, and he hurried off to do the chores he had promised his mother he would do. Mr. Hay stood in the doorway of the school and his heart seemed full of love for this adult child.

Chapter 23

Mr. Hay had been a schoolteacher most of his life, it seemed. He had started teaching in the country schools when he was only 18 years old. He wanted to teach children who had no other opportunity to learn. He had been born in Morehead, Kentucky, to a family whose breadwinner had been an underground miner. His father toiled many long hours in the underground caverns that gave birth to the product that the Eastern Mountains' inhabitants thrived on. Coal was a necessary commodity for everything from the power plants to the steam engines that pulled a lot of freight across a sparsely inhabited region of the United States. It was the land that "time forgot". Ryan Hay's mother had been a hard working woman who only had one child. She toiled in the fields and attempted to eke out enough vegetation to last them all winter while her husband eked out a living under the earth. They had lived in a tiny two room house, not unlike the cabin that Emily had inherited. When Mr. Hay had begun teaching he was paid very little, but he gladly gave most of his earnings to the family to help defray the expenses. His father died when Ryan was only twenty years old, leaving his mother alone and destitute. He became the breadwinner and the caretaker of his mother. She gradually became more and more frail from trying to continue to work the fields without any help. In the last few years she had become an invalid, and Mr. Hay had cared for her and still made the trip to his school every day on horseback. She died in 1944 leaving her only child the house and about 4 acres of land near Morehead. Mr. Hay had always dreamed of going back to school, but there had never been an opportunity to do so. He felt that following his mother's death, he would be able to concentrate on his own life patterns or career path. After all, a man of 36 years of age should be able to pursue his own life. He had never married because the burdens at home had been too demanding. He felt that he was married to his school. He had never experienced a serious romance because there had never been any time for such a focus. Nevertheless, his life had been very full, and his love for children was so overwhelming that it had seemed to be the prerequisite for being a good teacher. He was that.

Buddy had continued his trip to the store and got the supplies, then hurried home to see what else needed to be done. As he drove up the winding drive, he was surprised to see a familiar horse tied to the tree. He smiled to himself and thought that his one friend in the entire world was waiting for him. Little did he realize just who his friend wanted to see.

Bursting through the screen door with its familiar "whap" he saw Mr. Hay and Emily sitting at the table going over the remodeling plans that they had drawn while they had still been in Erie. Mr. Hay was offering his ideas and thoughts about what they might consider doing. He assured them that he had been talking with carpenters and plumbers about what could be done. The REA had brought the electric lines to the road below the cabin, so it would now be easy to get electricity to the house.

Emily was filled with lots of news regarding their three years absence. She shared with Mr. Hay how she had been attending school in order to fulfill her own desires as well as his suggestion that she become a teacher. She also told him about the wedding of Mrs. Thompson and Uncle Russell, making them Grammy and Grampy to Buddy. She talked about the time she had been able to spend with Charlotte and of her work at the hospital. Mr. Hay listened to all their stories and as noon approached he mentioned that he would like to treat them to a lunch at the café downtown. Buddy was anxious to drive him in their car. Emily and Buddy began to laugh as they related to him the story of the "forbidden café" that Papa talked about. Mr. Hay rose to leave the kitchen when he turned and looked at both of them and stated that his name was Ryan, and not Mr. Hay. They all laughed at the formality they had been holding to for more than 12 years.

Chapter 24

Emily and Buddy spent the rest of the summer vacation at the cabin. Ryan came to the house in the early spring shortly after they had discussed how they would go about the work to make the cabin "modern". Ryan also briefly told them about the death of his mother suggesting that he now would have time to help with the work. Emily assured him that they would gladly pay him for his time. Together, they worked most of the summer trying to improve the cabin. Buddy also managed to get Mr. Baker to plow the garden spot so they might have some vegetables to eat. In addition to what they could raise on their own, each time Mr. Baker went to town, he dropped by the cabin and brought more vegetables and fresh eggs so that they seemed to have a bounty of food for everyone. Emily learned to put together a meal and then return to the ladder to paint quicker than you could imagine. Buddy, too, was learning all that he could about being a carpenter by working alongside Ryan in building the front porch and the new room. The plumbing for the bathroom would have to come later since their helper was doing other jobs and couldn't come as soon as they would have liked.

Emily and Buddy finally returned to Erie in late August. They had put electricity in the house and the bathroom had been "roughed in" awaiting installation of the plumbing. A septic tank had successfully been installed after Ryan and Buddy had labored in the hot sun digging the 8' deep hole to house the concrete block walls. The lines had been dug through the hillside for the leech line, and it seemed to Emily that it represented a giant snake weaving back and forth across the former tobacco patch. The porch had also been rebuilt. Emily had insisted that it remain a long front porch with room for chairs and a swing. Another bedroom had been added and the kitchen had been enlarged. Emily had seen white cabinets in a store in Huntington, West Virginia, called a "Youngstown Kitchen". She determined that she would have them in her cabin. The cabinets had not been delivered by the time they left, but Ryan assured her that he would have them all installed when she came back the following summer. She could not imagine what she was thinking when she left the cabin to go back to Erie. She had spent nearly $3000.00 on a cabin in a desolate mountain area that was many miles from any civilization, especially since she anticipated only being there from April to September each year.

They said their goodbyes to Ryan and began the return trip to Erie. Buddy drove the car in silence for many miles. Finally he spoke up to say how much he already missed leaving the mountains. He felt that Erie was too big to be "homey" and that he was isolated in the city. Emily pondered that thought for a moment and mentioned that the mountains were also an isolated area. Buddy quickly countered with the fact that Ryan was part of the mountain life, and he was also his best friend. Emily had not really noticed how much Buddy had attached himself to Ryan, although she noticed how they worked together every day and seemed to have developed a bond.

She also cautiously admitted to herself that she enjoyed having Ryan around during the day as he was working. They had eaten every meal together for the entire summer so he had become their constant companion. Although they had enjoyed little time in reading, Ryan had continually talked about the books they had already read and the things that she was studying in school. He also had mentioned that Buddy would soon be entering college. He had spoken of the things that Buddy should include in his curriculum. Ryan had also told Emily the entire story of his own family and their life in Morehead. When there was a free moment, Emily had also related her own story from the day of the birth of the twins to the present day of being a widow. She lamented the fact that she was always being moved about and still had no real roots. Her pride and joy was and had always been her son, Buddy. He had been her constant companion since his birth. She wanted always to do what was best for him. She really felt a kinship to Ryan and she had always felt he was a good friend to her even though they remained many miles apart.

As she continued reminiscing, she remembered her first trip to the schoolhouse on the ridge to get books for Papa more than 12 years earlier, then she dozed off as they drove toward Pennsylvania.

Chapter 25

They stopped in at Meadville to see Grammy and Grampy. As Emily expected, they were more frail than they had been in the Spring. It seemed that they were aging rapidly. Emily babbled about the repairs on the cabin and how Buddy had helped Ryan as they worked on the septic tank. Buddy spoke up and related to them how his friend had helped with the knowledge he didn't have and yet he let him lead in many of the projects. Grampy smiled and mentioned that Buddy was going to be the engineer that his father had wanted to be.

After a short rest Buddy and Emily continued their trip to Erie and arrived home late on Saturday night. Emily knew that Charlotte would be over for lunch the next day, so they carried in their bounty from the cabin, then quickly went to bed. It had been a hard trip and Emily had many things going through her head. She wanted to share her plans and ideas with Charlotte about the cabin, yet she wondered if a part of her stayed in Sandy Fork, Kentucky. As she lay awake in the bed, she had to admit that she missed being able to talk to Ryan. She wondered if he would always live in Morehead or would he leave for a bigger city and more money now that his parents were both gone. Suddenly she came to grips with the fact that she didn't want him to go away. Then, the thought occurred to her that maybe he was not even currently including her in his future plans. How could she be so selfish? Maybe, it was time for her to reveal to Ryan that she hoped, that he would remain close to Sandy Fork. She had to wrestle with her own emotions that were coming alive in her mind and body as they had so long ago with Eustis. It was 1:00 A.M. She got out of bed, went to her desk, and penned Ryan a note.

Dear Ryan:

We arrived home this evening around 10:00 P.M. and unloaded the car before collapsing into bed for a good night's sleep. However, I found I could not sleep because I realized I had not expressed my gratitude to you for your kind friendship to us. Buddy loves you very much and could hardly stop talking about you to everyone he met. But aside from that I need to tell you how much I miss you. I am sure I did not express my feelings to you or for you as we labored to make the cabin livable, but in my solitude this evening, I wished that I had you here to talk to again.

Please accept my heartfelt thanks for all your efforts, but more than anything else, please understand how much I miss you.

Emily

After she had written the note and addressed it for mailing, she crawled back into bed and fell asleep immediately, feeling as if a big load had been lifted from her shoulders.

Morning came too early, but they ate their breakfast together while Buddy was still talking about their trip to the farm. They went to church, had a joyful reunion with Charlotte, and decided that they would eat their lunch in the local café before going home for their session of catching up.

Emily also mailed her letter to Ryan at the post office before going home following lunch. She hoped that he would get it the next day.

Meanwhile, Emily went about her routine and readied her wardrobe and Buddy's for going back to school. She reviewed her upcoming studies and purchased the books that she would need for the coming school year. She was going through the motions, but could think of little else except what Ryan would think about her letter or how he would respond.

When the postman came by the house on Friday morning, she gathered the mail and went inside to see what bills needed to be paid and if there was a letter from Ryan. First there was a letter from the Navy with the death certificate for Eustis and a confirmation of her pension as well as the stipend for Buddy. She laid all those documents aside and carefully examined the rest of the mail. At the bottom of the stack was a letter from Ryan. She tore it open as quickly as she could, then suddenly stopped! Did she really want to read it or was it bad news? She carefully opened the envelope and carefully read every word:

My dear Emily:

I was so very glad to receive your letter. I, too, miss you very much. I can hardly believe that we have been friends for so long. You have always been special to me. From the first day I met you at the school, I wondered how I could have been so lucky to find such a fine young woman to be a friend. You mean so very much to me. I simply can not bear the thought of your being in Erie when I really want you here with me.

I love Buddy as if he were my own son and I see that he has a need for a father image. I don't mean to imply that I want to take his father's place in his heart. I only mean that he needs a man to lean on during his time of maturing.

Thank you again for writing to me to express your feelings. I assure you that I, too, spent a sleepless night after you left.

I will have some time off at Thanksgiving. I would like to visit you in Erie if that might be acceptable to you and Buddy.

Please write soon and often.

Your loving friend,

Ryan Hay

There was also a letter to Buddy from Ryan. Emily ran to find him and gave him his letter. Buddy went to his room and read the letter in private. He never disclosed to her what it said, nor did she ask.

Emily announced that Ryan would visit them during the holiday season and that they needed to prepare for his arrival even if it were almost 2 months away. She glanced around their house and decided that they would need to do a few things prior to his arrival. She and Buddy listed their projects and completed them as they proceeded to prepare for Ryan's visit. It was hard to guess who was anticipating his arrival the most; Emily or Buddy!

Ryan's visit might just tell their future home and life choices.

Epilogue

Emily really did finish college and became a teacher. She applied for a job in the Elliott County of Kentucky school system and accepted a job at a school in nearby Newfoundland. She and Buddy moved to the cabin when school was out in 1946.

In the fall of 1946, Grammy died, leaving a grieving husband. Emily had long considered her a mother and she too grieved the loss of a long-term friend. Grampy died before winter that same year stating that he did not want to live without his beloved wife. He simply grieved himself to death. Mrs. Thompson Garland left her home to Emily. Grampy left his home to Buddy, the sale of which was to be used for his college education if he chose not to live in it.

June 1947, Emily became Mrs. Ryan Hay. She had never been so loved. Ryan adored his beautiful wife and doted on her every whim. Together they went hand in hand everywhere. They became active in the Baptist Church where Emily returned to playing the piano. Buddy never looked at Ryan as a step-father but soon called him "dad".

On June 14, 1948, Emily gave birth to a beautiful baby girl whom she named Vivian Charlotte after the two most important women in her life. The child was born at the hospital in Morehead, Kentucky where Charlotte had transferred, becoming head nurse there. Charlotte had made the move to be near her only relative in the world.

Ryan Hay could hardly believe his good fortune. He knew that God had answered his prayers for a companion, but he hardly expected to get a wife, a son, a daughter, and a sister all in one year. But he did!

THE END